The Cost of Survival

An Apocalyptic LitRPG
Book 3 of the System Apocalypse

By

Tao Wong

Copyright

This is a work of fiction. Names, characters, businesses, places, events and incidents are either the products of the author's imagination or used in a fictitious manner. Any resemblance to actual persons, living or dead, or actual events is purely coincidental.

This book is licensed for your personal enjoyment only. This book may not be re-sold or given away to other people. If you would like to share this book with another person, please purchase an additional copy for each recipient. If you're reading this book and did not purchase it, or it was not purchased for your use only, then please return to your favorite book retailer and purchase your own copy. Thank you for respecting the hard work of this author.

Books in

The System Apocalypse series

Main Storyline

Life in the North

Redeemer of the Dead

The Cost of Survival

Cities in Chains

Coast on Fire

World Unbound

Stars Awoken

Rebel Star

Stars Asunder

Broken Council

Forbidden Zone

System Finale

System Apocalypse – Relentless

A Fist Full of Credits

System Apocalypse – Australia

Town Under

Flat Out

Anthologies & Shorts

System Apocalypse Short Story Anthology Volume 1

Valentines in an Apocalypse

A New Script

Daily Jobs, Coffee and an Awfully Big Adventure

Adventures in Clothing

Questing for Titles

Blue Screens of Death

My Grandmother's Tea Club

The Great Black Sea

A Game of Koopash (Newsletter exclusive)

Lana's story (Newsletter exclusive)

Debts and Dances (Newsletter exclusive)

Comic Series

The System Apocalypse Comics (7 Issues)

Contents

What Has Gone Before

Ten months ago, the System came to Earth, bringing with it monsters, aliens and glowing blue boxes of notifications that detailed their lives in this new Galactic System. Humanity was forced to evolve, their lives dictated by statistic screens, Classes and Skills that gave them strength and abilities beyond the norm, providing them a fighting chance to survive. Still, the apocalypse saw the death of nearly 90% of humanity, the malfunctioning of everything electronic and a new, blood-filled existence.

John Lee was camping in the Yukon when the change occurred. Gifted with perks beyond the normal, he journeyed to Whitehorse and aided in the establishment of the city under the rule of the alien Truinnar, Lord Graxan Roxley. With the help of other survivors, the Village of Whitehorse was quickly established to provide a stable environment for growth.

But the System was not done with them yet, with increasing number of monsters and the introduction of 'dungeons' onto Earth, giving truth to the Galactic term 'Dungeon World'. Together, the survivors in Whitehorse and the Yukon managed to destroy an infected dungeon, saving the Village and most of the Yukon from further dangers. This destruction was not without cost, with numerous friends falling by the wayside.

Now, the survivors retreat to Whitehorse as they await the next System generated crisis.

Chapter 1

Regrets are a part of life, one that we all bear in different forms. Words that should never have been said, punches that should never have been thrown, anger that should never have been swallowed. Actions and inactions can lead to regret, making your entire world nothing but pain and disappointment over things you should have done or not done.

Right about now, I'm regretting getting out of bed and making this meeting.

"You going to help?" I snarl as I snap-kick a weird snake-cow hybrid away from me, then shoot the one that follows it in the gut. Standing in the middle of a monster swarm in the Carcross Cutoff, surrounded by Hakarta who are barely bothering to do anything, is not happy making. It really isn't. Of course, if I'd known the swarm would happen while we were talking, I would never have come out but some things you just can't control.

Major Labashi Ruka, the space-marine mercenary Orc and my erstwhile semi-employer, grins at me in response. Labashi flicks a pebble with his off-hand so hard that the impromptu projectile pierces a Snow Caribou in the head, dropping it instantly. The major and most of his people out-level the swarm of monsters around us by a significant amount. Which would be great for me if they decided to actually help. Instead, Labashi seems insistent on continuing my debrief.

"This is the fifth swarm then?" Labashi says in that System-given upper-class British accent of his.

Another of the deer swerves rather than rush him, heading in my direction. Behind it, even more monsters cluster and charge over the snow, the swarm running, jumping, and flying away as they abandon old zones for newer, less dangerous ones. Monster swarms are part and parcel of our life since the System designated Earth as a Dungeon World. Mana begets monsters who vie for control of mana-rich zones. Leave the monsters alone in any one zone too long and the most powerful eventually drive away the lower-level ones, kicking off a giant domino effect.

I sidestep the deer whose head butts up against Sabre's—my mecha-cum-motorcycle—shield before I snap off a shot with the Inlin machine gun at another threat. "Just about."

"Just about?"

Beside Labashi, the rest of his squad are taking bets and fighting bare-handed in a casual display of strength while they wait.

"Yes. The fifth! Things have been a bit busy lately," I snap as I shoot the next three deer in quick succession. High-explosive projectile rounds from the Inlin tear holes into the monsters, sufficient to deter their advance. "The swarms are coming faster and faster."

"Not surprising. Your defenses?"

"Improving. The first were ultra-low levels. These guys," I snarl and catch the Level 24 wolverine before it can clamp its jaws around my helmet. A powered-armor-assisted throw sends the monster flying into the distance to be gored by another as it lands. "Are a bit more of a challenge than the last swarm."

"Your hunters leveling?" Labashi continues with his questioning about the city.

Months ago, I ended up with a System-enforced Contract with the major, forcing me to feed him information about Whitehorse whenever he wants it. I do get paid in Credits, but even if everyone knows I'm spying for him, I still feel a little dirty about it all.

Above us, Ali sits cross-legged in his usual orange jumpsuit, holding a bowl of popcorn and staring at a System screen only he can see. I'd ask what my brown-skinned System Companion is watching, but it's likely some cheesy reality TV show. The last time I checked, he was into house hunting and renovations, but I'm pretty sure he's moved on by now. I'd be annoyed by his antics if I wasn't so damn used to them. Actually, never mind. I am annoyed.

"Decently. Most are in their mid-30s now and they've gotten pretty serious about training. The displacement has made it a lot easier to find level-appropriate monsters." I duck beneath a magpie that's literally on fire. "This swarm might be a bit of a push, but they should be able to handle it."

That also explains why I'm doing my best to kill, maim, and otherwise redirect as many of them as I can before they reach Whitehorse. The fewer of these monsters there are, the fewer the city will have to deal with and the easier they'll have it. Especially since in monster swarms, the damn System reduces our experience gains while it's happening, so no one is leveling up from this. On the other hand, the system-generated quests for safeguarding the city can compensate for the loss in experience—if I had been in town.

Ten months since the world changed under a series of blue System notification windows and we've lost nearly ninety percent of the human population and all our electronics. The earth had plunged back into the early 1900s, since delicate electronics don't mix well with high levels of Mana—unless they've been specially constructed. I'd been caught up in the change while I was camping in Kluane National Park and, luckily, ended up with a few additional System-generated Perks due to my location.

Without electricity, without most of our machinery, and with monsters spawning all across the world, staying alive became a mad scramble for everyone. Unfortunately, keeping as many people as possible alive meant making some deals with people I shouldn't have.

"What are you doing here anyway?" I say as I spin and chop the head off a monster, my soulbound sword appearing in my hand. One of the nice things about my Class was I got to bind a weapon to me. It levels as I level, giving it greater strength and sharpness. It also appears and disappears on command, which can lead to some really interesting fighting techniques.

"I'm out of those Belgium chocolates."

Bullshit. Considering I buy my chocolates from the Shop, he could get some just as easily as I do. Which is trivial, so long you have enough Credits. Heck, you can buy anything in the Shop—and I do mean anything. Secrets, Classes, Skills, equipment, and more. I've even heard that there are sections in the Shop that include sentient contracts. Serfdom, if not slavery.

"Bullshit."

"Again, I am not Yerick," Labashi says, referring to the minotaurs that have taken up residence in the city. "And your other visitors?

"Xev and Sally?" I play dumb, not that I expect it'll work. Xev's a giant arachnid that makes grown men cry, and Sally's a tiny cheerful gnome with a very sharp tongue. Both Galactics are well known to Labashi and his employer.

"No. The Kapre."

"Oh. Them." I sigh.

The Kapre are recent immigrants, another race of disenfranchised aliens who have been ground under the System's heel. Unlike the Yerick, they never had a whole planet of their own—they were one of four races on their home planet. When their planet integrated into the System, they spread across the Galactic core in a desperate race to remain relevant and level up. All of the Kapre are tall—like, a good seven feet tall—with elongated faces and brown bark-like skin. Weirdly enough, they all have beards and are, at least to human eyes, male. All of them.

"They're doing well. I think. Hard to tell. They've taken over the hills along Long Lake behind Riverdale and don't mix much with us. Humans aren't excluded from going in, but we're not exactly welcome either."

"Us?"

"The city."

"So you have become an us," Labashi muses, absently holding a tiger-like monster by its face as it attempts to claw him. Razor-sharp claws just bounce off his armor, which is impressive, considering most armor takes damage from attacks like that. I have a feeling a Skill of some type is being applied to increase the armor's strength and durability. Might be something for me to look into.

"Yeah." I flick my blade wide, calling forth a Skill of my own and sending a wave of power flowing forward in its wake, cutting through monsters and throwing the tougher ones aside. Blade Strike, my anime-inspired—or really, the other way around if I understand how this works—System-generated Skill.

"Interesting. Well, I believe this is all that we needed," Labashi says then raises his hand. Light plays along it for a moment, then he calls down the sky.

Lightning flashes from clear skies to destroy the swarm. My helmet automatically flickers, compensating for the overload of light, and by the time I've stopped flinching, the Hakarta are already walking away.

"Oy! Boy-o, they're still coming," Ali shouts, and I bring myself back to the present.

The monsters that were present are dead, giving the Hakarta more than enough time to wander away without harassment, but more are coming and I know what I need to do. I call my sword back into my hand and I wait, smiling at the monsters as they come. Time to get back to work.

***

Two hours later, the swarm is finally gone and I sigh, triggering the mental command that retracts my helmet into a black ring around my neck. The cold air is bracing and pleasant as I lean against the wooden wall of my fort. Well, not mine, since the Council has finally taken it over. Funny thing—once the

General Council in the city was ratified by Lord Roxley, the people they sent out to take control of the fort made it part of the city. I didn't even know you could do that—and neither did they. The Council also made it clear to me that they would like me to not take the structure back, which is more than fair enough. I don't really have the resources to make the fort all it can be, all it will need to be.

It takes a single mental command and Sabre comes apart, switching back to bike mode. I step away from it, staring at the clear winter skies before taking a deep breath of the crisp air. It is -20 Celsius—cold enough that I should feel it. However, I don't and I won't. Just another damn gift from the System. That and the ability to kill and kill and kill without thought or hesitation or regret.

I lean back, watching the sky and glancing occasionally at Ali as he loots the bodies for me, pulling System-generated loot then dumping the corpses into my pocket dimension. I lean back and try to figure out when I stopped feeling anything for the monsters I killed. My hands move, pulling forth a chocolate and popping it into my mouth. I barely even taste it as I stare into the sky, body and soul numb. Silence descends over the fort. It's a brief moment of peace that I know won't be here long, because with Labashi's appearance, matters are definitely coming to a head.

Chapter 2

"Your boss in?" I ask Vir, the lieutenant of the guard who glares at me as I stare around the blue, utilitarian waiting room just before Roxley's office.

The black-skinned, white-haired Tuinnar in his silver-and-white guard uniform glares at me and I wonder what has him playing receptionist. Or did I just catch him while he was coming out? It's possible that Vir was just finishing up his report over the swarm.

"*Lord Roxley* is busy. You may tell me what you wish to tell him," Vir answers coldly. I get the feeling he's not a big fan of mine, especially not since learning about my involvement with the Hakarta.

"Well, I could. But then I'd have to go into exhaustive detail about the tongue hockey we did," I say, grinning.

Vir stares at me before his face goes even flatter than normal. "Adventurer Lee, do you actually have anything relevant to say?"

"Fee fii foo fum…" I stop, shaking my head. "Sorry. I'm feeling a bit silly right now. Might be the swarm I was fighting in in the outskirts of town. Or the talk I had with Labashi."

"You spoke with Major Ruka?" Vir says, interest piquing his voice despite his best efforts. "Directly, I assume?"

"Face to snout." I nod. "Wanna see?"

"I…" Vir tilts his head for a second before he steps sideways, gesturing to the blank wall that hides the door to Roxley's office. "Lord Roxley will see us now."

"Figures," Ali mutters, flying alongside us as we enter Lord Graxan Roxley's, current holder of the Key to Whitehorse and Baron of the Seven Seas, office.

Virtual reality software, floating blue screens from the System, and the ability to share information directly means his office mostly consists of a series of really comfortable chairs and a single black marble desk. The man—dark elf/Tuinnar—stands there relaxed, smiling with the left side of his face slightly higher than the right in that endearing way that he has, all muscley and good-looking and…

Mental Influence Resisted

Right. I push my hormones down and my lustful thoughts aside as the System reminds me of Roxley's effect. I'd be annoyed, but he doesn't even do it on purpose. He just has a series of Skills, Stats, and modifications that makes everyone more susceptible to his charms. Lucky for me, my Class comes with extremely high level resistances, so I'm pretty safe from the direct effects. It doesn't stop me from wanting to jump his bones, but that's more personal.

I think.

"John," Roxley says, and his voice is like dark chocolate rubbing over my skin.

"*Wakey wakey. Stop drooling.* Lord Roxley. Perhaps you'd care to see this?" Ali slides in while I get myself under control as he projects a video of our meeting in a series of blue windows.

"Thank you," Roxley says.

Vir steps closer, both of them falling silent as they listen to the edited video.

"You edited this?" Vir says, looking at Ali.

"Yup. Left the relevant points in. No point watching John get his ass kicked."

"I would like the unedited videos for my files," Vir states.

"And I'd like a Nymph," Ali answers.

I glare at Ali and the Spirit snorts, waggling a finger, which I assume is him sending it on. After that, the pair stays silent till the video finishes.

"So it begins," Roxley finally says, exhaling slightly as he turns to me.

"Do you think it's time for you to explain what *it* is?" I answer.

Vir and Lord Roxley exchange a look before Roxley speaks. "You know most of it. Duchess Kangana owns much of the land north and to the west of us, the area that you once called Alaska. It is our belief that she intended to purchase Whitehorse as well, creating a monopoly in this region. We do not believe she has given up on those plans as yet."

"But why? That's the bit I don't get."

"High-level zones in a Dungeon World are extremely lucrative if well-managed. In your parlance, they're a high-risk, high-reward location. High-level monsters have more mana-dense bodies and loot, which allows the creation of more durable, powerful, and expensive equipment. Control over a single staging area is extremely valuable, and wars have been fought in established Dungeon Worlds for such locations."

Well, that explained the why. Especially if she could get a monopoly and build out. It also explained why the Duchess decided to go for the larger cities rather than our tiny town. On the other hand…

"Why hasn't she or someone else come yet? If it's so valuable."

"Why did your big companies not go into smaller developing countries?" Roxley asked rhetorically. After a moment, as he saw the blank look in my eyes, he added, "Too much risk during the initial development stage, for too little gain. While the returns can be high, until the flow of loot and resources have increased, the risk of losing one's capital entirely is too great. Most of the major players are already dedicated to other, more established regions. When the Dungeon World is established, when the flow of loot has increased sufficiently, then the largest groups step in."

"What's her play?" I ask as I digest the tacit admission that Roxley is considered a small fish in the Galactic pond.

"Unknown. She has the military resources to crush us, but that reduces the value of the city. It would be more optimal for her to win this without fighting, but we have no word on her plans as yet. However, I do not believe she will hold off much longer."

"No, I'm pretty sure you're right about that." I exhale, glancing between the two before I ask the next question, the one I've dreaded. "What can I do?"

Roxley and Vir share a look before Roxley replies. "As yet, nothing. We will inform you once your aid is required."

I have a feeling they aren't being entirely truthful with me. My actions have put me on the outside once again. I stare between the pair one last moment before nodding and turning away. Fine. I'll just do my own thing then.

***

I stare at Aiden as he crouches, drawing on the ground with a wand that bites into the asphalt, his signature manbun swaying as he works. I have to grunt in annoyance even as I watch the mage work. I'd looked the hipster up for another lesson and instead got dragged into some civic duty. I'll admit, I am learning a little about enchanting and Mana manipulation, but this really was not what I was hoping to learn. A new healing spell, maybe a combat one. Not how to enchant roads with an ongoing heating spell to keep the snow off.

"Battery."

I hand to him the Mana battery, which consists of a tiny Mana crystal and battery interfaces. Aiden grasps the intricately crafted battery, and I watch as he inserts it into the ground and closes off the enchantment. The moment he's done, Aiden moves smoothly to the side to give me space to work. I bend down and Mana flows from my hand, from the center of my body. I make sure to take the time to really feel it, to sense the changes in my body and the enchantment, the way the runes light up as Mana travels through them, focused through both the script and the intention behind the script. I sense my Mana drop precipitously as I charge the entire spell in one go and top-up the battery at the same time. Tapping into my skill of Mana Manipulation, watching the shift and flow of the blue energy through my body and in the environment, I do my best to take some learning from all this.

That's the thing about enchantments and magic in this crazy world—it's all about perception. Elemental Affinities like the one Ali shares with me actually require work. With those, you need to actually understand why and how you're going to make the changes you want. Mana, on the other hand, is the paint-by-numbers version of the Elemental Affinities, and the System is the art teacher holding your hand.

Once the battery is finally full, I catch up with Aiden, who is already working on the ground twenty meters away. Behind me, the snow's melting as the runes warm the earth. The battery and charge I've provided will last a good week or so, but with so many people running around, it'll be a simple thing for others to top it up as they go along their day. Or so we hope.

"How much have we gotten done?" I ask.

"We've mostly completed the Downtown core. Still need to stretch it out to the industrial district, but getting the main roads into Riverdale sorted was high on the list."

"That seems fast. You've been at this for what? Two weeks?"

"Two and a half. Once the others got trained up, we picked up speed quite a bit," Aiden answers, brow furrowed. "Biggest problem is getting the initial charge. Not that many people have enough Mana to do that."

"The hunters should."

"Har. Half of them are physical specced; the other half are mixed in between. Only a small number are actual Mages. Even those who have enough Mana don't have the recharge rates we need, so we end up waiting a lot," Aiden answers. "And don't forget, we still have to keep clearing the Dungeons and Bosses around the city. The Yerick might be bearing the brunt of that, but our hunters are almost always busy. Hard to justify clearing roads when the swarms keep coming."

I nod slightly, reminding myself that most Basic classes add three, maybe four attributes at most per level and only by a point, maybe two. The Erethran Honor Guard Class I have is both rare and an Advanced Class, which means I get a huge boost each time I level. Of course, I also level about twice as slowly as everyone else, which is why everyone around me looks as if they've got higher Levels than I do.

"How's the dungeon clearing for you guys?" Aiden asks as he stands, conjuring a flame between his fingers to warm them.

"About the usual. We could use a mage," I reply, smiling slightly. "We're a bit too smashy for my liking."

"Not happening. And Lana? How's she doing?"

"She's *going through the motions*," Ali sings from his spot above us.

"Why is there music?" Aiden says, looking around as he tries to spot the speakers.

"You can hear it too?" I glare at Ali. I've heard it a few times recently, but I figured it was something Ali was doing to mess with me. When the System first came into play, I gave him full access to my settings, the backend of all this. I've since come to realize my experience with the System has been somewhat different from others because of that.

"Like it?" Ali flashes a wide grin. "It's a new ability."

"You got the ability to play atmospheric music?" I say, disbelief in my voice. "How? Why? When? We haven't leveled in weeks."

"What? A Spirit can't take his time choosing?" Ali points at his clothing. "I got a few different changes of clothing too."

I look. And then I'm not entirely sure I'm seeing it right. "Are those shoulder pads? And a purple suit?"

"Yup," Ali says proudly.

Aiden stops even trying to hide his amusement, laughing his ass off, and I close my eyes, breathing deeply. It's when I'm calmer that I realize maybe having this conversation in front of Aiden wasn't the best idea—most Companions are purchased or gained at a specific Level. They don't improve, not without spending more money at the Shop. Ali, on the other hand, is a Linked Companion, which means he does Level at pretty much the same rate I do. I grimace at the thought and finally just shrug. Ah hell, not much I can do about it now.

"So Lana still not doing well?" Aiden says after he recovers from his bout of laughter.

"No. Not really." I open my mouth to say more, then shut it. I'm not sure it's my place to explain what I'm thinking, what I fear. "But she's functioning."

"Well, tell her we've missed her presence on the Council," Aiden says then gestures to the enchantment. "Your turn."

"Of course it is." I bend down.

***

A trio of beautiful women come walking down the street, flanked by an equal number of huskies the size of ponies and a fiery fox the size of a large dog whose very presence melts the snow around it. Call me crazy, but I know trouble when I see it. That two of the three are members of my usual hunting party lends credence to my thoughts. Lana, on the left, is a buxom redhead whose pets flank the group and whose once-smiling demeanor is now shadowed with loss. Mikito walks in the center, which emphasizes how short the Japanese woman is, her naginata held loosely in one hand. Amelia's the odd one out. The ex-Constable is often too busy keeping the peace in town, as one of the few human members of the Guard.

"Ladies," I greet them, glancing at Aiden as I add to him, "I'm nearly out of Mana."

"Fair enough. We got more done than I expected anyway," Aiden replies before smiling in greeting at the three.

"John. Aiden," Mikito says. The Japanese woman has a very faint Japanese accent, one that is nearly drowned out by the System. Accents are one of those weird little idiosyncrasies of purchasing Skills from the System to cover gaps in your own skillset. Labashi for example has a strong British accent. "You done?"

"Done and done," Ali answers, brushing his hands together. "And not a moment too soon."

"Good," Lana says. Like the others, she's dressed in post-apocalyptic hunter chic—a one-piece armored jumpsuit. She's switched up her usual colors; instead of the mixed brown and yellow that she used to wear, it's all black. I have to admit, it's hot in a 1960s Catwoman way. "We just received some information about a new Boss. One of the hunting groups ran into it. Level 48."

I grunt, my mind already calling Sabre to me, courtesy of a neural link I got implanted via the Shop. Haven't actually made great use of the link recently, but it does make certain things easier. Shadow growls quietly as the mecha rolls past it silently, the husky's shadow shifting on its own accord to chase the bike as it comes to a stop at my side.

"You know, that's just freaky," Amelia says, pointing at Sabre. She's dressed in a red that is reminiscent of her old uniform and has pistols slung low on her hips.

"Don't be jealous." I flash her a grin, walking over to the bike. "You coming?"

"No. I'm just here to grab Aiden. There's another meeting," Amelia replies, and Aiden groans slightly.

"Offer's still open," I say.

"You know how people say they'd rather get shot at than do another meeting? That's not me. Take me away, m'lady," Aiden says as he walks over to Amelia quickly.

Ali, to punctuate the last of Aiden's words, plays a series of drum beats.

Amelia's eyes widen. "Is that…?"

I sigh. "Don't ask."

"No one appreciates me," laments Ali as Lana beckons Shadow for her and Howard for Mikito to ride.

The moment the pair are on, they take off, and I gun Sabre to follow.

Whitehorse has changed somewhat since the apocalypse. On the surface, Downtown Whitehorse is much the same as it was before, 1960s-era two-to-three-story storefronts mixed with some early 1920s pioneer buildings. All but the single, ten-story silver building that dominates the middle of Main Street where Lord Roxley rules over us all. On cursory inspection, it seems the same. But we didn't use to have weapon stores, armor stores, or alchemists. Our clothing stores didn't prominently display the level of protection they provide against monsters. And let's just say that the sashimi from the Japanese restaurant is now non-traditional and much more gamey.

The people are the most surprising change. Not that the city was ever that crowded, but now, the few who are on the streets have an edge you didn't see in North America. At least, not in the nice parts of most cities. They have a certain wariness, an awareness of their surroundings from constantly looking around for threats, and the all-too-casual weapon check as they go about their daily business. Constant danger and the need to kill has given everyone a hard edge and a penchant for violence as their first solution.

The drive up Two Mile Hill is fast, since most vehicles are still owned by the hunters, who are all out. Ahead of us are the walls that block off the city, gleaming metal with a pair of vehicle gates and gun towers. Those are the visible defenses—hidden force fields and mines are just some of the less obvious safety measures. As we reach the gates, humans bearing futuristic beam rifles and old-school melee weapons mingle with dark-skinned, white-haired, pointed-eared Tuinnar guards, watching for the next swarm.

Once we're out of the gates, the puppies pick up speed. In a few minutes, they swerve off the road and I hit a switch, making the bike jump. Another mental command and the bike switches, wheels rotating, and suddenly I'm hovering as the anti-gravity engines kick in. They're not actually anti-gravity engines, but once again, my physics and engineering knowledge failed me when Ali tried to explain it.

Bikes are fun, but they aren't particularly practical when the snow's sitting at least three feet deep. Driving with the anti-gravity engines is interesting, but I've gotten quite used to it. A few minutes later, my Mana's back to full, which is good—fighting a Boss without Mana is never a good idea. We move fast, cutting through the trees and leaving the few monsters that try to stop our group bleeding and dead behind us. Anna, who is strapped to Howard in a sling, yawns through most of it, barely shifting unless she is forced to throw a bolt of fire.

Our first major problem comes in the form of a large, humanoid white-furred creature.

Alpha Yeti (Boss) Level 48

HP: 7730/7730

A furry paw comes up, and the next thing we know, we're hit by a blizzard that whites out the entire area. The vision assistance in my helmet tells me what my body has already let me know—the temperature's dropping like a rock, crossing -40°C within seconds. With a thought, Sabre comes apart, armored pieces sliding across my body even as the helmet keeps shifting vision options, trying to find something that can cut through the blizzard. It ends up on a hazy, weird mixture of thermal imaging and visual magnification which lets me see that the Yeti's gone.

Crouching low, I snarl and look around even as Lana and Mikito get off the huskies. Mikito's flipping the naginata in swirling patterns around her the moment she gets clear, ensuring that anything that tries to sneak up on her gets caught in it. Lana's crouched, hair streaming out behind her as she cranes her head, turning occasionally at a new noise. Her pets spread out, encircling her in a defensive formation.

It's a futile effort. Ice spikes erupt from the ground without warning, catching Howard on his back foot and spearing Lana directly in her stomach. The spike erupts out of her back, lifting her into the air and leaving her impaled, her scream of pain setting the huskies howling.

"*ALI. Where is he?*" I scream, rage coloring my vision.

"*Give me a second, this blizzard is messing with my sensors,*" the Spirit thinks back over our mental link.

Even my own ability to sense the monster is drawing a blank. I spin, searching as I edge toward the struggling Lana, but there's nothing but the howl of the wind and the creaking of ice. Damn it, I should have thrown the Soul Shield on her immediately.

Instinct throws me sideways moments before more ice spears erupt from the ground. Superhuman reflexes and a hell of a lot of combat hours gets me most of the way out, my armor absorbing the glancing impact. Rolling, I come to my feet in the flattened snow and catch sight of Lana falling, the ice spear hacked apart. A second later, she's got Elsa, her pet turtle, out of its carry-on and pointed. Elsa begins to breathe fire. Anna, released from Howard, heats up too, breaking formation as she dashes near trees and lights them on fire by sheer proximity.

I catch all this and the tail end of Mikito being hit by a four-foot-wide snowball that picks her up and sends her rolling down the hill like Wil. E. Coyote with a bad plan. I'd laugh, and I'm sure I will when I view the recordings later, but I'm still looking for our attacker.

"Got you!" Ali snarls.

Suddenly, there's a yellow outline to my left. I raise the Inlin, barrel already spitting high-explosive death and tearing up the earth in gouts of flame. Surprisingly, Lana turns too, and I wonder if Ali's sharing data now. Either way, blood blooms as explosive rounds impact, throwing the monster back.

Even as it falls, the Yeti raises its hand and a wall of ice appears, blocking our view. The fox darts in a wide circle while Lana points Elsa at the wall, burning it down. I run forward and jump above the melting wall, but the damn Yeti's gone.

"Boy-o, every time it gets colder, the Yeti drops from my sense."

Fine. I raise my hands, pointing in two different directions, and call forth my Fireball spell. It's pretty much everything that you'd expect it to be—a ball of flame that explodes after a pre-determined distance. The fire melts snow, burns up the trees, and sets the Yeti alight, highlighting the monster for all our eyes. The puppies rush the monster, and Lana, dropping Elsa to the side, opens up with a beam pistol.

By the time Mikito gets back from rolling down the hill, the Yeti's down and in a number of unappetizing pieces. Even on fire, it managed to spike Howard and Anna, but with all of us ganging up on it, the Boss doesn't stand a chance. Somehow, the idea of dragging the remains back to the butchering yard seems wrong—whatever else it was, it fought smart. It might even have been somewhat sentient—and eating a sentient creature just seems wrong. Lana loots the body without a word, hunched over slightly as she walks back to me. I eye her injury, note that it seems to have stopped leaking blood, and leave it alone. The pain is real, but the System helps our bodies heal at an accelerated rate, which makes injuries transitory. Even if the mental scarring that might occur from getting ripped apart repeatedly isn't. That's why tanks are all just a little insane.

"Whitehorse?" I inquire, looking around.

"Let's hunt. We're out this far. The monsters are a decent level out here," Lana says immediately.

I swear, it's like I've warped back in time and replaced Lana with Mikito. She has the same desire to be in the wilderness, killing and killing and killing.

"Okay," Mikito agrees of course. She might be on a more even keel, but that's not to say Mikito's ever going to turn down a chance to exact a little payback for her dead husband.

"Fine. You want to lead the way?" I gesture for Lana. I'm outvoted after all, and frankly, I'm not that interested in arguing for not killing monsters when we can. I can always use the experience and Credits.

Hunting over the next few hours is interesting. The monsters haven't really settled down after the swarm, and even if we're quite a distance out, the mix and numbers are just weird for the newly created zone. Good news is that the low-level monsters avoid us and vice versa. That leaves a wide mixture of more level-appropriate monsters, from Level 30 to 40 bumming around, attempting to get themselves sorted.

Anyone who has gone hunting or hell, even taken a walk in the woods would be very clear on the idea that you just don't stumble over animals every few meters. Well, unless it's a bunch of squirrels. The coming of the System altered that in a few ways.

Firstly, it evolved most creatures, so even insects and ants can sometimes be the size of a dog. Add in the fact that some of the trees have become deadly monsters and you can see how the population of "nasty things that want to eat me" have increased in the wilderness.

Secondly, the increase in Mana has actually increased fertility rates and growth rates for most creatures. While it doesn't seem to have changed the incubation period for human women, we've certainly seen a spike in pregnancies—including among women who swear they're on the pill or have been using other contraceptive methods. I recall lipreading a particularly gruesome conversation about an IUD that the nurse could no longer find no matter how hard they tried. Whitehorse has seen a large number of pregnancies, many of which have resulted in births with very few complications. This effect seems even more pronounced with the animals and monsters that lurk outside the city.

Thirdly, when the System builds up too high a level of Mana in any one zone and can't locate an appropriate monster to dump the excess Mana into, it does one of two things. It either creates a new dungeon or it will "spawn" a new monster. Technically, the System uses the Mana buildup to teleport new monsters from another location in the System, often another Dungeon World, to the affected zone. It's how some of the weirdest monsters we have have made an appearance.

And as any good biologist will tell you, an invasive species that doesn't have a natural predator will grow unchecked more often than not. So what would be explosive growth anyway becomes a tsunami of monsters.

Lastly, Bosses are often Alpha monsters and their presence adds to the growth rates and strength of any group they lead. More often than not, a couple of unchecked Bosses are what triggers a swarm and why they're the hunting target of choice. Of course, there's some futility in all that—killing the Bosses doesn't reduce the flow of Mana. It just means that the System ends up having to pick another method to control the Mana flow.

In fully transitioned Dungeon Worlds, Mana flows are much more stable. Zones and the monsters that live in each zone rarely shift as the Mana-soaked ecosystem stabilizes among a few dominant species. Swarms do happen but are much rarer because Adventurers and the local populace are out much more frequently and are more level appropriate, dealing with the monster buildups before they become an issue.

I end up thinking about all of this as I watch Mikito, Lana, and the puppies do most of the damage. I step in occasionally, but other than keeping Thousand Steps—a shared movement skill of mine—active, I'm somewhat superfluous. Until we hit something in the Level 60s, this pair can more than handle themselves. Even using Thousand Steps is a waste, other than as a small chance for me to train in its use. It doesn't mean that I don't have to occasionally kill a few monsters myself, mind you. Stupid levels of aggression are another System addition that results in the increase in danger while we're hunting.

As I bend to loot another body, tossing the System-generated loot directly into my inventory without looking at it, I can't help but take a look at the pair's Levels again, studying them in more detail. It's the first time I've done it in a while, and I have to say I'm slightly surprised by how much information Ali can display now.

Mikito Sato (Samurai Level 42)

HP: 590/590

MP: 250/250

Conditions: Thousand Steps, Hasted

Lana Pearson (Beast Tamer Level 40)

HP: 280/280

MP: 560/560

Conditions: Thousand Steps, Bestial Senses, Linked x 4

"That's new," I mutter, staring at the information display before glancing at Ali.

"Like it?" The Spirit floats over, waving, and suddenly all but the Hit Points disappear. "Could keep it simpler too."

"Mixture maybe? Remove everything but the hit points in a fight? And maybe Mana. Though how accurate is that?" I frown.

Ali raises his hand, waggling his hands sideways. "So-so. Depends on whether they've got any counter-measures in place. Anyone playing at the higher levels will have purchased at least a minimum obfuscation package. Can't pierce those just yet, not at my level. Hit Points are a lot easier to gauge."

"Right, Hit Points only then. The Conditions might be good, Resistances would be better," I add.

"I could pull those from the party sheet, but not for opponents. Not yet anyways," Ali answers, shrugging. "Though I've got wider access to general monster databases now, so I'll be able to provide that information if it becomes important."

"Come on, we should catch up," I say, realizing the pair has waded deeper into the group of half-horse, half-mantis armor-plated creatures. I can barely see them as they get swarmed, the pets and Mikito fighting to keep Lana safe in the center. I hit the group with Polar Zone, slowing everyone—including my friends. Truth is, a Fireball would have been the better choice, but something about getting toasted alive makes people grumpy.

Whine, whine, whine.

***

My sword glows red, the attack enhanced for a second by my Skill Cleave. It slices apart the hand-sized monster with ease, dropping separate pieces to the ground. I stomp on them before they can begin wiggling toward each other. Too small finally to reform, the Frazak Beast dies. Already, the ladies and Ali are swooping around, scooping up System-generated loot. We leave the bodies. I'm not sure even the hungry would want to eat the slimy, ectoplasmic remains of the Frazak. Definitely not carrying them back in my Altered Space.

"Well, that was weird," I sigh and shake my head.

I step aside as a root from a nearby tree humps to the slime before it drains it from the ground at an astounding rate. Following the root back to the ash tree it originated from, I make a note of it for future reference. Might be that Sally, our resident gnome Alchemist, would want to know about it.

I'm silently grateful for the visual aid my helmet gives me. It's still not as good as bright daylight, but between the automatic motion detection software, light enhancement, and infrared layering, it's more than good enough to stay out here after sunset. Which is a good thing, considering how little daylight we're getting as the solstice approaches. That being said…

"How are you ladies seeing?" I ask.

"Beast Master enhancement," Lana replies, and I nod. Like her enhanced sense of smell and hearing, Lana seems to be picking up certain traits from her connection with her pets as she levels. Wonder if she'll ever gain the ability to fly. Or a tail?

"Gene Therapy," Mikito adds as she flicks her armor plate into bare space, the plate disappearing into thin air. Of course, I know she's just putting it into inventory, but it does seem like magic.

Sometimes, I wonder how much of us is still human. Certainly, the things we can do, the changes made to and on our bodies, has shifted us far from baseline human. Add things like gene therapy, cyberware, and other enhancements and you have to wonder, are we even human anymore? The way we all handle pain and injury is so different—these days, safety standards are significantly laxer. Who cares if you break a bone if it heals within a few minutes? Even chopped off limbs can be regrown or replaced.

With a thought, my status information forms in front of me and once more I survey the "new" me.

Status Screen			
Name	John Lee	Class	Erethran Honor Guard
Race	Human (Male)	Level	34
Titles			
Monster's Bane, Redeemer of the Dead			
Health	1580	Stamina	1580
Mana	1220	Mana Regeneration	89 / minute

Attributes			
Strength	88	Agility	149
Constitution	158	Perception	55
Intelligence	122	Willpower	124
Charisma	16	Luck	27
Class Skills			
Mana Imbue	1	Blade Strike	2
Thousand Steps	1	Altered Space	2
Two are One	1	The Body's Resolve	3
Greater Detection	1	Instantaneous Inventory*	1
Soul Shield	2	Blink Step	2
Cleave*	2	Frenzy*	1
Elemental Strike*	1 (Ice)	Tech Link*	2
Combat Spells			
Improved Minor Healing (II)		Greater Regeneration	
Greater Healing		Mana Drip	
Improved Mana Dart (IV)		Enhanced Lightning Strike	
Fireball		Polar Zone	

Since the Onlivik Spore Dungeon, I picked up a few new toys for my combat arsenal. In particular, I upgraded some of my attacks and spells. The first new, out-of-Class Skill I purchased was an upgrade to Cleave. The nice thing about the upgrade is that while it only increases my basic strikes by another 25%, the Mana cost has stayed the same. It isn't all-powerful, but it's certainly a useful upgrade.

Elemental Strike gives me another way of layering damage. As monsters go up in levels, their resistances to basic damage increases, which means layering damage types becomes more and more important. Fire might be more generically popular, but the damn collateral damage of unchecked flames has a tendency to make me leery of using it too often. There are weirder elemental options, like radiation or darkness, but for now, I'll stick to the traditional elements.

Lastly, I picked up a support Skill from the basic Erethran Guard tree. I really should have gone poking into their specialized Skill set beforehand, just to see what I had been missing out on, but I'd been lost in the shiny of the numerous other Skills available. While most of their Skills aren't much better than what's available to other Classes—or in a few cases, worse—Tech Link is particularly interesting. For each level, I can designate a specific tech and enhance its performance and connection to me. No surprise, but I designated both my Neural Link and Sabre. The boost in performance and my connection to Sabre was impressive, and given enough time and Levels, it could be a major game changer. Sadly, the next Level up is pretty expensive in the Shop.

To round out my purchases and my usefulness, I now have a more powerful healing spell and a Mana regeneration buff, both of which I figure will be useful for longer fights. I could do with a combat spell or two more, but the good stuff is extremely expensive. Better to save up the Credits for something great rather than a couple of goods.

I've been holding back on adding to my Class Skills with my free Skill Points. I'm still uncertain of which route to go down, and if at all possible, I want to save enough points so that when the third tier of my Skill Tree unlocks at Level 40, I can pick up a bunch of those Skills at once. Portal and Army of One look amazing, while Sanctum might make a huge difference one of these days. A skill that basically blocks every type of attack for a set time limit seems rather overpowered. Then again, I have a Skill that teleports people. If you look at it that way, there must be a bunch of Skills that teleport attacks past barriers. Heck, would a line of sight spell just require me to see them to cast?

That's one of the problems about the way we get abilities and Skills through the System. We learn them instinctively, the same way we grow up knowing how to make our hearts beat. A purchased Skill just is—something you can use but not necessarily improve. Most people are happy with that, but then you hit questions like mine, where a better understanding of a spell and what it does would probably answer my question.

That's the thing about the System. While I won't say there's a Dungeon Master or something out there balancing the System, with the sheer number of people, Skills, and abilities out there, it's impossible to say that any single Skill, piece of equipment, or Class is the trump card to beat all trump cards. At least, none that I've come across yet.

When the ladies break off, heading for another set of tracks Lana has spotted, I tag along. The System continues to puzzle and infuriate me. It works incredibly well as a seamless integration that constantly enhances our bodies and lives. However, once you're in, you're in. Surviving the System and the Dungeon World without its benefits is impossible. On top of that, Classes, Skills, spells, all of those fade away the farther you are from the System Core. At the edges of System-occupied space, you can only rely on your existing Mana pools.

It's why we never had various aliens visit us before our introduction to the System—no one wants to go from Superman to Clark Kent. Well, except for bad writers who have run out of stories to tell. If the System is Apple—industry leader but a closed ecosystem—then you've got to wonder about the Windows and Linux options out there and how to access them. Certainly, accessing methods of gaining power outside of the System would be heavily discouraged—if not potentially lethal.

As much as I have learnt about the System, I still have more questions. Each answer just generates more questions. I don't have even the beginning of an explanation of why the System can so casually break the laws of physics and common sense. Nor do I know why the System was coded to create Dungeon Worlds on populated planets or why it automatically conscripts everyone. Sure, more people equals more loot which means more Credits and gear, but Credits seem like such a prosaic reason. At least when you're talking about something that affects entire galaxies. Power and control make more sense, but it doesn't explain the abilities and Classes that allow anyone to level. If you want to control the populace, you don't hand out plutonium and a nuclear bomb DIY kit. It's a puzzle and one that I've even got a Quest for.

The System Quest

You've begun to grasp the very edges of the meaning of the System. However, there is much more to learn with an uncertain reward at the end. Will you continue the journey?

The fact that hundreds of thousands of people have tried to complete the System Quest and failed is rather discouraging. The System Quest is also known as the Fool's Quest among the Galactics. Hundreds, maybe even millions, of scholars, adventurers, and explorers have tried and failed over the years. Ali himself got exasperated with me when I started poking into it. Yet something in my gut tells me that the System Quest is the key to it all and that the more I understand the System, the more I'll understand this insane world I live in.

Problem is, none of these musings are actually relevant to my day-to-day life. My current problem is the Duchess and whatever else she has planned for the city. I have to admit it grates on my nerves that my help was dismissed so casually, but in this, I have to trust Roxley. Unfortunately, it's hard to do so when the man's just too damn good-looking.

"Penny for your thoughts?" Lana says as she taps her foot and I realize I've been lagging again.

"Just thinking about Roxley," I reply without thought. For a moment, I see a tightening in her eyes before she smiles.

"Enjoying the fact that your boyfriend's back?" Lana says.

"Not my boyfriend. And no, not that. I'm wondering about the Duchess and Roxley and what's the plan," I say.

"Does it matter? They're all the same," Lana replies, her voice suddenly bitter. "We're just pawns to them. Toys to play with and, when we're broken, to be thrown away."

"Lana…" I fall silent. I'm not even sure where to start. Truthfully, I sometimes have my doubts about the Tuinnar but… "Roxley's better than most of the other options."

She grunts, clearly irritated by my words, and looks away.

Mikito looks between us for a second before she spins her naginata to lop off a reaching vine. "It's late. We should consider resting. Carcross is closer."

I grunt, glancing at the minimap in the corner of my eyes. We're actually not much closer to Carcross than Whitehorse. Carcross has the distinction of being the last existing human settlement outside of Whitehorse in the Yukon, even if it is barely more than a couple dozen buildings and a couple hundred people. Still, the town has well-defended walls and friends we haven't seen in a while. If that's the reason why Mikito wants us to go, I'm not complaining.

"Whatever," Lana says dismissively. "Let's just get this over with. There's probably some decent hunting on the way there."

"Just follow me, toots, I got this," Ali says, waving us forward.

Well, I guess we're headed to Carcross.

Chapter 3

It's been nearly a month and a half since I've visited Carcross. I'll admit, I've been concerned about Lana's state of mind. Then of course, Roxley came back, and after that, the Kapre arrived and I decided to keep an eye on them, just in case. Trust but verify, you know. And well, time flies when your time is spent fighting and killing and training.

It's no excuse, not really. I have friends here, survivors who have lost friends and family to the System and fought by my side through the worst of it. Then again, who hasn't lost someone? I might not have seen my family's bodies, but I checked with the Shop. It took me a long time to get the courage to do so, and sometimes, I wish I didn't. The faint hope was comforting, like a child's baby blanket. Having it ripped away made me want to scream and cry. Luckily, I channeled the grief into a more mature, considered response and went on a forty-eight-hour genocidal rampage outside of town with Lana and Mikito.

The party ends up coming toward the city at an angle and we have to skirt around the wall until we hit the gates. We could easily jump the fifteen-foot concrete barrier—the bigger problem is the automated defenses and the force field surrounding the town. As we traverse the edge of the wall in their clear zone, I can't help but note the slightly scrunched up faces that peer down at us, most of them sporting a beard. Dwarves. Funnily enough, they're pretty much everything you'd expect them to be—outside of the smithing thing. As I understand it, this is a small Clan who's fallen on hard times, so their presence here is as much a matter of colonizing as guarding. Either way, their presence adds a seasoned, professional force to the civilian guards within Carcross. It was something they desperately needed when the swarms increased in intensity.

Surprisingly, the gates are open and we're not the only ones arriving. A group of five, carrying an assortment of swords, guns, and bows, walk in ahead of us, towing a sled piled with corpses. None of the five look human, though three could pass if you squinted and ignored skin color, additional appendages, and frill. One looks very much like a traditional Klingon with a weird frill on its face and arms so thick around, you'd need a pair of hands to grasp them. A second is short at four and a half feet but makes up for its size with its additional four arms located in the center of its bulbous body. An extra pair of eyes stare at us from its torso, while the last humanoid creature is bright blue with scales all across its body. Mostly though, I'm staring at the spherical creature that totters above them on too-thin legs, four eyes rolling along tracks across its body. The humanoid velociraptor barely gets a glance after that.

The Dwarves on duty wave the Galactics in as a matter of routine before they turn back to their own conversations. They speak in a language that I don't understand until Ali does his thing and the gibberish becomes English. In this case, they're mostly discussing how pretty Mikito is, if a touch too tall for a proper Dwarf spouse.

"Oy. Stop staring like yokels," Ali calls out to our group, and we start, realizing we've all come to a standstill in front of the gates.

Out of the corner of my eye, I see some of the Dwarves laughing at us. I growl slightly, and Mikito places a hand on my arm, shaking her head.

Right. Friendly territory. No starting fights.

"What the hell is going on?" I mutter as I gun the bike, drifting inward.

One of the Dwarves moves to cut me off and I shoot him a look that has him reaching for his weapon. Good sense prevails as one of the other Dwarves waves down the overeager bunny.

Inside, the town has grown. What used to be only a dozen or so buildings has sprawled with the addition of a baker's dozen of new buildings, each of them at least four stories tall. Residences and stores seem to make up the most of them, with the new construction having that weird silvery sheen of default

System-created construction. Right next to the city center, a large six-story building dwarfs the old log buildings. It's this large building that the Galactics approach and enter with their kills.

As much as the layout of the city has changed, what's more surprising is the mixture of individuals tramping around the town. While humans still dominate, clumps of aliens are easy to spot, none of them seeming to elicit even a nasty look from the locals. Considering one of them looks like a typical horned devil with tail, that's pretty impressive.

"Huh. An official Guild house," Ali says as the puppies come up next to me. I look at him, and he points at the big building the group went into. "Carcross managed to seal a deal with the Rolling Sea Guild. That's where most of these Galactics are from."

"You know that you're just saying words right now, right?" I mutter, shaking my head. "Context, man."

"Right, right. Ignorant human." Ali rotates himself upside down while he continues to talk. "Guilds are like, well, guilds. Corporations, I guess, in your parlance. Just, you know, more individual? Anyway, powerful Guilds can rival countries in size and members. The Rolling Sea Guild is a Tier IV Adventuring Guild with about two thousand members and an average level of 36.7."

All three of us stare at him, waiting for him to continue.

The annoying, shoulder-pad-dressed brown Spirit draws the silence out until I'm almost about to shout at him. "Adventuring Guilds are always looking for unexploited, unclaimed leveling zones. Finding one and getting the right to set up a guild hall here gives them a huge advantage."

"Halls are limited?" Lana asks immediately, and Ali nods.

"Yup, by size and ranking of the safe zone. It's why Carcross has one and Whitehorse doesn't."

I grunt, nodding slowly. Our lack of a safe zone arises from the fact that we've yet to exit Village stage, which is due to us not hitting the minimum threshold required to stabilize the Mana flows in Whitehorse. Carcross, being an initially smaller town, had fewer buildings to purchase, which gave them a significant advantage over Whitehorse.

"Adventuring Guilds build guild halls. Got it. What do they do?" I ask.

"A variety of things. Reduced teleportation costs for guild members between guild halls, access to guild storage, training halls for increased experience gain, and safe areas for rest are the main things. Guilds sometimes also have contracts with smaller Shops, which set up physical stores in their halls, letting them bypass the System Shop," Ali answers.

"Let me get this straight. Carcross made a deal with this guild to use their only…?" At Ali's nod, I continue with more confidence. "Only guild hall space for them. They provide additional defense and, of course, killing of monsters. That sound about right?"

"Pretty much, boy-o."

"That just sounds like they've painted a target on their back," I mutter.

"Just about,' Ali confirms.

Mikito looks puzzled and Lana's face is blank, so I fill them in. I guess they don't have as much experience with Galactic politics as I do. "The other guilds aren't going to like it because it means the Rollers will get more powerful if they aren't kept in check. That means they'll likely take steps to hurt both Carcross and the Rollers. Ali, they must have known that was going to happen."

"Of course. Best guess? They're gambling. Just like Roxley. If they can hang on long enough to power up their people and the city, they'll be able to get to the next tier and upgrade themselves again. If they can keep upgrading, everyone who might want a place this small will be left in the dust. And the bigger fish will be angling for Whitehorse rather than Carcross."

"And if they fail?" Lana asks, her brows drawn together.

"Then they might die. At the very least, they'll lose a lot of prestige and Credits."

"I meant the city."

"Same thing." Ali shrugs disinterestedly.

"Dangerous," I say, and Mikito nods. Still, I can see why the Carcross City Council did it. They couldn't hold the town, not with the few hunters they have left. Even with the Dwarven clan, the number of swarms must have been pressuring them significantly. And if you're refusing to leave, then better to act—however bad it might be in the future—than sit around doing nothing.

Still, the guild presence here explains why the monster numbers around the city were lower than we expected. It also explains why I haven't been getting subtle suggestions from Jason or the Elder to come visit. The Carcross City Council might not even want us here—I'm not entirely sure Roxley will be happy with this development. That being said, the Tuinnar might already know about this.

"Well, are we going to say hi or not?" Lana finally says, pointing forward.

I open my mouth then shut it with a snap. She's right. We're here, so we might as well say hi and get something to drink. Whatever decisions they've made, it's done and over with. Time to see some old friends.

***

"Jason. Rachel," I greet the pair when we finally track them down.

Surprisingly, they're in a rather spacious condo on the top floor of one of the new buildings. Inside, floor-to-ceiling windows give us a nearly complete view of the walls. A good thing too, considering Jason is the town's most powerful Mage and Rachel's only a short hop behind him. The wiry teenager is grinning with an arm around his First Nation girlfriend as he waits for us to troop in and take off our shoes.

Surprisingly—and thankfully—when we poked our heads into the City Center, Elder Badger was out, resting. It wasn't uncommon to find her working late into the evenings before, so it's obvious that the new additions to the city seem to have taken some of the burden off her. Even with our boosted Constitutions, most of us needed at least a few hours of sleep a day to reset our brains and not completely crash.

Not finding the Elder meant that our next stop was locating Jason and Rachel. Being the local celebrity he is, that wasn't difficult.

From the way Jason is holding his robe closed, I'm assuming we interrupted some naughty time. Either that or he likes to sleep in his boxers. Idly, I check him out. He's filled out even more, leaving behind the scrawny teenager I once knew. He's no gym rat, but he doesn't look as though he'd get blown away by a stiff wind either.

Rachel, on the other hand, looks, well, older. The sixteen-year-old teenage girl has matured, her face slightly chubbier with new bags under her eyes. There's no bounce in her step, and there are new lines on her face as she clings to Jason's arm. The scars from losing first her village then most of her team seem to linger, and the once-tough teen seems more fragile, more prone to shatter.

"You do know it's, like, eleven, right?" Jason grumbles good-naturedly as he plops himself into a chair, Rachel curling up in his arms immediately.

"Yeah, yeah. We can leave if you want." I turn, and he flicks a glowing blue ball at my head that shocks me ever so slightly.

"What John is trying to say is it's good to see you too." Lana sits next to the pair on the spare space on the couch. "How are you two doing?"

"Not bad. Things have been pretty good actually, ever since the Guild came. You saw, right?" Jason waves in the general direction of the city.

"Hard to miss," Ali says.

"How is that going?" I ask.

"Mike's been grumbling a bit, but they've been a real help, you know?" Jason answers.

I nod slightly. I'm sure Gadsby's grumbling is the same as Andrea's. Both the ex-RCMP members have a long list of complaints about civilians wandering around with the ability to destroy houses in their fingers. I know the pair spend long hours talking about ways to reconcile Canadian and Galactic laws. Personally, I think they're wasting a lot of effort, but no one's asking me.

As Jason and I chat, Lana murmurs something to Rachel, who shakes her head.

"Right. Girl talk time. You boys get out," Lana abruptly announces, pointing at us.

"Huh?"

"Out," Lana repeats.

Jason lets out a sigh, pulling his hand away from Rachel, who squeezes it for a second before finally releasing him, and beckons me to follow. A short jaunt later, we're out of the walls and wandering the night-time woods, idly patrolling for potential monsters. Jason calls up a series of bright yellow-green lights that hover around him and attack threats without warning as we walk. One thing Carcross still doesn't have is a bar—the Elder's insistence of keeping the place "dry" seems to hold, even with the new Guild in place. Understandable, even if annoying.

I finally break the silence as the smell of roasting owl assaults my nose. "What was that about?"

"Ah. Well. That. I'm going to be a father," Jason says. "Thought we had that covered—literally—but..."

"Yeah, we worked that one out from Richard's..." *Exploits*. I never finish the sentence though, the memory of the friend we've lost darkening the conversation.

"Seems self-defeating. The Shop sells alterations that let you neuter yourself, but it constantly breaks down. I've even heard of some women, older women, umm..." Jason stutters, blushing.

"Older women...? Having sex?" I tease. "You know, older people are humans too."

He glares at me even as the redness in his face grows. "Menstrual cycle reversing."

"You mean meno-pause becoming meno-start?" Ali says, cackling.

I glare at the Spirit. "Don't make me banish you."

"Yeah, that." Jason brushes at his face, pushing up non-existent glasses. He tilts his head and waves, refreshing his attack spell in a casual display of power.

"Cute spell. They look like guided Mana Bolts sort of."

Jason nods. "Tinkered with the formula a bit." As a bolt slams into a nearby tree and then another and then another, he sighs and recasts the spell. "Of course, it's still a work in progress."

"Uh huh. Think the tree's dead."

In the back of my mind, I'm thinking about what he said about the Shop. The way it keeps regenerating people, fixing them, even reversing old biology. As if it's attempting to increase our population whether we want it to or not. Almost like a self-replicating virus, continuously infecting host computers every time it can, searching for flaws in the operating system and copying itself into new storage devices. Except in this case, it's attempting to create the computers it needs to use.

System Quest Update (+500 XP)

The System continually replicates itself, creating new host bodies. Why would it do that?

Really? A quest update over that? I shake my head, dismissing the notification as I glance at Ali, who is busy bopping the Mana Darts with his finger. Now why the hell would I get that?

"Congratulations, by the way," I add belatedly.

"Thanks," Jason answers, his face growing serious.

Right, he's still a kid himself, and being a dad this young can't be easy. For a moment, I wonder what education will be like in this world. After all, purchasing skills for things like basic mathematics, science, and other social sciences isn't that expensive in the System. Why bother with formal schooling? Would schools in the future involve combat and Skill applications rather than classes on physics and English? Or would we continue with the old traditions since then we'd at least know they understood the basics. Really understood them.

"So tell me about the spell. Maybe I can learn something," I ask.

Jason brightens up as he explains what he did. Distractions. Always useful.

A couple of hours and circuits around the town to the river and back later, a pair of cloaked figures fade into sight in front of us. It's slow and gentle enough that it doesn't trigger an automatic attack from Jason's spell or myself. The first of the newcomers is a semi-transparent humanoid that floats, clad in tight leather that leaves little to the imagination. I find myself staring at its groin, the pair of cylinders that jut out fascinating in a disturbing way. Looking away from him (it?), its humanoid friend has four arms, its skin a yellow-green metallic sheen. Instead of a head, it has a variety of tubular connections with shining lights.

Eilon Lindrak (Level 7 Eldritch Knight)

HP: 1530/1530

MP: 320/320

Conditions: Insubstantial

Ixlimin Ldrik (Level 49 Mecaniservant)

HP: 570/570

MP: 740/740

Conditions: None

"You are not on the patrol schedule today, Jason," Ixlimin speaks. His voice sounds canned and just a little too high, the noise setting my teeth on edge.

"*Boy-o, the Knight's an Advanced Class, by the way,*" Ali mutters.

I blink, staring at the pair. Jesus, it'd be nice if there was a way to tell a bit easier. Then again, Squire, Knight… I guess that works.

"Just out for a walk with a friend," Jason replies, his body angled slightly away from them.

"Who is your friend?" Ixlimin says, and again, I feel my body tensing. It's the kind of voice you'd hear if you watched a bad 80s science-fiction movie filled with evil AIs and robots.

"Don't say it. The walking blender already knows," Ali says, glaring at Ixlimin.

"A Spirit Companion. How novel," Ixlimin says, staring at Ali.

Ali glares back, his eyes narrowing, and an uncomfortable silence falls as the pair stare at each other.

"So…" I add a smile. "I'm John Lee."

Thank the gods the language purchases include body language so they know what I mean when I smile. Otherwise, who knows—I might be challenging them to an eating contest.

"You are from Whitehorse," Eilon states, and I nod. "Has the city achieved its next rank yet?"

"No." As far as I know, the only thing holding us back is the lack of purchased spaces. We're actually pretty close now, and once that's done, I'm sure we'll rank up. After all, Carcross did.

"Aaargh!" Ali shouts, glaring at Ixlimin, and I reach sideways. Jason shoots a look between us, his hand curling up slightly while Ixlimin stands there smiling. "You damn blender!"

"What's going on, Ali?" I ask tensely. I really don't want to try fighting these two. No guarantee that Jason will back me up and together, they might be really pushing things for me.

"Freaking blender's a M453-X. They're sort of like the Spores—shared central consciousness through data uploads. I was trying to figure out if the computer here had a connection. He blocked me. And stole some information about you," Ali said tensely.

"Stole?" I growl softly.

"An exaggeration of facts. Your Spirit is lax and dropped his defenses while he assaulted my data sectors. Certain information leaked," Ixlimin says. "My system, I am programmed to acquire information. Any information."

"So you grabbed what you found?"

"Yes."

"And now you've uploaded it to this shared database?"

"No," Ixlimin says, his voice still flat and toneless. "I have yet to earn the necessary uploading privileges. Direct upload is reserved for those Rank III and above."

"You guys rank yourself?" I tilt my head, curious about the robot. Android? Cyborg? I'm not entirely sure. I'll have to clarify with Ali later.

"The Program has grown such that individuals must be ranked. It is the only logical option to ensure the optimal in-flow of information. My reports are still provided on a regular basis, but it has been determined that those below Rank III have insufficiently important information to require the burden on resources a direct connection would accrue," Ixlimin replies.

"Thanks. You're being quite helpful here," I say, glancing at Ali, who still seethes with a rather constipated expression on his face. "*You're being quiet.*"

"*Updating my firewalls. Bastard cut through my base ones like butter,*" Ali thinks back at me. "*Don't trust him. The Ixlimin are like your Borg. Or maybe Mormons might be a better fit. Unrelenting in their goal of expanding the Program. If it weren't for the System's interference in their Program, they'd probably be running around in giant cubes.*"

"It has been decided that providing clear, concise information about the Program when asked is the most efficient method of removing concerns about our goals," Ixlimin says.

"And that's when I say enough," Eilon adds, holding up a hand. "If I let him, Ixlimin will talk your ear off about the Program and we're still on patrol. Not that there's been much to do."

"Noticed that. You guys didn't get hit much by the Swarm, did you?" I ask.

"No, passed us by. We tracked it on the scanners, but outside of a few outliers, the general level around Carcross is too high to be affected. Yet," Eilon says, then adds, "Peace out."

"*Did he just say what he said?*"

"Translation error. The Eilon have a somewhat similar saying, just without the hippie connotations. Properly translated, it'd be 'May the rains of peace fall and the winds of war blow past till our next meeting'," Ali helpfully says, and I nod slightly.

"Peace out," I repeat, smiling slightly. Well, when in Rome.

Jason, of course, stares at me as the pair leave, but I give him a grin. When they're gone, I prod him to get back to teaching since he doesn't seem inclined to talk about his feelings.

***

The next time we see the girls awake, it's morning and Lana's hogging the bathroom. Thankfully, the Clean spell works just as well for our purpose, so Jason and I end up doing the cooking for breakfast. The sheer volume of food we need to feed five Adventurers with enhanced metabolisms is staggering— we probably could have fed a few Sumo wrestlers in the meantime. Amusingly enough, Jason has a Skill that allows him to throw together our breakfast extra fast, which relegates me to doing prep work. I'm okay with that—my cooking is, as best, edible.

When Lana finally makes her way out of the bathroom, Mikito steps in from the balcony, where she's been running through her forms. I'm amazed she manages to swing her polearm on the tiny balcony and not destroy anything, but I guess that's why she's a master martial artist and I'm just a hack with a pointy piece of metal. I try not to be too bitter about it—it's not as if I haven't gotten a lot better in the last few months, especially for a rank beginner. Between her lessons and Roxley's, I've even gotten a veneer of skill. Doesn't hurt that the System seems to boost my understanding of what I need to do whether or not I want it to.

Frankly, the sheer amount of changes the System makes on both a physical, mental, and somewhat social level is frightening. While the exact changes might not be as bad as the numbers on our stat sheets make it seem, it's still clear that the System is reaching right into us and making changes on a daily basis. If I were a spiritual man, I might even be a bit afraid for my soul. I know that the churches and the remaining spiritual figures in town have been somewhat stretched in explaining both the System and the apocalypse. I don't envy them that. I wonder how many have done the spiritual equivalent of sticking their fingers in their ears and going "na-na-na-nah"?

"Earth to tall, dumb, and brooding," Ali says as he buzzes in front of me.

I blink, realizing I've gotten lost in my thoughts once again. It's a bit of a worrying habit, one that I used to do a lot of pre-apocalypse. Mostly when I was under a lot of stress at work or avoiding thinking about uncomfortable facts—like the amount of time my now-ex spent on the phone with her "friend" in Whitehorse. I haven't done that in ages, so finding myself doing so again is a bit concerning.

"Sorry." I wave guiltily and look around. "I miss anything?"

"Just a discussion of what we're going to do. We can sell our loot and the bodies in Carcross at the Guild. It will work out to be a minor loss in most cases and a decent gain in others. If we do that, we can hit the nearby mountain range and go hunting for something more Level appropriate," Mikito says.

I grunt and look at Lana, who nods firmly. I'm not thrilled with the idea of running around killing even more monsters for the heck of it, but it does need to be done and we might find something interesting. Maybe a Dungeon or two.

"Coming?" I ask Jason. I know from our talks last night he's been raring to do a bit more challenging hunting. I wasn't so horrible of a friend to not actually chat about things he might need or want.

"Can't. I have a couple of meetings today. Andrea wants to go over the development plans for the city, see if we can chart out the best upgrades to buy," Jason says.

"Huh." I rub my chin before shrugging. Teaches him to volunteer the fact that he was a huge gamer beforehand. Now that the world plays similar to some of our old computer games, figuring out how to streamline your development options is something he'd be pretty good at. Even if he does need to be reminded once in a while that his choices have real-world consequences. The optimal route might not be the best route, not when there aren't any extra lives or game restarts. "Your loss. We'll hit the Guild then and get hunting."

I wish I could say the Guild was mind-blowingly awesome, a mixture of the streets in Harry Potter and Valerian's floating alien city. Instead, it's more akin to visiting a pawnshop. We dump our stock, there's a brief argument between the counter attendant and Ali, and we're on our way. The Shop when I first visited it, with its holographic walls, modern furniture, and glowing blue screens, was a lot closer to a science fiction shopping experience than this.

On the road again, the puppies take off at a speed I'm hard-pressed to keep up with, even with Sabre in mecha mode. We head toward Tagish, starting on the highway but quickly enough diverting into the tree line and the mountainside. Lana and Ali converse together at the front, using the extended senses of the puppies and Ali's direct link into the System's backend to hunt down threats for us.

It's the usual plethora of the weird and nasty. Mutated Earth animals like an Arctic Fox or a Snow Owl, both of which wield impressive control over the lower end of the temperature spectrum. An Ice Bear that is busy freezing trees then eating them as popsicles. And then of course there're the aliens. Elemental Salamanders whose bodies are so transparent, you can see the light blue lines of frozen blood that pump in greater haste as they throw icicles at us. Fluffy

Snow Elementals that refuse to die no matter how many times we cut them, till we figure out it is their core we need to shatter. A flock of Crystal Birds that kamikaze us as they dive, shattering on our bodies before reforming and flying again, ever smaller till they finally can't reform anymore.

Post-apocalypse Earth is filled with the weird and dangerous, and our job is to kill them all. I find myself tossing Fireballs and Mana Darts constantly, rotating between the two spells because it's easier than cutting apart most of these creatures. I almost regret not purchasing a damn flamethrower for Sabre, until I remember that burning down forests is one of the things we're desperately trying not to do before the onset of winter.

Still would be useful right now.

Fighting monsters in their mid-40s to low 50s means I'm not bored anymore, that I have to focus and pay attention and do damage. It's not thrilling, not "flying by the seat of your pants and make a mistake and die" fighting, but it's better. I'm awake again, focused. Kind of worrying that I've been getting a bit jaded with fighting for my life.

Our trip takes us up, up toward the top of the mountain ranges, and on a whim more than practical sense, it seems, we find ourselves climbing to the top of the range. A hike that should have taken us hours and left us winded, we finish in an hour and a bit and only because we have to stop and kill more monsters. There aren't many up here, so we mostly just run, jump, and bounce our way up.

For a time, we stand and survey the lands around us. The snow-covered forests look so pristine and peaceful from a distance. A winding river, portions of it iced over, and frozen lakes, many of which look no different than the ground surrounding them but for a minor depression spread out before us as we relax. The skies are mostly clear, outside of a few flying gryphons and silver-colored avians. Oh, and the Dragon.

"Dragon!" I hiss, ducking and cursing.

It's a hell of a distance away, so far that it's mostly a dive-bombing speck, but there's no such thing as far enough away when it comes to those creatures. The last thing we want to do is have it notice us and lead it back to our home. Bringing burning death to towns is bad. Lana and Mikito drop too, hunkering down low to the ground, and Ali stops hovering.

Dragons come in variations—from the almost-Dragons of Drakes and Wyrms to full-on, fire-breathing flying monsters of legend. Thus far, the ones we've spotted look like a cross between a Chinese Dragon and your typical western one with a long serpent body with giant wings that lift the creature. Real Dragons start at Level 100 for the juveniles, and an elder Dragon can easily cross Level 300. Ali once told me a story of Praxard, one of seven legendary Dragons that had been attacked by the Empire of Kingul. In retaliation for the attack, Praxard decided to destroy Morix IV, a sparsely populated planet that had just reached stage two of its terraforming under the aegis of the Empire. It had taken Praxard four hours to do the job.

Thankfully, Dragons seem to run by the manliest of reptile codes and don't band together or support one another. It's probably the only reason why they haven't overrun everyone else and become the de facto rulers of everything. I sometimes regret not taking the Dragon Knight class when I had the option. When it comes down to one-on-one battle prowess, their Class Skills are significantly more powerful than the Erethran Honor Guards. Even if the Dragon Knights mostly fight lesser versions of the Dragons on their home world, they still kick ass.

"What is it doing?" Lana mutters, staring into the distance.

Vision magnified as much as possible, I watch as the Dragon swoops down again, breathing a spray of white smoke that dissipates quickly. Humanoid figures freeze in their tracks as the smoke touches them.

"Picking up a meal…" I mutter, watching as the Dragon wheels back casually and picks up a pair of the humanoid popsicles before winging away. As its wings beat, I note how the trees only seem to reach the humanoids' chests. Chest-high trees, big Dragon… "Those are Giants!"

"Frost Giants. Must be a clan that moved in recently. Average height of about forty feet," Ali adds.

Mikito's squinting, probably watching it all through the contact lenses she's purchased.

"Is it carrying the Giants off in its feet? Like a raven with a ground squirrel?" Lana says, unable to pick out details like we can. Even her Skill-enhanced eyes are unable to keep up with our technological tools.

"Yes," Mikito says, her face pale.

I'm probably not looking too good either. That Dragon must be enormous.

"Let's not fight that one," I say, and there are rapid nods from all around.

We wait and watch as the Dragon wings away, never once glancing our way. In fact, it barely seems to pay attention to anything around it, arrogantly flying back to its nest. Then again, I can't think of anything that could hurt it.

"*Ali, is it headed back to Kluane?*"

"*Yes. The icefields down that way are probably its nesting grounds. My guess, it's taken Mount Seymour as its home. Biggest icefields, tallest mountain, deepest inflow of Mana. Dragons are arrogant like that.*"

"*Not sure it's arrogance when it can back it up.*"

"*Point, boy-o, point.*"

When the Dragon is no more than a speck, we scurry down from the mountain, tails between our legs. Literally in the puppies' cases. Our hunting is more subdued and focused, all of us probably thinking the same thought.

We've got a long way to go.

Chapter 4

By common consensus, we spend the next few days working from Carcross, hunting and killing in the higher-level zones that dot the surroundings. After our distant encounter with the Dragon, the rest of our hunting trips are routine. Lots of blood and violence, lots of monsters killed and looted, and even the occasional injury, but nothing surprising. I'll admit, I get bored once again and start testing out new fighting techniques in the middle of battle just to liven things up. Forming a sword and kicking it straight through a monster is a lot more difficult than it looks in the animes.

Eventually, Rachel and Jason's subtle hints that they'd like their home back stop being subtle. Surprisingly, now that we're out of Whitehorse, Lana seems intent on not going back, at times almost rudely ignoring the couple. I have to admit, I'm getting a little antsy myself, considering what might be coming down the road for Whitehorse. In the end, it's a message passed on through the Carcross City Council that gets us moving—a new, high-level dungeon has been found.

The moment we get the notice, we dump most of the extra loot that we've been keeping for sale in Whitehorse's Shop with the Guild. There's no point—the single monster they located in the dungeon was level 55, so if we survive, the dungeon will give us better loot overall. Theoretically we could swing by Whitehorse, but Lana's insistent that we just do the dungeon. We acquiesce to her request and head straight for the coordinates, a hacked-together job of old GPS data and map coordinates that, thankfully, everyone with System access can figure out.

Up a mountain and around a series of trees, we're greeted by an interesting sight. A quintet of muscular humanoid bulls clad in white, modern battle armor stand opposite another group of humans. Even from a distance, the tension between the groups crackles in the air. No surprise—Bill's party has been one of the most outspoken against the Yerick.

"Capstan, Nelia, Aron," I call out a greeting to the three Yerick I know.

The other two are known, but I can't recall their names. I mean, I could look it up and read it off their nameplates and I do, but within moments, I've blanked again. You'd think that all the points I have in Intelligence would have made things like that easy to remember, but it might have as much to do with what I consider important or not. Their names, thus far, don't register on any scale. Funny thing is, the Yerick might look like minotaurs from Greek legends, but I don't think anyone ever envisioned an anatomically correct female minotaur. Not that you can really tell with Nelia, but could you imagine Greek statues of that?

Even as I muse on stupid things like that, I let my gaze roam over their group, noting a decent increase in Levels since the last time we fought together. That thought makes me look at Lana who, even with her face mostly hidden by Howard's fur, is showing conflicting emotions.

"Redeemer," Capstan rumbles, his voice like stones grating together. The leader of the Yerick towers over his group. "Are we all here?"

"I think so. Bill." I tilt my head toward the leader of the other group.

Outside of ours, Bill's group holds the highest number of high-Level humans in Whitehorse, so it's not surprising that he's here. Especially for an unknown, high-level dungeon. We might not see eye to eye on many things, but after our time in the Spore dungeon, we've gotten along better. Fighting beside someone has a tendency to do that. I'm also not surprised he didn't tell the council to bugger off. The experience bonus from completion alone is hard to turn down. My eyes rake over his group, studiously ignoring Luthien, my ex, and noting that Kevin, the son of a bitch she cheated on me with, isn't around.

__Bill Cross (Level 7 Clipper)__

HP: 1660/1660

MP: 930/930

__Luthien Celbrindal (Level 47 Sorceress)__

HP: 680/680

MP: 2,300/2,300

Damn. He's gotten an Advanced Class now. I'm really curious about what the experience was like, but I'm even more curious about his actual Class title.

"You a barber now?" I ask Bill, who frowns at me then laughs, shaking his head.

"You can read Classes," Bill says.

"It's a cheapish purchase in the Shop," I answer. Evasive, but truthful.

"It's just the term the System gave my class," Bill says.

"Any useful Class Skills?" I ask.

Bill shrugs with a half-smile. "I didn't realize we were at that point."

"Har. You've seen my tricks," I say. "And you never know what might be needed in the dungeon."

"No group Skills. I can layer damage on a single target significantly, and I have a 'go away' Skill now. It pushes back attackers. The rest are just Resistances," Bill says, and I nod in thanks. "You?"

"Not much new. More spells—Fireball you might see more of if it's not too tight in there. Otherwise, I can switch between playing defense or offense pretty fast."

Bill nods then glances at the Yerick, his lips twisting wryly. "Well, I think they've got defense sewn up pretty well. Might not like them, but they're tough fuckers. As we know."

"Capstan especially," I say. Tension or not, we've had to work together often enough that when the blood meets the blade, we're all professional.

"I don't think I ever told you, but I'm sorry to hear about Richard. I liked him," Bill says, nodding toward Lana. "I tried to tell her but… well…"

"She thinks you're an exploitive asshole."

"And I think she's a close-minded dreamer," Bill says. "I'm just filling a need."

I shake my head, glancing around. Not the time to get into this.

"Ingrid." I nod at the assassin/rogue-Classed individual as my eyes finally find her.

It's only because I'm watching for it that I note when my eyes skip over the raven-haired woman who stands to Bill's left. She's listened to every single bit of our conversation, unlike Luthien, who moved away. I still owe Ingrid for her part in keeping me alive during the last dungeon run.

"So who's leading?" Bill says, having noticed my desire to not engage further.

"Capstan?"

"I believe my group is most suited to this, Redeemer," Capstan rumbles, having heard us.

Bill looks dissatisfied for a second before he waves dismissively.

"Drones first though," I say and hold out a hand, pulling them from my inventory. I throw the three I own into the sky and send them to scout ahead with a thought.

I'd send Ali too, but without entering the dungeon myself, he's stuck out here. And even in the dungeon, he's going to be tethered a lot closer than normal. The higher the Mana density, the closer he has to be to me; otherwise he'd be banished. Thus far, I haven't figured out if there's anything that can actually kill him, but Ali's hinted that the process of being banished and summoned is actually quite painful.

While my drones are working on getting us a map, Lana moves over to speak with Capstan, getting a briefing on the kinds of monsters we might meet. Rather than get my information secondhand, I focus on the images the drones are sending back. I get about a hundred feet in before the Mana interference cuts in and I lose my connection. After that, all I can do is wait for the on-board programs to bring back the drones, hopefully undamaged.

"You know, most people don't even see me when I don't want them to," Ingrid says when I finally stop staring at my screens.

I'll admit it, I jumped a little and was in the process of calling my sword to me when I realized who it was. I glare at the raven-haired woman, and she smirks at me.

Yes. Smirks.

Ingrid Starling (??? Level ???)

HP: ???/???

MP: ???/???

"That's a good way of getting stabbed, you know," I grouse at her, absently noting that Ali still can't pull up information on her in the System.

She laughs. Ingrid's got a good laugh, one of those infectious ones that makes other people want to join in. Of course, she's laughing at me, so I'm a little less likely to laugh with her but still, good laugh. "As if you could hit me."

"You're not that fast," I point out, and she smirks again.

"And you're not that good."

"Uh huh." I find myself getting grumpy, so I force myself to draw a deep breath. "You know, I'm actually working here."

"No, you're not. You're waiting for the drones to get back. Right now, you're just like the rest of us, waiting around with a stick up your butt. So, you going to share?" Ingrid asks.

At my frown, she points at my right hand. I look down and blink, seeing the bar of chocolate in it. I hand it to her without a word, pulling another for myself from my inventory.

"Think it'll be as bad as our first?" Ingrid says around the chocolate bar that's in her mouth.

"Our first?" I smile slightly, shaking my head. "Sounds improper the way you say it."

"Down, boy," Ingrid says.

Before I can say anything else, I find myself distracted, the feeds from the drones flickering to life. The download comes soon after, and I'm lost in reviewing everything I can about the dungeon. Long minutes of footage and radar readings give us a floor plan, but no sign of the monsters that reside in the cave. I flip through infrared then enhanced imaging and find nothing. It's only when I go into watching in ultraviolet that the monsters jump out. I hiss, the sparking and jumping from the creatures a dead giveaway of the kind of trouble we're going to see.

"That monster you fought, Capstan. It use any special powers?" I ask.

"None. Other than its ability to camouflage itself, it showed no additional abilities," the Yerick answers.

"All right then." I sigh and wave my hands.

Ali sends the information to everyone, both the incomplete map and the pictures we've taken. While everyone's busy looking it over, I take to storing my drones.

"What are these white sparks?" Bill says, frowning.

"You're looking at everything in enhanced visioning with ultraviolet light layering from the drones. The flashing white sparks come from the ultraviolet light that the monsters are giving off," I answer.

It's Mikito who gets it first, probably because she uses her lenses almost continuously. "Electricity. You think they might wield electricity."

"Yes. No reason for the sparks to jump unless they've got a huge current running through them." I glance into the ice cave with its hanging icicles. Outside of fire, lightning works well at killing. And it'll avoid doing any significant damage to the ice cave itself.

"It makes no difference," Capstan says, waving his group forward. "We shall kill them as they come."

Nelia walks behind him, raising her staff and whispering words under her breath as she casts some support spells. Hopefully she has an electrical resistance one in there.

"Ali, anything you can do? Maybe layer your Elemental Affinity on us?"

"Sure. But I can only do it for four. That's you, Lana, and Mikito. Who's the last? That tall drink of darkness? Or your furry friend?"

"The healer. Always the healer, asshole."

Even after my admonishment, I hear Ali chuckling. However, he's also slowly extending his gift, layering a shield around the four of us. Between my Class abilities, Sabre's armored resistances, and Ali's gift, I should be pretty immune to anything those monsters can throw. I almost offer to go ahead, but keep my mouth shut at the last instant. Bull-headed is both a literal and figurative appellation for Capstan—if he says they're going in first, they're going in first.

***

Caves are, by their very nature, temperature-controlled habitats. Stepping in from the -30°C should make the cave feel warm, even if it's filled with ice. Instead, the temperature drops again, and the humans who still have skin exposed hiss at the sudden cold. Everyone slaps, twists, and otherwise commands their body armor and clothing to seal off completely, removing bare flesh from sub-arctic air. Everyone except for Ali, of course, who decides to change into a speedo.

"No one needs to see that," Lana says.

Luthien raises a slim hand and throws a glowing blue spell at Ali, one that the Spirit actually bothers to dodge. Mana-based spells will hurt anything, even Spirits who aren't fully in our dimension.

Capstan and the rest of the Yerick ignore the byplay, stalking deeper into the dungeon, firing small glow-balls into the ceiling periodically to light up the area. Most of us have one form or another of enhanced vision, but it's always a decent idea to light up your surroundings when you can. Never know what kind of spell or damage you might take.

A trio of monsters surge out of hiding from behind a stalagmite icicle, their low-slung webbed feet contrasting to the humongous heads and thick tails they use to attack. Pure white, with just the barest edging of crystal blue on their scales, the monsters look like a prehistoric version of a crocodile and are about thrice as mean. Capstan catches the first on his axe, his blade crushing and tearing apart scales before sliding off while the second clamps its mouth around his leg. It rears backward and throws the large Yerick aside while the last neocroc rushes Aron. Aron hops backward, dodging the snap by millimeters while firing his pistol from his hip, each bullet opening bleeding wounds on the monster.

Their initial attack over, Nelia has her hands in the air as she finishes her spell and glowing green lines spring into existence, trapping two of the monsters and locking them into place. Now that the combatants are mostly out of melee range, the rest of us open up on the trapped pair while Aron duels with his own monster, straight-arming and kicking it before firing at it again and again. Unlike what anime and other TV shows might show you, it's really a bad idea to shoot into a melee fight unless you don't have a choice. You never know who will jinx when they should have juxed.

I layer shots on the trapped and thrashing monsters while I take in their Status Screen that Ali has finally tossed up.

Postosuchus (Level 52)

HP: 2799/3480

MP: 340/350

Postosuchus (Level 53)

HP 2477/3290

MP: 420/420

Tough but not overwhelming. Groups of three are doable, especially when we outnumber them so significantly. By the time Capstan gets back, the Postosuchus are dealt with.

"I left Whitehorse for this?" Bill says, disdain in his tone.

"You're welcome to go," Lana replies, waving toward the cave opening. "No one invited you."

"Incorrect. I did," Capstan rumbles. "This is but the entrance. More challenges await us within."

"Well, let's get on with it then," Bill says, and Capstan nods.

Lana clenches her fist and Nelia's tail curls up in what I've learnt is anger, but Capstan walks forward, beckoning his team. I stay silent for now. Capstan's a big, big boy and knows what he's dealing with.

An hour and five fights later, beyond a slow increase in the number of monsters and the use of a freeze ray trap, this dungeon hasn't gotten more dangerous. The lightning attacks never appear, which is a bit worrying. Perhaps I was wrong about what the sparks were meant for? Still, everyone else thought I was correct, and while the humans might not have much more experience than I do, the Yerick come from a long line of Adventurers. Whatever. Less trouble is good.

As usual, the dungeon morphs the actual dimensions of the cave, doing the "bigger on the inside" thing and letting us wander around for hours when we should have hit an ending already. Spatial dimensions, along with considerations like airflow and temperature, are an afterthought when it comes to Mana-infused dungeons. So when we hit an ice-filled cavern so large you could fit a couple of houses in it, no one's surprised, though we end up squinting a bit from the reflected light from the hundreds of ice crystals.

While we're squinting, a full fifteen Postosuchus hit us. Capstan swings automatically, his axe blade shearing through the air and passing right through the monster's body without stop, throwing his balance off for a precious second, and without doing any damage. It's enough for a pair of monsters to dog-pile him. Aron's bullets do no damage either, tearing up the ground as the Postosuchus rip into him. All along the line, the monsters attack and only a few weapons seem to work—Mikito's naginata, Luthien's guardian Mana blades, and Anna's flames, which flare and drive the monsters away.

Standing just in front of Lana, I don't have much time to pay attention as a pair surge toward me, their mouths wide and tearing as they crack against the force field Sabre generates. The shield drops by a third with just those attacks and I hiss, focusing for a second to cast Soul Shield on Lana. It lacks the auto-regeneration of Sabre's shielding, but it's certainly better than nothing.

"They're phased. Energy weapons and Mana spells!" Ali shouts as he floats high above us, pain lacing his voice as he clutches at the remains of his left arm. Blue lights float around where the stump ends, slowly filling out his form again.

I thrust out my hand, calling forth my Mana Dart spell, and watch as four appear around my hand. They fly straight out, slamming into a Postosuchus that's still trying to get past my shield. Sadly, Mana Darts might be cheap and fast to cast, but they're not particularly powerful.

"*Use your sword, boy-o. It'll hurt them,*" Ali shouts at me mentally. Now he tells me!

Not needing another invitation, I duck forward, calling forth the sword to lop off part of a nose that comes too close before making the sword reappear in my other hand, where I stab it down a throat. Between the pair of attackers and dancing deeper into the swarm, I keep my sword and my body moving. There's a trick to making a soulbound melee weapon appear and disappear around you, a certain sense of timing and motion that makes full use of its ability. Why take the half-second to pull a blade out of a body when you can just make it reappear outside? The Honor Guard have a fighting style built around their soulbound weapons and I've done the best I can to imitate them. It's effective, though often silly-looking.

Ingrid, in her shadow form, is fighting the monsters on their own turf, a pair of knives flashing as she cuts and stabs to keep the monsters from overwhelming Bill's line. Luthien, her Mana-blades on defense, wields whips of fire that pass through but injure the monsters, leaving her other teammates to lay down cover fire. Bill's pair of beam pistols kick out searing death, punching holes even through phased forms. The Yerick have switched weapons as well, converging and covering Nelia. All but Capstan, whose axe glows red under the effect of a Skill.

It's not all going our way of course. We suffer more than one injury, but Ali's warning has shifted the momentum in our favor. At least until the Postosuchus play their next card. They shift, dropping into our reality fully, and charge us. Attacks that once dug into their bodies and injured them glance off. They hit our line like wrecking balls and what was an ordered defense disappears as everyone ends up fighting for themselves.

I'm about the only one who isn't affected—mostly because I broke ranks a while ago to draw more to me. Doesn't mean I'm doing much better at hurting them, mind you, but when they come at me, I trigger Blink Step and appear behind them to grab the Postosuchus off Lana as she holds it off with one arm underneath its neck. I twist, making sure to put my hips into it, and watch the monster fly into its friends, who have just about turned around.

I lay into the four with Blade Strikes, blue lines of force rippling from my sword as I cut again and again. Each strike might not be as powerful as a hand-held cut, but at this distance, each blow is hitting more than one. Lana, on her knees now, adds to my attack with her shotgun, tearing holes into the monsters, blood and meat spraying from wounds.

"Go! I've got this," I snap at Lana.

She jerks a nod, spinning to where her pets, other than Anna, are fighting a losing battle. The puppies are just not strong enough to deal with the added resistance of the monsters. Dashing forward and sideways, Lana unloads her shotgun again and again at an outlying monster as it rips and tears at Shadow's foot. I don't have time to watch, stealing glances as I work to keep my four on their back feet and away from me. The last sight I have of Lana and her pets is of Mikito dashing over, her own attacker a cooling corpse. Then I'm too busy to watch.

***

Minutes that seem like hours later, I pull the last corpse of my quartet of attackers into my storage dimension after looting it and sit up. I don't bother moving faster—the last couple of dots on my minimap are a good indication that the party has things well in hand. Nice thing about the System is that if someone who's wounded doesn't have an on-going status effect, they'll live and heal. Looking around, I edge over to the puppies. Lana has a bandage over Shadow's leg while Mikito casts a healing spell on Anna.

"This more your speed?" Ali's sarcastic tone can be heard in the distance as he taunts Bill, who is standing still as one of his teammates casts a regeneration spell on his hand, restoring a pair of lost fingers.

Ali's only answer comes from Luthien, who tosses a ball of sickly green energy at Ali.

"Need some help?" I ask Lana, who nods. I squat, casting to help speed up the healing process. It's not necessary, but there's no point in wasting time either—you never know what might attack next. Which reminds me…

I look up, spotting the guards that Capstan has posted, all of them glowing with green light as Nelia's healing spells work on the Yerick. Always nice to have someone with a little more experience in play.

"So those lights—part of their shifting properties?" I ask Ali mentally as I work on Shadow, Lana stroking the whimpering puppy.

"Best I can figure it, yeah. Want me to scout ahead?" Ali asks.

I send confirmation to him. No reason to ask him to be careful. The Postosuchus might be able to injure him, but he won't die.

"You okay?" I ask Lana, eyeing the redhead with trepidation as she strokes the puppy. I notice the slight tremble in her fingers, the way she holds the black husky just a little too tightly.

"I'm fine," Lana says. "Did you loot the bodies yet?"

I consider pushing her, but over the last few weeks, the wall between us has gotten so high, I'm not even sure how to breach it. "Not yet."

"Go. We need the Credits," she says.

I frown. She's never been this obsessed with money. My hesitation draws an irritated glance from her and I stand to loot and store more corpses. Nothing I can do about it, at least for now. The others let me store the bodies, knowing it's easier than the "usual" routine of digging through the corpses for the bits that the alchemists, smiths, and other crafters can use. As I said, the Guard Skills are useful in other, less direct ways.

A few minutes later, the group's ready to get going, and I relay the new information sent back by Ali to Capstan. We head deeper, being more careful this time. Definitely not boring.

***

Nearly nine hours later, we finally come toward the end. If it wasn't for the fact that Ali had found the Boss room, we probably would have taken a break already. Hell, if it wasn't for the fact that we all had upgraded Stats, we would have *had* to take a break already. I can still recall my first day after the System came, when running, hiding, and occasionally fighting drained me completely—if not physically, at least mentally. But finding the Boss room gave us enough of a push to keep the group going, tired and cranky as we all were.

When we cross into the room, the Postosuchus Boss is curled up, head poking above its tail and staring at the only entrance. Violet eyes the size of dinner plates stare at us balefully as we enter, spreading out as we get ready. It doesn't move, just watching us, and something in the pit of my stomach drops. It's never a good thing when the monsters don't attack immediately. It means they're either smart or have something else nasty planned.

Capstan, Aron, Mikito, the huskies, and the large lunk who is Bill's tank move to circle the monster, our first line of defense. The rest of us hang back, charging up our attacks. And still, nothing happens. Capstan chops his hand down and we let loose, opening fire with bullets, beams, spells, and more—and that's when things go sideways.

One moment it's there, the next it's gone. All our firepower is wasted and we're left looking around, searching for trouble.

"He's shifted over comple—" Ali shouts, his sentence cut off as he's ripped apart. No blood, but body parts fly apart, and then Ali's banished. And still we can't see anything.

Ali's words are enough though, and I check through the QSM's settings. Assuming the Boss is using the same dimension as the rest of his team, I should be able to slide right in. A flicker and I'm in, the world around me becoming a ghostly outline. The QSM shifts me partly into the other dimension—not fully, since I wouldn't be able to see where I was if it did—but it's enough to let me see the Boss. The time I've taken is enough for it to shift positions again, getting behind our line and readying itself for the attack. I open up with the Inlin.

I've never tried before to fire the Inlin at a monster who's all the way in another dimension. Rather than tearing new holes into the monster, the bullets lose their place in the dimensional shift quickly, dropping back into my default dimension. Thankfully, the monster's so big, my shots tear up the walls rather than my friends. My shots landing so near the group sends everyone scrambling, making the Postosuchus shift and subsequent attack miss. A few attacks from my friends later and the Boss shifts back again, its minor wounds already fading.

Too bad for it that I'm waiting over here. Lightning greets it as I unload the spell I've been charging, white light so bright that even with flare compensation, I'm squinting. As before, energy crosses all dimensions—or stays in all dimensions, maybe. Either way, the Postosuchus writhes on its stubby legs, tail lashing as it attempts to hit me, but the lightning rips into it, tearing through its body and injuring it. I've got it on the ropes, its body writhing as electricity cascades through it, making muscles clench and neurons fire—and that's when the grenades go off.

Quantum grenades are the high-tech answer to dimensional shifting. Being not fully in any particular dimension, the focused energy of the quantum grenades deal a significant amount of damage and can, if used properly, throw the dimensional shifter back into reality. That's pretty much what happens to me as energy bombards my body, damaging me and Sabre in equal measure and ripping me away. I'm lucky that I wasn't at the epicenter of the blast.

I lie on the ground, smoking and groaning, knowing that the Boss was barely affected by the attacks. After all, unlike me, it was fully shifted to the other dimension. The grenades were useful against its brethren, but against the Boss, they'd be no more useful than a warm shower. Even as I lie there, I feel Sabre re-routing around damaged components, restoring functionality as quickly as my Skill and its on-board processes can.

"Sorry!" Aron shouts at me, eyes raking over our surroundings as he awaits the next attack.

I answer him with a groan, casting a quick Greater Healing spell while Sabre finishes rebooting.

I'm too slow for what comes next. The Boss reappears next to Bill's meathead and clamps down with its teeth. Luthien's defensive blades strike out, plunging into the monster's body, while spears of shadow erupt from the ground, impaling the monster even as the Boss attempts to bite the poor man in half. Bill is firing his pistols at point-blank range, each shot opening the wound wider and wider. Nelia and Bill's healer tosses healing spell after healing spell in a futile attempt to keep the tank alive, but a last crunch splits his top half from the bottom.

A chime tells me Sabre's up, so I'm up, a hand raised to add my spells to the mix, but the Boss is gone, back into the other dimension. I snarl, "It's fully in the other dimension but somehow still seeing into this one. Quantum grenades are useless."

I get nods and I scan around, glancing at the QSM. Nearly two thirds of the charge is drained, leaving enough to pop over and fight a little bit, but not really enough to kill. Probably. Better to stay here, add to the damage and healing. Maybe I can stop another person from being torn into pieces.

It pops into existence right behind Mikito, mouth snapping out toward the tiny Japanese woman. Bad idea, since she sticks her polearm into its mouth and jams it there. Halfway through her polearm, the Boss gives up on trying to eat her as the pain finally reaches its tiny brain. The rest of us are busy tearing into it, unloading shots into its body before it disappears, taking Mikito's naginata with it.

Mikito cries out angrily, hands twitching as she pulls a pair of short, curved swords from her inventory. Silence ensues as we wait for the next attack, silence that stretches for minutes before it reappears, giant tail sweeping the Yerick aside. The Yerick might be big for humanoids, but weight and momentum win out and the group is thrown into the nearby walls, cracking icicles on their way through the air. Spells made of ice, fire, and shadows rip into it while beams cook its flesh and bullets add to its injuries. Mikito dances through the fire, ducking in low and cutting at its foot, severing a tendon before she's brushed aside as the monster turns.

Twice more, the monster pops in and out, the second time catching Luthien and nearly killing her. Only a series of hasty healing spells and the fact that the monster is injured stops it from killing her, though it does take a foot from her as it dies. And then it's over, the mutilated body lying in a pile of freezing blood while the rest of us begin the process of patching ourselves together.

Congratulations! Dungeon Cleared

+10,000 XP

First Clear Bonus

Having cleared the dungeon for the first time, you have been rewarded an additional +5,000XP +1,000 Credits. Bonus for being the first explorer +5,000 XP +5,000 Credits.

Bent Knee Ice Cave Dungeon classified as Level 65+ and above.

Level Up!

You have reached Level 35 as an Erethran Honor Guard. Stat Points automatically distributed. You have 3 Free Attribute Points and 4 Class Skills to distribute.

I stare at the man we lost and the flat, emotionless faces Ingrid and Bill sport, and I grimace. I have no idea what they're thinking—perhaps someone like Rachel could understand the level of loss they must feel as another person from their town dies. So few of them managed to get out of Dawson. Selfishly, I can't help but think that losing another person is a blow to Whitehorse.

Especially when it's someone this high level. The damn dungeons are getting tougher and tougher each day.

Chapter 5

"I hate being banished. The headaches really, really suck," Ali grumbles when I pull him back into our world, watching my Mana pool drop like a rock when I do so. The biggest issue with Ali being linked to me is that the cost of summoning him keeps going up too.

"Do you even get headaches?" I wonder.

"Something close enough to it." Ali shakes his head. "Sorry about the loss, boy-o."

I glance backward at the reduced group trekking down the mountain and nod dumbly. Just another damn corpse to lay at the feet of the System. And mine. If I'd remembered to tell them not to use the grenades, if I'd purchased a Skill or some tech to talk between dimensions, if I had cast a Healing Spell… If. If. If. So many ifs. The ifs can pull you down, throw you into a whirlpool of self-doubt, and drown you in the past. You'll freeze in the future and ignore the present if you let it.

What is is. I push aside the thoughts, the doubts, and the mental recriminations. Too many battles, too many bodies, too many deaths. I know the rest are doing much the same in their own ways, processing the battle so that we can go on. Because in the end, all you can do is go on.

"*At least you got another level, boy-o,*" Ali says, switching back to our private channel.

"*Yeah. Going to have to assign those attributes soon.*"

"*Still keeping the Skill points for Level 40?*"

"*Yup. Third-tier Skills look pretty good. I'll make up the difference with tech and Credits for now.*"

"*Just be careful. Might not always get time to assign them.*"

"*I know. Speaking of Credits, what's with Lana's obsession?*"

"*Well… I have a few ideas, but you aren't going to like them.*"

Before I can say anything else, Mikito sidles up to me and prods me. I look at her as she speaks. "I'm nearing Level 50. I was hoping Ali could tell me what happens then."

Ali blinks and looks between the two of us. I shrug, and the Spirit rubs his chin. "Well, there are a few ways things can go. The easiest method is to take the Classes offered to you by the System. They're derived from your initial Basic Class, mostly direct upgrades. Not a bad choice if you've already got a good base Class. If you want access to specialized Advanced Classes, there are Quests you can complete to open them up. Not really viable here though, but for the Galactics with the Credits and time, it's a popular thing to do.

"Lastly, you can skip the entire issue and just buy an option via the Shop. Gives you access to a more powerful Advanced Class when you hit Level 50, but that's pretty expensive. Those are the most common options. The change can get more complicated too, like Classes and Skills that give you options to get better Classes, but again, that requires planning and access to the options."

"I'm assuming that's the same for Master Classes?" I say and get a nod from Ali.

"Is there a way to find out what I might get offered?" Mikito asks.

Ali snorts. "Duh. Buy it from the Shop. Normally isn't too expensive either."

Mikito nods, taking the rebuke in stride. Of course it was that simple. The damn System always wants you to buy something from it. Always.

"What's going on with Lana?" I mutter to Mikito, and she looks at me, opening her mouth to answer.

"I can hear you two," Lana calls, striding forward and glaring at us. "If you have something to say, say it."

Mikito blushes, ducking her head at getting caught.

I shift slightly, uncomfortable with the direct confrontation, but I grit my teeth and ask. Better to get it said and done. "What's going on with you? You've changed."

"I'm not allowed to?" Lana says, glaring at us.

"Not what I said. I'm trying to understand your actions. I'm worried about you," I say.

Lana snorts, scratching at Howard's grey fur as he moves up beside her. "I'm fine. I've got it handled out there, don't I?"

"So far…" I admit reluctantly.

"I'm not the one who broke ranks earlier today. Or disappeared without letting us know why. Or has been reporting everything we're doing to the Hakarta. Don't you try to guilt me over what I'm doing. I'm fine," Lana snaps. "I got this."

I open my mouth and shut it as she swings up onto Howard, leaning down close to the puppy as it takes off. Well, shit.

"Thanks for the backup," I mutter to Mikito, who shrugs, keeping her eyes on the ground. I can't blame her—emotional confrontations aren't easy.

We watch together as Lana and her pets take off, streaming away from the group, and we just shake our heads at the inquisitive glances we get from the others.

"Well, that went well…"

***

It's no triumphant return when we finally make it to Whitehorse hours later, though the Boss's body that I drop off gets more than a few wide-eyed stares at the butchering yard. It'll be a damn good bump to our food stocks. One nice thing about the System—pretty much anything that moves is edible, if it's not poisonous by nature. Not as if anyone's going to try to eat a Mercury Elemental of course.

It takes a short few minutes to get everything sold and the Credits distributed. Simple enough to send Credits via the System, so Mikito and Lana don't even need to be there, a fact that Mikito took full advantage of the moment we got back.

I'm standing outside the city center building with Ali, trying to figure out what to do next, when the day decides to take another turn for the worse. Out of the building comes a pair of tall Tuinnar in red and yellow who carry themselves with that ramrod-straight bearing you see in soldiers. They quickly spread out, one of them watching Ali and me closely while the other scans the streets for more threats. They jabber so fast that even Ali's translation doesn't work, not while he's busy with other things like getting their Status information for me.

A short while later, another pair of guards comes out, leading a tall Tuinnar woman and a shorter male Tuinnar, probably only five feet, three inches tall but with that predatory grace and unconscious confidence I've come to associate with the really dangerous. The woman is more interesting, beautiful in that dark-skinned, Elven way they have, long mossy-green hair contrasting with the gold and red of her dress. She walks the way the powerful do, certain with the knowledge that everything will work out just the way they want it to because that's the way it has always been. Standing next to her, Roxley, pretty as he is, is overshadowed, even with his Skills and attributes. Not because she's beautiful, but because her presence itself makes you want to watch her. Surprisingly, bringing up the rear of this motley group is Labashi, the Hakarta an ugly green contrast in the group of beautiful black Elves.

"Ah, John!" Roxley says, smiling as he waves me in through the security cordon. The guards tense slightly but don't move to stop me as I walk forward.

"May I introduce the Duchess Kangana's Envoy—the Lady Priya Kangana and her escort, Weaponmaster Hondo Ehrish."

Lady Priya Kangana (??? Level ???, Lady of the Seven Marshes, Mistress of the Kitchen, Savant of the Realm)
HP: ???
MP: ???

Hondo Ehrish (Weaponmaster Level 43, Master of Blades and Guns, Slayer of Orcs, Goblins and Unika, Destroyer of Monsters, The Unbroken Warrior)
HP: 4,340/4,340
MP: 1,900/1,900

"Evening," I greet them, smiling slightly even as my eyes narrow. Envoy… deep politics for sure. Deeper than anything I've ever swum in. I'm not surprised her levels are hidden. Those titles on the other hand… it's interesting what titles can tell you about a person. For example, Hondo's are pretty clearly "don't fuck with me" titles. Hers are more ambiguous. "What brings you to our little town?"

"Our visit to this *village* is a courtesy," Priya says, smiling tightly. "We're here to understand the scope of improvements the Duchess's nephew has completed."

Nephew. I still my face, knowing that going completely blank is as good a tell as shouting, but it's the best I can do. Well, isn't that interesting. "That's nice. I hope you enjoy the visit."

"I'm sure we will," Priya says.

"This is one of your human Adventurers you have cultivated?" Hondo says, his eyes traveling over my body and flicking up in an all-too-familiar gesture. "I am not impressed."

My smile widens at the casual insult, but I don't make a move. Standing here, alone and in my light armor, surrounded by his guards, it's not a good idea. Never mind the fact that he's a Level 39 Advanced Class at least, if not Master.

"*Advanced.*"

And it's just a bad idea. He got up to those levels the hard way, and kicking my ass would be all too simple for him. Better to smile. I'm a big boy. Words can hurt and annoy me, but swords and spears can impale me.

"Come, I'm sure Graxan has more he wishes to show us," Priya says and waves for Roxley to carry on.

The Dark Elf Lord does, leading them away, and other than a familiar nod from Labashi, the group doesn't pay me any further attention as they troop after him. I stare as the group departs, my brain trying to work out what this all means. It's kind of like seeing the Queen in Whitehorse—weird and without any real context but definitely important. Either way, at least the shoe has dropped at last.

***

I find Vir upstairs, watching over the group in the anteroom that leads to Roxley's offices, pretty much standing exactly where I expected him to be.

"Care to explain?" I growl softly.

"Lord Roxley mentioned you might be coming." Vir waves me to a seat, his attention only partly on me. The rest I'm guessing is on the various security windows he's got pulled up that only he can see.

"Why are they here?" I slump in the chair, waiting for an answer that would make sense.

"To take over the city, obviously," Vir says.

"That I got, but I expected more, you know, guns. And spells."

"That might come later, but it is not the way we operate," Vir says. "Too wasteful. Better to start soft, come in diplomatic, and play things quietly. Leave the fighting for later when that fails."

I frown. "So what, they're asking Roxley to leave?"

"That would be too gauche. No, they will explain how he is not doing well enough, how the city might be better managed under some other, more resourceful individuals. They will pressure him, personally and familially, and when that does not work, well… I'm sure there are more plans in play," Vir says, rubbing his chin. "Do keep watch. I expect there to be more plans in play at this time."

"Not worried I'd report what I see to them?" I ask Vir, and he smiles slightly.

"No. Worrying does little in such situations."

"Why aren't you down there anyway?"

"Mmmm?"

"Well, you're the spymaster, aren't you?"

"No. Lord Roxley has designated another as such."

"Bullshit."

"I speak the truth. You may request the information from the Shop. I understand it is quite cheap," Vir says, smiling slightly.

"But you handle all this spying and political shit, right?" I frown, staring at Vir. I'm pretty sure Labashi as much as confirmed it during our meetings.

"Yes, though I do not hold the title."

I frown. "Oh…"

Vir does the job but doesn't have the title. Which makes sense, since if someone wanted to know who Roxley's spymaster was, if they didn't word the question properly, they'd get a different name. On the other hand, the fact that anyone who pays attention can figure out he's the actual spymaster means that it's not something they're really trying to hide. Probably, again, because of the Shop.

"This is making my head hurt. If everyone knows you're doing the job anyway, why bother?"

Vir falls silent for a time, staring at me before he answers. "Because the information you so casually toss around might not be true. Many groups have run double, even triple bluffs. Designating a spymaster but not giving them any responsibility can often just be the first cover, while the second might have the individual receiving such information later. Each layer of deception requires Credits to acquire in the Shop or knowledge to bypass the questions."

"And the Shop varies the amount of Credits cost dependent on how much information you have beforehand, right? So if I wanted to learn who the real spymaster was without knowing anything beforehand, it'd be pretty expensive to just buy the information straight out."

Vir nods, and I sigh. It does explain why so much is kept hidden or if not hidden, obfuscated in layers. No secret is safe if it's been written down, spoken about, or transferred somehow through the System, but the cost of the secrets varies depending on how easy the information is to acquire. About the only secret truly safe is the one that stays in your head.

All in all, it makes for a paranoid world.

Chapter 6

A few days later, I find myself eating lunch at the Golden Nugget, working through the plates of ribs, steaks, and rice while waiting for the rest of my party to make an appearance. We're having a late start to the day since Mikito and Lana were on newbie hunter training duty this morning. I ran my own group through a night course, which as usual ended up with a series of wannabe hunters moaning and griping about injuries. Really, you'd think they'd get over getting impaled after a few hours.

After spending the last few hours working with Aiden on adapting my Fireball spell into an Iceball spell—or whatever you want the equivalent spell to be called—I made my way into town, still devoid of a new toy to add to my arsenal. Learning spells the hard way is painful, but it's useful for increasing my understanding of Mana. Problem is, even with my increased intelligence and knowledge, I only have so much time to devote to things like this. In the end, it'd almost be better for me to just earn the Credits to buy the spell from the Shop, but once again, that stubborn part of me actually does want to understand what the hell I'm doing.

"John!" Amelia, a broad-shouldered, big-boned lady, plops down in a vacant seat with a sigh.

"Constable," I answer, smiling slightly. She's dressed in Roxley's guard uniform, the shoulders straining as she moves. I swear, each time I see her, she's gotten larger and larger as her Class builds upon her physique. I'm sure, at some point, it'll stop, but I am curious when that will happen. Right now, professional bodybuilders would be envious of her physique. "Good to see you."

"Nice to see you too. Are you going to the meeting?" Amelia says brusquely.

I raise an eyebrow. "What meeting?"

"Of course, you don't know." Amelia rolls her eyes. "You really need to stop pissing everyone off."

"Oh come on…"

"You're actually going to deny it!" Amelia snorts and raises her hand, ticking things off. "Telling Eric off, calling Miranda Battleaxe to her face…"

"That was complimentary!" I protest.

Amelia doesn't even stop. "Recommending that the alchemists devote part of their time to making potions for free as their taxes. Asking the Council to their face when they would grow a pair." She shakes her head. "And that's in the last month."

"They needed to make the decision about the land claims. Dragging it out for another few months wasn't going to make a damn bit of difference. The people who would be upset would still be upset," I point out.

"I'm not saying you were wrong, but there are ways of doing things—"

"Politics you mean."

"Yes, politics. Diplomacy. Being nice. Lana's not around to smooth the feathers you ruffle anymore, you know," Amelia growls, gripping the newly delivered pint glass. She drains it before she slams it down. "Never mind. I'm not here to argue with you about this. I'm here to tell you that the Council— the human City Council—is meeting with Lady Priya."

"Interesting. I didn't think we had a human council," I say.

A few months ago, the City Council that had ruled over humanity pretty much imploded when a stupid plan by the current Mayor fell apart. It ended with the creation of the General Council—one that consisted of both humans and aliens.

"It's not official, but pretty much anyone who's anyone who's human is on it," Amelia says. "Richard was. So's Lana when she bothers to turn up."

"Huh." I shake my head again. I wish I could say I'm surprised I've been left out, but I probably wouldn't have turned up even if I was invited. It's a little surprising that they've gone and created an unofficial government, but only just a little. Humans will be humans and a surprising number of politicians seemed to have survived, at least in Whitehorse. "And you're telling me 'cause you think I should go?"

"Of course. Since I'm working for Lord Roxley, they don't want me there but…"

"But I'm rude and ignorant and no one is about to throw me out," I finish for her and sigh. Politics. But I have to admit, I'm curious. "When is it?"

"At noon." Amelia smirks slightly. "Might want to get on the move."

I grimace, looking at the clock in the corner of my vision that Ali hacked into the System for me, and I sigh. If I want to get to the meeting, I'll have to get going. Which means I won't have time to finish the rest of my lunch. Amelia already knows this, of course, which is why she's stolen a plate and is digging in without prompting. I frown at her and she grins at me, waving a pair of fingers as I stand.

***

The meeting is being held in the old city building. Thankfully, Ali's able to quickly guide me to where they are; otherwise I'd be wandering the large building, looking like a fool. The room looks like a typical conference room, large tables with an array of office chairs filled with pretentious and self-important people. Surprising how some things have managed to make its way through the apocalypse largely untouched.

All the usual suspects are here. Eric Roth in his suit flanks the matronly Miranda Lafollet, who sits at the head of the table, while Norman Blockwell and a few other council members sit about, chatting. Jim Calbery and a few other hunters sit across from the politicians in their own cluster, with Bill and Luthien seated close by but separate. There are even a few businessmen, clustered closer to the politicians than hunters, who I recognize by sight, if not name. It's a microcosm of the city—at least the human side. The tension in the room is high and grows even higher when I walk in.

"What are you doing here?" Eric says, lips curled up.

My lips tug up, the "smile" never reaching my eyes as I take a seat near the door and put my feet up on the table. "I thought I'd pay you guys a visit. Been missing your sunny disposition."

"John, we actually try to do real work here," Miranda butts in before things get too heated between the two of us. "Your presence wasn't requested because, well…"

"I'm an ornery bastard who gets bored?"

"You have no understanding about the difficulties involved in running a city!" snaps Eric.

"True."

That answer makes Eric blink, his mouth working as he tries to find a comeback to the unexpected declaration of incompetence. Hell, I was a (bad) computer programmer back in the old world. Ask me to put together a website? Sure, I could do that. Running a business, much less a city, is well out of my skillhouse. No shame in admitting that.

"So why are you here?" Bill asks.

Luthien stares at me for a second, sparks dancing along her fingers as she eyes Ali.

"I want to hear what your guest has to say," I reply, eyes tracking the red dots approaching our door.

I smile slightly, tilting my head as the Envoy's guards step in, clearing the room. In a few moments, the Envoy herself makes her way in. Lady Priya, flanked by her Weaponmaster, stares at the group of lounging humans. A few people nod to her in greeting, and some smile as we wait.

"You will stand in the presence of the Lady!" snarls Hondo as he stalks forward, eyes glinting bloody murder. He radiates danger and anger.

Almost as once, the politicians and most of the hunters scramble to their feet. Jim hesitates for a moment before he stands, and Bill compresses his lips in anger but eventually complies as Hondo glares at him. Which leaves me, seated with my feet on the table. Hondo shoots me a glare, and for a second, I feel my stomach drop.

Mental Influence Resisted

"Get the fuck up, boy-o!" Ali shouts at me mentally as I continue to sit there. My behavior is intensely rude, but I'm curious.

When Hondo moves, it's so fast that it puts Mikito to shame. One hand grabs my ankle, another my arm even as I twist to the side and attempt to straight-arm him away. I don't have the grounding to do that, and his momentum is enough to keep pushing me forward into the wall. He shifts slightly, blocking my leg before I can throw the kick, and snaps a series of punches into my short-ribs that crack them before he pins me with his forearm.

Most impressively, he punches me through most of the wall but not all the way in. With the amount of force we're throwing around, accidentally punching through the drywall completely would not be hard. Instead, Hondo perfectly controls the amount of pressure he's using, keeping me in the room. I grit my teeth as ribs grate against one another as they heal forcefully. Damn, he's good.

"Greetings, Lady Kangana. Weaponmaster Ehrish," I say from the wall, doing the best I can to keep my voice calm and controlled around the pain and budding anger. It's been ages since I've been manhandled like this, and even if I was egging him on, that spark of anger at the loss of control continues to burn.

"You casually insult my lady then offer greeting to her?" Hondo growls, his grip tightening. His voice lowers as he says softly, "What game do you play, boy?"

"No game with her," I answer him just as softly. Truth there. I was more curious about him.

"It is Lady Priya," the Tuinnar says as she glides over to where Miranda is. The matronly human blinks then edges away, whereupon the Tuinnar sits down in her seat at the head of the table while continuing to speak to me. "A common mistake among your kind. Only my mother would be Lady Kangana. Now, do let him go, Hondo. I'm sure the Adventurer has learnt his lesson."

Hondo drops me at her command, and with that dealt with, the lady's secretary comes forward, announcing the lady and her titles formally. I note more than a few puzzled expressions at the titles. Titles are weird and seem to be gifted by the System for exceptional deeds or when we reach certain thresholds or gain certain Skills or lands. Most of the humans don't have any, which leaves me with my two as a rare exception.

Most of the Lady Priya's don't matter as far as we're concerned, though the Savant indicates a deep understanding of something. Unfortunately, the title itself doesn't give more details than that and Ali's still digging. More interesting is the fact that they don't bother to announce Hondo. Not that his little demonstration didn't get the point across.

"I understand you humans are much more… informal than my people. Is this not correct?" Lady Priya says, turning to speak with Miranda, who has made Eric give up his seat.

The entire table has rotated one down, leaving only Hondo, the guards, and myself still standing. When I shift my weight, Hondo shoots me a glare that keeps me standing next to the wrecked wall where he dropped me.

"Well, I don't really know that much about Tuinnar culture, but we are informal here in Whitehorse," Miranda says, flicking a glance at Eric. "As much as it pains some of us."

"Well, as it is your city, I shall follow your customs. I am here to review the work that Graxan has done in his time in Whitehorse."

"Assuming you're talking about Lord Roxley," Bill chimes in, leaning forward, "it sounds like you're his boss or something."

"No. Just a stakeholder. Graxan did borrow heavily to finance his purchase of the Village key. We are but ensuring that our investment is being handled well," Lady Priya says, and more than a few humans look thoughtful. "Tell me, what do you think of Graxan's leadership?"

With just those words, she opens the floodgates and suddenly people are speaking. I stand there, keeping my mouth shut while my brain picks over the information I've been given. I guess I've seen one angle of their game now.

***

Listening to the group, I'm somewhat amused to note that Roxley gets both praise and complaints in equal amounts. Considering Roxley's a public persona, you'd have to figure he's doing well. The fact that the praising and bitching comes from the same people, often in back-to-back sentences, is even more amusing.

It's not to say I don't know that they're giving the young lady—old elf?—ammunition for later.

"Are Tuinnar ageless like the stories or is this just a case of Mana translation gone wrong?"

"Exaggerated. They're longer lived than humans—figure between four to six hundred years generally. The System keeps them ticking over pretty well, but well, it's also pretty lethal," Ali answers.

I nod dumbly, returning to listening. All these complaints are probably not helping Roxley's case. The fact that none of Roxley's people are here to guide the conversation or otherwise report on what's said is interesting too. On the other hand—I can just see Vir guiding Amelia to get me to come to listen in on all this.

The Lady Priya is good, the way she guides the conversations to raise issues and rile up the group. I'm not the only one who has noticed this—both Eric and Miranda occasionally look as if they've bitten into something bitter. Still, experienced politicians though they may be, the council is putty in the Envoy's hands. Issues that were laid to rest months ago are brought up. Complaints about the lack of a safe space, the tents we had to stay in, and the way the hunters are given preferential treatment are just the start. Other complaints, like shortages and lack of variety in our food sources and the lack of emotional support and counseling, are par for the course. When the talk of emotional support and counseling gets brought up, I spot the way Hondo's face flickers. I guess it must seem strange for someone who has grown up in the System to hear people talk about PTSD and stress from killing monsters.

"Thank you so much for your time," Lady Priya eventually says, standing and calling the meeting to an end. "I will take all that you have said into consideration. You've given us much to think about. If you do have further thoughts about this or how the city might be served better, do let me know."

Well. That's a nice little ending—just another way to keep the council chewing over the things that Roxley hasn't managed to make perfect. I note that she's not promised them anything, made no indications that if she or her Lady took over, things would get better. It's a smart play, since nothing she has said or done could be directly considered acting against Roxley. Just a stirring of the pot.

Hondo watches in silence, and when she's finally done, he follows her out with one last, long look at me. I grin back at him, which makes his eyes narrow. Yeah, taunting the guy who kicked my ass is probably not a good idea, but I never said I was smart.

"What the hell was that about anyway?" Ali says.

"Mmm… testing. I wanted to see how far they'd push it if I pushed them," I answered Ali.

"Learn anything?" Ali says dryly.

I send a mental shrug. Not really. I'd have preferred it if Hondo or Lady Priya were a bit more of a loose cannon. Smart, disciplined, and controlled are a tough combination to beat.

"Mr. Lee, we'll be billing you for the damages," Eric says, pointing at the wall, and I chuckle.

"Sure. Go ahead. Take it out of my next delivery of parts," I drawl.

Eric's lips tighten at my casual dismissal of his threat. Really, with the System in place, fixing up internal walls probably wouldn't even cost a hundred Credits.

Luthien sniffs as she and Bill get up to leave. "Always causing a scene, aren't you, John? Can't just play along." She falls silent when Bill puts a hand on her arm, silencing her before they walk out.

I grunt, ignoring her. I do play along. I've always played along—with my father, with the "yes man" culture I was brought up in, hell, even at my previous job. I played along so well till I got fired and my girlfriend left me. Well. I guess I do have a few issues I need to deal with.

Miranda makes her way to me, followed closely by Jim, my only real friends on the council. And with Miranda, I'd be more inclined to call her a sometime ally. Which is good, because while the lady might not be a fighter, she's fierce and determined and ruthless, willing to do what it takes to keep her kid alive in this new world.

"John," Miranda says. "Tell me, how much of what we said will you report to Lord Roxley?"

"All or none, depends on what he asks," I answer, shrugging. "I doubt anything said here was secret."

"There are no secrets in this world," Jim rumbles, and I nod.

"I meant secret as in you wouldn't want this to get back to Roxley. I am curious about why you said as much as you did to her," I ask Miranda directly.

"Sometimes, things need to be said in a different way for others to hear," Miranda says, her face grim.

All that was to put pressure on Roxley to improve things? Don't they know he's already doing the best he can? Anger flaring, I shake my head, staring at the pair.

"It doesn't matter does it? One owner is like the other," Jim says, his husky smoker's voice growling out his words. "We're still owned by them."

I open my mouth to answer him, then shut it. After all, it's not as if I actually have any proof of what life's like in the other demenses. I just have Capstan's word that Roxley is better than the others. Which, when you get down to it, isn't particularly convincing for others. I trust Capstan, but that's because we've fought and bled together.

"You're a bit too close to this, John," Miranda says, putting a hand on my arm. "Things aren't that great for your average resident. We've still got mutations in the city itself, everyone's complaining about the sheer amount of protein we eat all day—and the strange tastes!—and there just isn't much to do. No television, no plays, no music except for the occasional band. Sure, we could get some of these System entertainment options, but that's just more Credits and no one really has that much extra floating around.

"People are hurting, and all Lord Roxley seems to care about is how many Credits we can make him and when we're buying the next building."

My lips purse, and I have to admit, she has a point. The funny thing is that because we've finally had time to breathe, to relax a little and consider what has happened, everything we've lost is hitting harder. The friends, the family, the small luxuries are all gone, and all the wonders of the System aren't available to most. And the few times we see those luxuries in use by others, it just makes us angrier. When we were all scrambling and fighting to get through the day, everyone was happier because we were all equal. Now, that equality is gone and the fractures are widening.

"It's not that simple…" I say.

"I—we know. But it is that simple for most others," Miranda states.

"You could talk to him yourself."

"We've tried, but it's hard. His… Skill makes it hard to think around him," Miranda points out.

I sigh. "Fine. I'll talk to him."

She nods in thanks, letting my arm go. Jim grunts, following soon after, and I find myself staring at their backs, watched only by a distrustful Eric. I wonder if he's thinking I'm going to break something else or steal the flat screen. It is a nice flat screen…

"*Are they right?*" I ask my Spirit as I head out the door.

"*About what?*"

"*That Roxley's screwing it up?*"

After a moment's hesitation, Ali says, *'Maybe. Roxley's stretched thin. He could have, he should have, bought up the buildings a while ago and resold them. That's what they did in Carcross and Fairbanks. It's what anyone with good sense would do.'*

"And someone with more funding could fix things up faster eh?"

"Could. If they would… well, that'd depend on how useful you are to them."

I nod. Damn. Perhaps it is time to have a real chat with Roxley.

***

Of course, it's not that easy. It never is. I have to schedule an appointment for later that evening, which leaves me with nothing to do for hours. Mikito and Lana are nowhere to be found when I get out, so I just spend the time walking around the town, getting a feeling for the city again. Even though I live here, I don't actually spend any real time in the city itself. That leaves me somewhat startled by the significant changes I see. Main Street is buzzing again, every single store filled. Instead of a single pub or restaurant, now there are a half dozen that cater to everyone with any Credits. Which in this case is mostly hunters.

And that's the thing—the majority of the money in the city comes from hunting. Sure, crafters and makers pull together some small Credits from the goods they produce, but other than our beer, we've got nothing that special for the Galactic community. Nothing that would make others purchase our potions or armor from the Shop, no large trade deals. Eventually some of the materials we're getting and altering will be in demand, but for now, we're mostly just selling raw goods.

It's the hunters who generate those raw goods, the hunters who get Credits from System-generated loot and hauling bits of monster back and clearing dungeons. Everything revolves around them, and everyone knows it. I have a bad feeling that this might be how knights and lords got started, but I'm not an anthropology major. It's never a good thing when there's such a big power imbalance, and even if people aren't thinking of it in these terms, they certainly understand it on an intrinsic level. We've all grown up with the belief that at some level we're equal, but reality and the System are kicking that right in the face.

The few hunters I see prowl the streets as if they own them, and everyone gets out of their way. Or tries to sell them something, whether it's a new potion, piece of armor, or in some cases, themselves. Not everyone's set up to be a fighter, but support personnel can be useful too. Even if that support is in the bedroom.

I don't see much in terms of Yerick or Kapre, mostly because both races keep to themselves in their respective neighborhoods. In fact, the only Kapre I spot is down at the butchering yard, dickering for and purchasing the offal being thrown away. The Yerick are a bit more common, little bull-children running around, picking up flowers to chew on and being watched over by bored teenagers. Tensions might not be as high, but the aliens have their own lives to live.

Compared to Carcross, Whitehorse is plain dull. It makes the Tuinnar guards in red and yellow stand out all the more, the way they casually throw around Credits as they buy whatever catches their eye and wander around in a single layer of clothing. Probably some form of high-tech fiber, alongside natural resistances to the cold, is keeping them nice and warm. More than a few have little drones following them to store their purchases, the guards obviously not caring if the drones get stolen. About the only thing they store in their System-generated inventory is beer, which is amusing in its own form.

Eventually I end up back at Roxley's building, ready for our chat. Surprisingly, I'm directed into his dining room rather than office and find

Roxley's personal chef, with his spherical, bulbous body, waiting for me, our places set and served. A moment later, Roxley walks in alone.

"Roxley," I growl, staring at the plates that smell so damn good. Strips of green and purple vegetables lay alongside meat pieces and a carb dish similar to but sweeter than potatoes. "What's going on?"

"I thought our discussion could be had in a more informal setting. You haven't eaten, have you?" Roxley smiles at me, walking over.

I can't help but follow the line of his lips down to his broad chest.

Mental Influence Resisted

A bit late on that one. It's why, as much as I'm attracted to the man, I can't, won't act on it. I don't like not knowing why I like him, and I don't trust the emotions I feel around him. Even if I can resist his ability most of the time, most isn't enough. Even if I know some of this attraction is natural. Or you know, alien natural. There's a thing to be said about tall, dark-skinned, pointy-eared, muscular men.

"John?"

"Sorry." I shake my head then glance at Ali, who's still hovering by my side. He's been quiet for the last little bit, play-acting as if he's watching some new reality TV show, but I know he's paying attention. "I was hoping to discuss something important, Roxley."

"And we will. But there's no reason not to eat as well," Roxley says, gesturing to the table again.

My stomach rumbles, reminding me that I never did finish brunch, and I give in. "*All right, go. Find out what you can from his companion, will you?*"

"*Next you'll be teaching me how to balance a neutron,*" Ali sends back sarcastically.

"Fine, I'll join you," I reply, taking a seat while Ali disappears.

As per Tuinnar custom, we don't speak about anything important while we dine, just a bunch of small talk about the city, Vir, and the food. Mostly, we talk about the food. It's only when dinner is drawing to a close and dessert is ready that I drag the conversation back to something a little more serious.

"This dinner is a bit nostalgic, isn't it?" I say, looking around.

"Good times. Simpler times," Roxley answers before sliding the mousse-like substance into his mouth.

"Things seem to have gotten more complex recently." I push my plate aside, and Roxley sighs.

"Thank you for waiting," Roxley says. "I know it's hard for you humans."

"Hard…" I huff and shake my head. "For some. My family didn't do much talking about work at dinner either. But Priya and her minion are dangerous."

"For many reasons," Roxley confirms.

"You know about the meeting with the humans today?"

"Was it eventful?"

"Complaining, bitching, and the like. The council wants you to push more funds into making the city better. At least stabilize the city mana flows and stop the spawnings."

"As if it was that easy…" I raise my eyebrow, and Roxley stares at me before he answers. "We've never talked about the Seven Seas, have we?"

"No."

"It is not a prosperous land. Not anymore. The cities, the lands surrounding it were destroyed when a Titan and an Aeldar Giant fought. They tore up our lands, our cities, and there were no Adventurers who could stop them. By the time they were done, my land was ruined." Roxley says all this in a deadpan tone, keeping his emotions in check. "I was not there. I'd brought my personal guard with me on a luxury trip, and by the time we learnt of it and found a Shop to teleport back from, it was too late."

"I'm sorry."

"It is the past. However, the barony has struggled since the fight. This, the new Dungeon World—it was, it is, a chance to finally turn the fortunes for my house and my land," Roxley says. "Ever since the battle, we've lost access to high-level zones and decent dungeons. The Titan drives away all but the lowest level of monster, and even when we hunt those, we must do so carefully. It is only due to its laziness that any of my people survive.

"To buy the Key for Whitehorse, I had to call in the many favors my house had accumulated over the years. In doing so, I have diverted the resources, the guards, and the Credits from my barony. I can do little more for either location. If we are to survive, if the city is to prosper, you humans must make it so."

I grunt, leaning back and staring at Roxley. It's the first time he's ever been this frank with me about the situation he's in. Not that I haven't gleaned some of it through previous talks, but it's the first time he's said it. "Capstan once said that compared to others, you're dealing us a fair hand."

Roxley stares at me, frowning. "That is a gambling metaphor, is it not?"

"Idiom maybe? Something like that. Sorry." Sometimes, the System-enabled translations miss things. "You're being fair to us and not attempting to screw the city over."

"Ah… yes."

"Why?"

"Enlightened self-interest. My understanding of human culture is that humans work better when their self-interest is engaged. So long as these benefits are coupled with significant downsides," Roxley says.

"Huh." I rub my nose. "And I guess the System provides all the downsides, eh?"

"For the most part. Though Whitehorse being taken over by the Duchess and being relegated to manual labor is hopefully a significant deterrent as well."

"Manual labor?"

"The Duchess has little use for those who produce little. Those that do not generate sufficient Credits are either removed from her lands or become her serfs. Financial slavery until such time as they have earned enough Levels to pay off their debt," Roxley says. "Though I must admit, the Duchess does provide training and keeps her interest rates at a justifiable level, unlike some others."

"How does all this land thing work? I mean, you own the city and can upgrade it, but I own my house in it."

"Ah… you are wondering how the System enforces our titles and ownership? It does not. Much like your own world's history, ownership and control of a location may be taken away at any time. It requires force of arms," Roxley explains then gestures downward. "In the end, control over a Shop and the City Center is most important, but many of my brethren also enact controls over movement and commerce. The level of each is up to the various forms of government to enact and, ultimately, enforce."

"Huh."

I fall silent for a time while Roxley sips his drink. It's a light blue beverage that tastes somewhat similar to coffee but with more intense sour notes. I'm served coffee, which I add a large dose of sugar and milk to, contemplating all that he's said. If I had to guess, it sounds as though our cities are basically ancient city states—more theoretical control than realistic in many ways, outside of where the guards march. Then again, I'm no history major—I just took a few classes during university. Some days, it's frustrating running into blind spots like this.

"What'll it take to upgrade from Village to Town?" I ask, returning to stare at the handsome lord.

"We have both the population and resident level requirements, along with the minimum number of registered building types. What we require in the end is the safe zones—and those are close. So very close." Roxley exhales, shaking his head. "If we had but another month, it would be fine."

"You don't expect to get that month?" I ask.

Roxley shakes his head. "No, the Lady is already pressing ahead with her plans."

"Which involves making you pay her back? And why the hell would you borrow from the Duchess anyway?"

"I did not. However, my creditors sold my notes to the Duchess when asked. She is… formidable and I'm sure offered more than the notes were worth," Roxley says bitingly, his tone saying "how dumb do you think I am." I take the rebuke quietly. "And she cannot use my notes for this. My contracts are very specific in this regard—I have until the end of the year to ensure Whitehorse is a Town. However…"

I somehow knew that Roxley had a however when he started speaking. I keep my mouth shut and let him talk.

"My liege lord has rescinded the reduced tax rate that was assigned to my barony. At this time, I have projected that I will have sufficient funds to either pay the taxes or my Credit notes if we are able to upgrade the town. Not both."

"What happens if you can't pay the taxes?" I ask, and he smiles wanly at me.

"A noble who cannot pay for the upkeep of gifted lands is no noble. I will be stripped of my title and the lands and, depending on the severity of my shortfall, be subject to further sanctions."

I wince. "Well, that sounds like they've got you in a bind."

"Indeed."

"Is that it then? Or are we looking at more?"

"Definitely more. To start, I expect she will ferment further insurrection. Slowing down the purchase of buildings would be the obvious step. To ensure I cannot meet either obligation, the Duchess is likely to exert additional financial pressure on the city, potentially manipulating the market for our materials. I am sure there are other plots in play, but those are the ones we have ascertained."

"And if all that fails, she sends in Labashi?"

"Yes," Roxley says grimly.

"Can we beat him?"

"If they sent his entire command? No. Even a small portion would be difficult."

"So..."

"The usual method to deal with mercenaries is to ensure that it is too costly for them to carry out their contract. Or for their employers to pay for the contract to be completed."

"Make them bleed on the beaches and streets, eh?"

"Whitehorse has no beaches we care to defend," Roxley says.

I sigh. Well, there goes my attempt at being smart.

We fall silent for a time before Roxley speaks again. "Do you have further questions?"

"No. Not right now," I answer, standing at the obvious dismissal. He's right—as fun and enlightening as this might have been, it's time to go. One hand still on the table, I stare at the Elf, lost in thought.

"John...?"

"Sorry. I just don't like being on the defensive."

The Tuinnar hisses and walks to me to grip my arm. "Don't, John. They are more powerful than you could believe. So long as we play the game as expected, they will not take further steps."

I feel the warmth of his fingers pushing through my sleeves, warming me up. "If we do that, we'll likely lose."

"If we break their rules, we'll likely lose anyway," Roxley says, growling softly. "Promise me you won't do anything stupid."

"Fine. I just don't like it," I grumble. Not as if I had any actual plans, just a feeling.

Roxley releases my arm, leaving me to flex it. It's only then that I realize how close he is, how I can almost sense his body inches away from mine. I turn toward him, and he tilts his head, the corner of his lips tugging up.

"Well. Time to go," I say hoarsely.

"But we haven't even trained yet," Roxley objects, pointing toward the training floor.

I blink, recalling previous sessions where we fought and trained together, times when he was shirtless and sweating, and find myself stirring.

"Definitely time to go," I mutter, but I find my feet refusing to move.

"Are you sure?" Roxley murmurs again, a hand lightly touching my arm.

I focus, pulling my attention and will to my feet to get them moving. Yes. Definitely time to go.

I leave to the soft, luxurious laughter that escapes way-too-kissable lips. Damn elf.

Chapter 7

Home is a short bike ride back, but long enough that I've cleared my head by the time I pull up. That's a good thing because the large, tusked Orc walking out of my house's door is not what I was expecting to see. In fact, a Hakarta coming out of my house was never something I expected. I almost go for a gun when I realize I know this particular Hakarta.

"Labashi," I greet the large green humanoid who looks briefly surprised to see me before he gives me a huge grin.

"John," Labashi says.

"Ali," Ali greets himself and, seeing that neither one of us is particularly interested in having him join the conversation, returns to staring at his screens.

"Why are you here?" I growl, the conversation with Roxley still ringing in my head.

"Visiting a friend." Labashi inclines his head inside. "I wanted to offer my commiserations to Lana for her brother."

"Really?" I say, doubt in my voice. That seems… well… strange for someone who only knew either of them for so little a time. Or maybe the fact that I find it strange says something about me, the way I can regret and hate the deaths but at the same time not really feel them. How my feelings are always just a touch remote—all but that bubble of anger that sits in my stomach.

"Yes," Labashi says. "I liked Richard and his sister. They are, were, strong individuals."

"How is she?" I tilt my head to the door, curious to see what the more experienced Hakarta might have to say. Dealing with grief might be something we've all had to learn, but Labashi and his people are experts at it.

"I have seen worse," Labashi says. "The first major loss is the most difficult. Some never recover."

I grimace, wishing he had something better to say. Yet I can't really blame him or discount what he said. I guess it's a good thing that for me, my first loss was decades ago when my mom died when I was a toddler. A late night, an inattentive driver, and our world changed. It took me years to truly understand the loss, and my father never did. What had been a strained relationship became something so acrimonious that even now, knowing he's dead, I can find little there but rage.

"John." Labashi's voice cuts through my ruminations as he steps past me, headed back to the city.

"Labashi," I call, making the Hakarta turn. "What are you doing here?"

"My job," Labashi replies then continues walking.

I say goodbye to his back, watching him leave while I mull over his words. Inside, I don't find Lana working in the kitchen or dining room, and the door to her room is closed. For a moment, I consider knocking but then push aside the thought. I don't know what else I could say that I haven't. Time. That's what she needs.

***

I wake to the *1812 Overture* blaring at thousands of decibels. I roll and snatch a pistol from a chair, my sword appearing in my other hand, only to find no visible threats. A quick scan of my minimap shows me nothing new either, even as I hear tramping and shouting above me as Lana, her pets, and Mikito waken.

"What the hell, Ali?" I shout as the music turns off.

"Incoming trouble. Need you to get dressed, boy-o." Ali shoots up, straight through the walls to even more screams and shouts.

Soon enough, the clamor calms down and Ali floats back through the floor with a shit-eating grin as I finish dressing.

"Did you have to use the cannons?" I grumble, slapping around my neck the circle that makes up my helmet.

"No." Ali smirks and points. "Come on, slowpoke. The girls are mostly dressed already."

And I bet he enjoyed buzzing on them. Seriously, he's a disembodied piece of energy and concepts in his home dimension—how the hell did he turn into a minor pervert? Then again, as I clip on my belt and head out the door, Ali did say he drew his "human" form from my mind, so perhaps I should stop asking those kinds of questions. I might not like the answer.

"John." Lana's face is washed, devoid of any form of makeup.

Mikito, on the other hand, seems to have found the time to put on the lightest of touches, which says something about her speed and priorities.

"Nice of all you to join us," Ali says, a giant blue screen blooming in front of all three of us. "We've got a swarm coming right down the river to hit Riverdale. They don't look like they're going to stop anytime soon."

"How?" I frown, staring at the details on the map. The way the purple dots bob and move, I figure we've got at least an hour before they arrive. Which makes no sense, since even with his greater scan radius, there's no way Ali's able to reach that far.

Mikito offers the screen the briefest of glances before she heads to the kitchen to raid the fridge.

"Tapped into the city's expanded sensor grid. The Kapre tied themselves to the city and the surrounding trees," Ali explains as he gestures us out. "Extended our sensor net, at least on this side of the river, a good few miles."

"Nice…" I admit. I grab the package of rice balls that Mikito hands out before we all exit, the puppies and Anna already gathered outside, waiting for us. I'd been wondering what the Kapre had added to the city and I guess now I've got my answer. "So the hunters have all been alerted?"

"Yup." Ali nods, gesturing to the lights flicking on all around us. Formerly dark houses are filling with light as the residents wake up to the new danger. "Plan six is already in play."

"Six?"

"Yes, John, six," Lana says bitingly as she climbs onto Howard. "We've been planning for an attack on this side of the river for a while now. Six is for when we've got enough warning to evacuate the non-combatants to the other side of the river."

"Oh…" I feel kind of foolish. Of course they've got plans. It's not as if the fact that Riverdale is pretty much our most unguarded flank is unknown, nor is the fact that we're seeing more and more swarms. Even if we do our best to cut down on the Bosses on this side of the river, it was bound to happen eventually.

"Now come on," Lana says to me irately, suiting action to words by kicking Howard into gear.

Mikito's already on Wynn, and the pair of them ride off, leaving me standing next to Sabre. *So it's like that, eh?* I get on hastily and get moving, the too-quiet Mana engine switching on without a sound. Still weird.

***

The problem with defending Riverdale is that there really isn't a natural chokepoint or even a simple demarcation of urban and nature. At best, there's the dirt road that cuts behind the suburb, but with the way most of the houses abut the forest, there's no real clear ground to fight from. We can, and probably have, thrown up Mana shields around the whole suburb, but the larger the shield, the less powerful it is. Unless, of course, you get a bigger Mana engine and battery to power it.

"Care to fill me in?" I send to the Spirit after a few moments of thought. Trying to figure out the plan seems silly, considering they have a plan.

"Pretty simple. We're hunkering down in a few houses along the line that have been reinforced for just this purpose. Long-range weaponry and casters being primary, a few melee supporters in the mix. Mobile troops here and here"—as Ali speaks, my map flashes in time—*"with a final reserve here. Mid-way fallback points are here and here with final fallback at the bridge."*

I grunt, tracking over the map. If we fall back to the bridge, the school and the last few people who haven't made it out of the tents are going to lose everything they've got. Again. Hopefully they've grabbed anything important and stuffed it into their inventory, but with the panic that's probably spreading in the school, it's unlikely they got it all. Still, things can be replaced. Us humans are getting a lot scarcer.

"Where am I?"

"We're in the middle house," Ali says, flashing it green.

Makes sense, we'll be able to… I clamp my mouth shut when I watch Lana and Mikito split to head to their own posts. Right. No use putting all of us in the same house. We'd hold that location and maybe lose the others. Better to split up the heavy hitters for where they can do the most good.

Glancing upward, I watch as the flood of purple dots continues to advance. *"Any data on levels yet?"*

"Drones are on their way. Data should be back in another ten." Before I can even ask, Ali continues. *"The Kapre had the choice of giving us range or accurate data. We picked range."*

Fair enough. I still wish we had more information sooner, but it is what it is. I'm pulling up to the designated house, another Riverdale special with its ground floor and partially-submerged basement. A long, deep backyard runs into the woods and a small bike path. A kid's playset and a pair of trees lie trampled on the ground, smashed apart by a metal dinosaur that shifts from foot to foot, moonlight gleaming off its body. I stare at it and its likely controller, a half-Dragon man, who's busy planting a series of explosives into the ground and directing others who are busy shooting, blasting, and chopping back the forest. A part of me wonders why we've never done that before, but I'm smart enough to keep my mouth shut. After all, it's not as if I did it either.

"Tim," I call to the lizardman.

He turns toward me, flashing a wide grin filled with shark-like teeth. I have to admit, it's a bit disturbing, but I don't let that show on my face. Tim's dealt with enough shit for the way he looks after he made the change. No point in adding to it, especially when I know from the other side what it's like to have others judge you based on your looks only. The number of times I've been shouted at to go "home" while in Vancouver isn't something I can be bothered to count.

"You in charge here?" I ask.

"Not anymore," Tim says, grinning. "Heard you were assigned here, so I'm handing this over to you."

"Nope." Ali floats over and shakes his head. "Boy-o here doesn't know the plan. Not really. You're in charge, Timmy's."

"Don't call me that!" Tim says, and I chuckle slightly while Ali smirks. Admittedly, the loss of our favorite donut place is more of a sore spot for some. Personally, I thought their coffee was okay and their donuts stopped tasting right a while ago. "And I don't want the responsibility."

"Suck it up, scaleycup," Ali retorts.

Before this can escalate any further, I point at the big dinosaur-shaped creature that stomps around on its clawed four legs, its extra-long neck twisting and turning as it scans for trouble, tail lashing out behind it. "What's with the dinosaur?"

"It's a Dragon. Sort of."

"It's kind of missing its wings. Or you know, ridges on the back and a much longer body if you're going Chinese," I point out.

"I haven't put the wings in yet. Do you know how expensive anti-gravity engines are?" Tim grumbles, and I just look at him, sitting on my hovering bike. He blinks and nods. "Well, yeah. Okay. Fine. I need to put a lot of them in to keep the entire thing stable."

"So you made a dinosaur," I point out.

"It's a wingless Dragon!"

"Di-no-saur."

"Go plant some mines!" Tim snaps.

I chuckle, transforming Sabre before walking toward the rest of the group to do as he says. Well, that settled that.

Let me be clear. When I say we planted mines and trapped the area, this wasn't a professional job. Sure, we'd picked up a few tricks along the way—maps of where all the mines were, secondary triggers just in case the first didn't work— but we mostly just stuck them in the ground and moved on. The mines and grenades aren't going to do much damage, so no one is willing to spend a ton of time on it. They'll add damage and hurt whatever comes, but conventional weaponry in general just isn't that powerful. It's why it's so cheap in the Shop. Anything mass-produced has a tendency to be reduced in effectiveness—or maybe it's more accurate to say it's not boosted—by the System. Still, if my experience in the Spore dungeon was anything to go by, explosions and flames do a lot in terms of sowing confusion. And I'll admit it, I add a couple of the more expensive Chaos mines as a tribute to Richard. The man always did love adding those to a fight.

By the time we pull back to the house to settle down for the fight, the data from the drones is streaming in. Not as good as anything Ali could get if he was there himself, but the images are enough to give us an idea of what we're looking at. Unsurprisingly, the first wave is comprised of the lower-level monsters that hang around the safety of the city. Most of these we leave to the automated defenses and Tim's dinosaur. The hunters that sit, squat, and peek out from the windows of the house add the weight of their own firepower once in a while, enough so that Tim shouts at them to slow down and conserve their Mana and charges.

Out on the lawn, there's just me and a man who looks like a cross between a lumberjack and a pro linebacker. I let him do most of the work with a sword the size of a spear, which he wields with ease at any monster that breaks past the defenses. Few enough right now, though I watch others flow into the city through blind spots between the front line.

"Ali…"

"Already on it, boy-o. We've got mobile shields on the way to plug the gaps."

With a thought, I'm floating a few feet, enough to get a better view of the forest in front without getting too high and blocking the shots of those behind me. A few feet isn't a lot, but it's enough for me to start adding the weight of my own firepower to the line. I let loose my newly upgraded Mana Darts, a half dozen glowing blue missiles of irritation. They hit, they hurt, then someone else's shot kills them..

All the while, I'm watching the dots in front of me shift from the purple of unknowns to the grays of low-level creatures, then to the blues of those only mildly below my level and the greens of those level appropriate. The fact that it's all based off my numerical level means the data isn't exactly accurate, but I've gotten used to reading it anyway. End of the day, blues are good, very good. It means that the hunters with me, the fighters, and the automated defenses can handle them. If we start seeing greens in any real numbers, then we're in trouble.

Minutes tick on. Monsters fall and pile up before me and always, always there are more. Conservative firing or not, the hunters behind me run out of beam rifle charges and have to switch batteries or to projectile weaponry. The slack in fire, the break in shooting, means more monsters make it through and the linebacker has to pick up the slack. I could look at his name, figure out who he is, but I'd forget it soon enough anyway.

"Tim," I shout over the mic, raising my hand and opening up with the Inlin attached to the mecha, watching as it spews death. "You want me to push them back?"

"We're good. Hold back on your Mana," Tim says over the com.

"My level's pretty good," I add, glancing at the bar that has barely shifted from three quarters down, even with the firepower I've thrown around. Tim's never fought with me before, and unlike me, he doesn't have Ali feeding him stats on everyone around.

Silence. Then Tim says, "Light them up."

My lips widen and I raise my hand, calling lightning to my fingers. I'll admit, months after I was able to summon the forces of nature for the first time, I still can't believe I'm doing this. As much as I bitch about the System, there are perks. I hold back for a second, reaching for that other sense that Ali awakened in me so long ago. An Elemental Affinity they call it, a sense for the forces that make up the world. Sensing it is only the first part. Making adjustments comes after that. Small ones, tiny enough by themselves, that build and build, then I let the lightning loose from my hands. There is no pain, just a slight shuddering as electrons pull through me and outward before I play the electricity across the forest and the monsters. The creatures twitch and fall from the attack, lightning sparking and cooking flesh as I float higher. I barely notice poorly aimed blasts to my back, Sabre's armor shielding me from the majority of the damage.

"Oy! Friendly there," Ali shouts for me while I cut off the lightning.

The Swarm lies twitching and smoking in front of me, the few still alive finished off by quick blasts. Simple. Easy.

And of course, that's when things go to hell.

Red dots, a lot of them.

"Tim, you seeing this?" I snap as I float back down.

"I see it. This…"

"I know. Pull back?"

"One second," Tim says, and I know he's consulting with whoever is running the whole show.

"*Ali. This seems… wrong. We've never had a Swarm in the middle of the night before. Doesn't make sense for it to happen—so far, it seems most of the major predators are day creatures, and they're the ones that dictate the Swarm movement. No reason for a Swarm to start if there isn't enough pressure, which shouldn't come at night. And reds? That's Level 40 plus.*"

"*I know, boy-o. I'm looking into it, but I ain't seeing anything strange. If someone, something screwed with the monsters around here, it's too far back for me to tell.*"

I don't have to wait long before the call for a general fallback comes over the radio. The mobile troops move into the street to lend their firepower to make pullout easier, allowing the linebacker and our hunters a chance to disengage. I don't move though, staring out into the distance, not firing.

"John! We're pulling back. Come on!" Tim shouts, but I shake my head, still staring into the distance.

"Shit. I know that look, boy-o. Forget it."

"Tim…"

"Here we go again," Ali says plaintively.

"John?" Tim's voice sounds a little harried.

"I'm going to check something out," I say then take off running straight into the woods.

"John!"

Tim's shout gets lost as I kill the audio connection. I leave him my video feed, though who knows if it'll still be transmitting by the time I get there. There being uncertain and unknown, since I'm working off a hunch. An educated hunch, but a hunch nonetheless.

***

This isn't the first time I've gone running through a Swarm. I figure it's, like, the third time. If you count the couple of runs through the Spore dungeon, it's my fifth time bouncing through clumps of monsters. All that is to say, there's a trick to it, one that can be acquired through experience, preservation, and a willingness to do incredibly stupid things.

First thing to know, always keep moving. Staying still is death. I'm pounding ground since the hover ability on the mecha can't keep up with the speed I'm moving at. I do use the anti-gravity engines in small measure, giving me additional distance on each leap, but it's all about momentum. Monsters in a Swarm aren't out to kill and maim. They're mostly running away from something, like a bear running from a forest fire. It isn't necessarily dangerous if you get out of its way. Of course, when they're running right into your house or city, getting out of the way is much harder.

"Yahoo!' Ali screams, laughing as he flies above me.

I can't help but grin, bouncing off the ground and bowling a giant slug-like creature out of the air through sheer momentum. It splats against a six-legged cat monster, then I'm gone.

Second lesson—sometimes, going through rather than around can be more efficient. Physics in a System world is messed up, but momentum is still momentum, which means a fast-moving heavy object is still more likely to smash apart a tree or monster than the other way around. Or you know, at least push it aside.

I skip across the ground, get into a slide, and pass under the giant rock monster that swings at me. I don't even bother opening fire on it, though Ali goes into a panicked climb as he tries to get away from one of the few monsters that can not only see but hurt him. Unfortunately, my slide keeps going long after I want to stop and the weird slime creature that glomps along looks to be interested in eating me.

Third lesson—always have another trick up your sleeve. I flick on Blink Step and teleport to the side, slamming my fist to the side to kick my entire body up and let me keep running. I toss a plasma grenade off-hand into the path of the slime monster just because I'm tired of getting eaten. Like, seriously, I'm not into slime monsters.

I keep running, dodging deeper and deeper into the Swarm, watching as the blue and green dots disappear from my map to be replaced by red dots. Many of these monsters are less panicked, more angry, and I find myself having to shoot, cast, and dodge more than ever. Frankly, it's getting dangerous, even for me, but whatever I'm looking for, I haven't seen it yet.

"Ali? Got anything?"

"Nope," the diminutive Spirit sends right back, probably expecting the question.

I call forth my sword, using it to impale an ugly horse-faced demon as I go by, it's sex dangling dangerously low. No city for you. I leave my sword in it, continuing on as I drop another pair of grenades behind me. As I said, they don't do a lot of damage, but the confusion and fire help.

When the sea of monsters around me becomes almost purely red, I know my time to cut and run is near. I need some results before turning back becomes an impossibility. Did I mention that Fate really doesn't like me?

Just about when I think that, I get an answer. It's just not the one I expected.

The halberd cuts through Sabre's armor and into me with ease, catching me mid-bounce and throwing me for a hundred or so feet and through a couple of trees. Pain racks my body as broken ribs grind in my chest, blood pouring from the wound and staining the mecha red. A part of me is wondering how the hell I got blindsided like that, but I'm already triggering Sabre's shield and my own. I'd have had them up earlier, but Sabre's shield drains her battery fast, which is why I try not to use it when I don't need to.

It's a good thing I've got the shields up though, because the follow-up attack crashes right into Sabre's shield and is stopped only by my own Skill. I stare at the glowing pale-blue blade in disbelief before I trigger Sabre's mini-missiles.

My attacker jumps back a short distance, his weapon spinning and slicing as he tears the missiles apart. While I struggle to my feet, the son of a bitch cuts my missiles apart. With a halberd. It's times like this that I hate the System. Still, he might have sliced the missiles in half, but I can remotely trigger them, so I do. The ensuing explosion is less useful for damage purposes—which sucks because those are expensive, hand-crafted missiles—and more useful for giving me time to actually assess what I'm seeing and feeling while I back away.

Feeling first. I'm not sliced in half. More like a third off my hit points. The cut itself was probably about four inches deep, but Sabre's automatic healing processes has clogged the bleeding and started injecting healing potions directly into my body. It's the usual mix of a regeneration booster and a direct healing potion. Sabre's nanites are also flowing toward the armor plate, patching the hole as fast as they can.

Seeing next. My attacker's tall, thin, fast, and deadly. He's dressed in high-tech camouflage gear that hides his face and body, but the way he moves and fights speaks of years of mastery at combat. Ali is flying back to catch up with us but circling wide as if the Spirit is scared of him.

"Sorry, boy-o. He dropped out of hiding just as you got near him." Ali squints at the figure before me. Data blooms on top of the figure, but it's not particularly useful. Just a lot of question marks.

Sneaky Bastard (Level ?? ???)

HP: ???/???

MP: ???/???

"And his data's all hidden."

"No shit," I answer. I raise my Inlin, tracking the masked figure with it while I keep my other hand down and to the side, ready to call forth and use my sword if he gets in too close. Of course, with that polearm, he's got the reach advantage on me.

Whatever internal debate my attacker was having, it's resolved when he flickers toward me. I'd say faster than I've ever seen, but that's a lie. Mikito, boosted by a Thousand Steps and her Haste Skill, is just as fast. Which is a good thing for me because I spar with her quite often.

I catch the polearm with my summoned sword's guard and lash out a kick to a kneecap. It's dodged easily, and his follow-up attack with the butt of his halberd crunches into my shield. I watch as the barely regenerated shield flickers and dies again, and I stop playing around.

I throw on Thousand Steps, Blink Step to the side of him, and cut fast. He's already moving, dodging backward to get back into his preferred range, but I expected that. I trigger Blade Strike with my cut, sending the blue edge of force outward and opening a cut on the man's armor. It's not a powerful strike, but it does score the armor, opening a wound on his body. I pile on the Blade Strikes, one after the other.

After the third attack, they stop hitting because the bastard is weaving between the strikes, shifting his body in weird angles as he closes the distance. Having shaken off the surprise, he's back in my face and attacking and it's my turn to retreat, dodge, and generally try to stay alive. It's not that simple though, as I realize I'm seriously out-matched. Every shot, every spell, every cut I throw is anticipated and I'm somehow never in the right place to land the hit. All the while, he's chipping away at my Soul Shield then Sabre's armor, the halberd a twirling blur that rocks me side to side.

Unable to get away, pushed into a corner, I open up with the barrage of missiles again now that they've reloaded. This time, my attacker doesn't bother to dodge them, tanking the damage to stay close. However, for that brief second when fire illuminates everything, I disappear.

As I said, always have an extra trick. And the QSM is mine.

Chapter 8

I crouch low by instinct as my body shifts over to the other dimension partially, the QSM holding me partway between each. Now that I'm hidden and untouchable—mostly—I back away. That glowing pale-blue Skill probably could hurt me, even through the dimensional wall, if it hit. One thing I learnt when I fought the Hakarta, the QSM might be powerful, but its shift is distinctive, which is why I waited until my attacker couldn't see before I used it. Now he's spinning around, searching for me on the wrong plane, probably thinking I Blink Stepped away.

As I back off, I have time to really study my opponent. There's something eerily familiar about the way he moves. I had gotten that feeling when we fought, and it strikes me again. I just can't put a finger on it. Not yet.

"Ali, anything you can tell me?"

"Well, I'm pretty sure he's the reason the Swarm happened. I think he's been pushing the Bosses around, creating the environment for one."

"You can do that?"

"Well, he can."

I hear the slight incredulity in Ali's thoughts as well. Jesus. Perhaps it's time to get out of here.

I really should remember not to tempt Fate like that. Pretty much the moment I think it, he shifts and moves, crossing to where I am, his polearm glowing with blue light. I throw myself to the side, but I'm too slow, too surprised to get out of the way properly. I feel the blue light tear through me, pulling apart atoms and locking up muscles in agony. My shields are down— can't keep them up in this state—so I'm just a sitting duck as he lashes out again and again and I scramble to get away. My hit points are falling like a waterfall, dropping below 40% in seconds.

I'm too exposed between dimensions. With a thought, I drop, fading back into reality. Before I can stand, he's on me, a hand clamping my arm. He grinds down, inhuman strength warping armor until he reaches the QSM embedded in my flesh, then he keeps squeezing. I hear the crack of my arm breaking, along with the QSM, but I'm too focused on his other hand. The polearm is held up overhand and stabbing down and I can't get away.

Ali swoops in, catching the blade at the edge and pushing it aside just enough that it misses my neck and rips apart the armor around it. I scream, pulling on my gift, and Blink away, stumbling. I don't hesitate this time, Blinking again and again. On the third, I drop a series of grenades before I Blink again, making Sabre inject a Mana potion into my body to give me the energy to do so.

In the corner of my eyes, I see Ali's dot flicker and vanish, banished. I snarl, but I can't stop, can't wait. Running isn't the best option, but it's the only option here. He's too fast to fight at range, too good to fight at melee, and my tricks don't seem to be working. I run, Thousand Steps and Blink Step taking me farther away with each breath, my ruined hand and QSM clutched to my chest. I run, because staying means my death.

***

"John!"

The shout brings me back to my senses, Sabre finally in contact with the city. Ali's still banished, so I'm limited to what on-board software and my Skills can provide in terms of information. It's not bad, mind you, and outside of the main path of the Swarm, I'm able to heal and kill on my way back. My left arm's fixed and working again, though the QSM is still broken. To say I'm angry about it is probably an understatement, but underlying the anger is fear. I've never had a fight be so one-sided before, have it dominated completely from start to finish.

"I'm here," I reply, glancing at my Mana bar. I have to admit, I've been keeping my Mana high just in case I need to run again. As much as I'd love to pull Ali back, I definitely don't want to be caught out here again.

"What the hell happened?" Tim's harried voice comes back. "And why the hell did you leave?"

"Had a hunch. It paid off. I'm coming in from the other side of the river. Think you guys can drop the shield for me?"

"One second…" Tim answers then falls silent.

Within minutes, I catch sight of the walls that make up the start of the defenses and the slightest shimmer in the sky that indicates the shield is still up. To my right, I see the bridge and the guard posts being swarmed by monsters, bolts of blue mana beams, red flames, and I hear the crack of projectiles erupting from the wall and the defenders. Behind the monstrous attackers, Riverdale is ablaze, houses and trees on fire. Thankfully, it seems to be relatively contained, the snow on the ground keeping it from becoming a full-out inferno.

"Redeemer," Capstan, the Yerick's First Fist and titular leader, rumbles over the communication channel. "We are not able to drop the shield for you. We do have some minor problems on the river. Can you deal with it?"

I grunt, looking at the low-running, half-frozen river, and see what they mean. The shield is holding up quite well, but the small pile-up of aquatic and semi-aquatic monsters on the water's surface are clawing and biting as they batter at the barrier. Their constant attacks are weakening the shield slowly, and if they aren't stopped, they'll eventually tear it open and leave us vulnerable to being flanked. Raising the Inlin, I target the monsters, picking them off from behind as I float forward.

An hour later, I'm done shooting and looting the corpses and have stuck most of them in my Altered Space, leaving me floating in the middle of the river, occasionally adding the weight of my spells to the pile of monsters still trying to cross the bridge. Luckily, the vast majority of the creatures can't fly—and those that can rarely bother us. Unfortunately, the corpse pile in front of the wall is so high that I can barely see the monsters I'm supposed to kill. I can shoot farther downriver, and I do, but that doesn't really help relieve the pressure at the wall itself. I'm mostly just stuck, floating and waiting, watching the pile of red dots slowly disappear, some being killed, others following the river farther north.

When the shield finally lowers, I breathe a sigh of relief and float up to the bridge. I'm already working my fingers, calling Ali back to this dimension. I doubt my attacker will make an attempt now. Ali shimmers into existence, purple, green, and yellow colors swirling before he arrives with an audible pop, clad in his usual orange jumpsuit and looking uncharacteristically serious. I guess getting killed can do that to a Spirit.

"Redeemer. Care to explain why you abandoned your post?" Capstan rumbles, hands on his hips and neck stretched forward as he stands on the wall with the rest of our fighters. I watch his short tail wave slowly, methodically.

"Had a hunch the Swarm wasn't natural. Thought I'd check it out," I explain, ignoring the threatening nature of his words. I like Capstan, but the Yerick is used to working with his clan where his word is law.

"Was it?" Mikito asks.

I look at the little Japanese woman, flicking a glance at her still-dripping naginata, before nodding slowly. It takes me only a second to spot Lana, knee deep in the bodies, looting. Surprisingly, Aiden's on the walls too, earphones on and staring away from the carnage with an indescribably sad expression. That man's bleeding heart is going to get him killed someday.

"Sort of," Ali answers for me while I look around. "We found the instigator. I'm sending you guys the data. Boy-o got his ass kicked though."

"So did you," I point out to Ali, who sticks his tongue out in reply before wincing at the movement.

I see worried looks cross more than one face. Outside of potentially Capstan, I'm stronger, faster, and tougher than anyone here.

"This seems to be information Lord Roxley should learn of," rumbles Capstan.

Ali snorts, about to retort, and I shoot the Spirit a look.

Capstan picks up on the byplay and inclines his head. "Do we know who this was?"

"No real proof. As you can see, he's all covered up," I reply then pause, considering adding my suspicions. Eventually, I choose to stay silent. Even an old dog like me can learn.

Capstan notes the hesitation and snorts, nostrils flaring, but he doesn't push. Leveling charges without proof is probably a good way of getting into real trouble.

"How'd the defense do?" I ask, glancing around. "We going to be able to reclaim Riverdale?"

"We held them at the wall with minimal issues. Allowing them into the chokepoint ensured that the shield was not over-burdened and allowed us to deal with the Swarm. No major injuries and no deaths," Capstan replies, shrugging broad shoulders. "We will be sending in groups to verify the damage and deal with the fires soon, once the Swarm fully disperses."

I nod and sigh. "I'll join them. I should check out my house too."

Capstan nods, and I glance at Mikito, who shakes her head at my unasked question, pointing at Lana. I stare at the redhead, who's focused on looting, and I nod. Yeah, best to have Mikito keep an eye on the lady. It's not as if I'm that worried about an attack in town. That would be a touch too blatant I think.

***

Coming home, I stare at the remains of my house. The good news is that it hasn't caught fire and the stand-alone workshop is mostly in one piece. Bad news is that, reinforced walls or not, the house didn't survive the Swarm. I don't know if it was one huge monster or a series of medium-sized ones that knocked down the walls, but I guess it really doesn't matter.

> *89 Alsek Rd.*
>
> *Current Owner: John Lee, Adventurer*
>
> *Purpose: Residence*
>
> *Status: 84% Structural Damage*

A thought is all I need to call up the next screen.

> *Cost for Repairs: 22,987 Credits*

Expensive. It's more expensive than buying the actual building initially, even if it was discounted. I've managed to upgrade it a few times, so the cost isn't completely out to lunch. If I get someone with skills or the right Class, I could have them do the repairs for a lot less. I raise my hand to pay for it, knowing that it'll take a chunk of my Credits, then hesitate, realization flowing through me.

Gods. Of course. That's what the Swarm was for. They weren't looking to kill us or hurt us. They were looking to make us waste our Credits, waste our time and effort rebuilding. Riverdale will never be particularly safe, not without a lot more effort put into developing walls, pits, and other defenses. It's just too spread out and exposed.

"First Fist. Lord Roxley," I greet both of them as they pick up my call. "I'm standing in front of my destroyed house and I'm thinking that this was the point. I could fix it but—"

"But it would be destroyed again in short order. Perfect plausible deniability," Roxley says. "Yes, we know."

"Oh…" I fall silent, shaking my head. I guess when it comes to the politics of this stuff, I'm still behind. Well, at least I figured it out. Not completely, of course. We could buy the identity of my attacker from the Shop, but considering he had Skills that hid his identity, I wouldn't be surprised if it was very expensive. And then what would we do? Accuse him and end up in a fight that we know we're already going to lose? Better to avoid that discussion for now.

"We have already informed many of the residents that we have arranged housing on this side of the river temporarily. The General Council has been informed of the likelihood of further damage to residences in Riverdale," Roxley says.

"The Yerick have offered to put up some of those displaced in our settlement," Capstan adds.

I blink, trying to figure out how many would actually take them up on the offer. Then again, most of these people were living in tents not so long ago. The Yukon winter isn't particularly comfortable to live in with only a single layer of thin polyester between you and the howling winds.

"I guess you guys have it figured out." I kill the channel before they can answer and look up at my Spirit. "Ali? Any suggestions of where we're going to crash?"

"Well, Capstan did say the Yerick are taking in strays."

"No."

"John…"

"No."

"Fine. Maybe ask the girls?"

I nod. True. If anyone has an extra space or know of any extra space, it'd be Lana. After all, between her involvement in the city and the foundation she's set up, she's probably got the best connections. Even if she's been shirking her responsibilities lately.

I cast one last look at the house, wondering if I should go into the ruins to pick up anything. In the end, I don't. There's nothing in there that I really need. Everything important, everything expensive or System-registered is on me. The rest—clothing, food, and furniture—doesn't matter. I was never one to put up photos, and when the electronics died, that destroyed everything else I kept. Now all I have are fading memories, glimpses of the past and flashes of what my sister looked and sounded like. Just ghosts in my soul.

"John?"

I blink, finding my hands aching from how tightly I've closed them. Damage monitors flicker, telling me that Sabre's gauntlets have taken damage while I was off thinking.

"Sorry. Thinking. You're right, let's talk to the girls."

***

I'm not sure it's a good thing or a bad thing that Ali was right. Lana did have a place for us to crash. The fact that it was the floor of the Nugget… well, that was just the way it was. I sigh, shaking my head as I lever myself straight after only a few hours of sleep. Not that I needed much more physically, but mentally, I could probably have used a few more hours. Still, the Nugget needs to open and at least breakfast is on its way. Looking around, I note that Lana's still in the office, probably crashed out on the couch inside.

"John," Mikito greets me as she walks out of the ladies' room. She looks all put together, shining with that weird too-clean look of a Clean spell.

"Morning." I push tables and chairs into place before seating myself. I cast a simple Clean spell on myself, twitching as a thousand feathery fingers run down my body and clear away the dirt and grime. Mana drops, and in a second, I'm clean but feeling slightly raw. Did I mention that it also exfoliates?

"I was reviewing the fight footage," Mikito dives right in, taking a seat next to me. "He uses a polearm too."

"Mmhmmm…" I answer as Sarah troops in.

Richard's ex dumps a pot of coffee and two cups in front of us. I smile my thanks and she inclines her head before heading back into the kitchen.

"He's good. Very good. Different style, more Chinese, but very good. You need more training if you wish to face him again," Mikito says, pulling a cup to her.

"Huh. I was hoping I'd just let you deal with him next time," I tease, stirring sugar into my coffee.

"Don't have the Levels," Mikito says, shaking her head.

I sigh. She's right. There's the thing—skill matters, but Levels really matter. "Recommendations?"

She purses her lips, thinking. "I'll review it more. Let you know." Mikito's black hair sways as she glances back at the closed office door. "John… Lana. I'm worried."

"Oh?" I raise an eyebrow, urging her on.

"She's not handling Richard's death well." Mikito looks down at her hands. Her voice drops as she continues to speak. "Not that there's a good way when you lose someone. But she's not talking. Or raging. No crying. She's just... focused."

"I've noticed." I look at the door again then glance upward, calling Ali's attention back to us. "You got anything to add?"

Ali's lips purse and he stares at us. "She's in denial."

"Figured that. She's obsessed with Credits right now. Why?"

"I can find out more, but she's a friend. If we do this…" Ali says hesitantly.

"Crossing a line?"

"Definitely." Ali nods firmly. "There's basic data searches and then there's this."

I look at Mikito, who returns my gaze. She considers for a moment before she nods firmly and I nod once. I guess we're committed to this then. Breach of privacy and all. I just hope what we learn is worth it.

Talk drops off as Sarah comes in with a plate of bacon, and I pour the coffee as we get ready for another great day in the city.

Chapter 9

Swarm or not, life goes on. In days, the city has fallen back into its new pattern. Our guests continue to make their presence known, poking around town and setting up a series of meetings with various individuals. Nothing that can ever be considered hindrances, but the background grumbling about the state of affairs in the city grows. Unsurprisingly, humans being humans, not everyone agrees to staying out of their homes in Riverdale or refusing to fix them up. Futile or not, I can understand clutching to something, anything that reminds you of your past. Understand, if not relate to.

Mikito and I pool our Credits and pick up a small apartment downtown once we realize there isn't a better option. Lana refuses to spend her Credits or stay with us, citing the pets as an excuse. She ends up staying in the Nugget's office, where we meet her for breakfast every day. The rings under her eyes have gotten darker and I know she's not sleeping as much as she needs. Enhanced constitution or not, we're still mostly human and need a few hours every day. Even her pets look a bit worn down. I have a sneaking suspicion she's been hunting with them at night, alone.

Lana refuses to speak about it, leaving Mikito and I to wonder and worry. Ali hasn't provided us any further details, just asking us to be patient. I'm not entirely sure what the holdup is, but then again, I don't have access to the System like he does.

Perhaps it's the constant death, the on-going pressure of annihilation, or just the Council's desire to give people something, anything to celebrate that has the streets decked out for Christmas day. Preparations took surprisingly little time. Skills and magic can make a lot of things, so giant Santa sculptures, thirty-foot-tall snow slides, bouncy castles, and party decorations litter the downtown. They've turned Main St. into the main party area, with tables full of food and drink and trapped Fire Elementals giving off light and heat in equal order. A good thing too, with temperatures sitting at -30°C tonight before the wind chill.

Everyone who can be spared from the city defenses are there, Yerick and Kapre mixing with humans. Most of the humans are busy explaining Christmas food and rituals to the aliens in stilted, uncomfortable conversations. As usual, the hunting groups mix the best—the shared danger and risk having broken down the barriers between the races.

Well, the hunting groups and the children. Kids, once they've realized that neither group is inherently dangerous, get along extremely well. Mixed groups of children race through the streets and the giant bouncy hall set up next to the bottom of 2nd St, playing with the wild abandon that only children have. It's good to see them, hear them laughing again. The first few months, there wasn't much laughter. Even now, the occasional human child will drop out of play as bad memories surface, but their minders are more than used to that, offering cuddles, kind words, and sweets as necessary.

Everyone's having fun in the main square, laughing and dancing and passing along small gifts. So of course, I'm out here on the walls, staring into the dark of the night. Other than Tim's dinosaur drone, I'm by myself, holding the south wall on the off-chance something might test our defenses tonight. I turn away from the party, commanding the magnification to drop off as I stare at the road before me. It's good that people are enjoying themselves, taking a break. Perhaps this will quiet some of the grumbling I've heard recently.

"John," Mikito greets me as she climbs up next to me.

"Mikito. What are you doing here?" I jerk my head back toward the city. "Why aren't you at the party?"

"I was. People were wondering where you were."

"Ah…" I fall silent, shaking my head. "I don't celebrate Christmas. Figured I might as well let others who do so have fun."

"Oh?" Mikito raises an eyebrow, propping her naginata up against the wall she leans on.

"Yeah. My family wasn't Christian. My dad thought the entire thing strange. He never had Christmas growing up. Actually made it difficult for us in school…" I sigh, recollections of taunts and awkward conversations as a kid coming back to me. I shake my head, pushing it aside. That life is gone now. The past is pain.

"I understand," Mikito answers, looking back, and sighs. "Last Christmas Eve, Shota and I, we spent it together. This year, we were supposed to celebrate it with his parents as a married couple. Our first…"

I hear her voice catch, the hitch in it. I ignore it, knowing Mikito hates to have us notice. For a time, we stand there in silence, staring into the dark. Even now, with the city slowly coming back to life, the darkness is barely pushed back by the ambient light. It's something that would have been impossible a short while ago, this inky blackness, and leaves no doubt about why our ancestors made fire a priority.

"You could join them," Mikito suggests after a while. She doesn't look surprised when I shake my head. Her next words come out as a statement. "You're planning on leaving."

I flinch slightly even though there is no accusation in her voice. "Yes."

"When?"

"After we've sorted the Envoy out. Once Whitehorse has settled, once the set-up time is over…"

"Where?"

"I'm… not sure," I admit, staring into the darkness. "Probably down to Fort Nelson first. Debating between Edmonton and Vancouver."

"Your family is—was—in Vancouver, was it not?" Mikito asks.

I nod. She frowns at me and I know what she's thinking—that I should go there to check it out. But I verified a while ago. They're dead. I paid the cost to the Shop, high as it was.

"Have you told Lana?"

"She knows." I figured that out a while ago, that she knew I'd be leaving one day.

"Did you tell her?" I shake my head, and the Japanese woman sighs and shakes her head. "You should."

"I will. When it's right." Not that it matters. Lana's focused on whatever she's up to, and everything else, everyone else, is secondary to that.

Mikito nods and lets the topic drop, and I exhale. Well, that went better than I thought it would. As much as I like Whitehorse, as proud as I am of the people here and what they've done, this isn't my home. Soon enough, I'll be gone. It's better for me, for the city, if I stay out of their way, out of their politics and institutions. Better to be the ghost in the system that no one remembers.

***

We're having an early breakfast a few days later, the sun still hidden beneath the horizon, when Amelia and Jim come in looking tired and depressed. At Mikito's wave, they join us, snagging a cup of coffee and orange juice respectively while they take a seat.

"What's up?" I ask, not bothering with pleasantries.

"We lost another team. The Killa Squad," Jim says, and I raise an eyebrow.

"Martial artists. Went around punching and kicking things mostly, though they carried guns too. One of the mid-range squads, they worked the level twenty to thirty zones," Amelia explains.

I nod. Right. I remember seeing them in the Nugget. Tattoos, mohawks, and wannabe fighters given life by the System. Nice guys actually, if loud. I cudgel my brain for more information but find nothing—I rarely interact with the majority of hunter parties. They weren't good enough to be part of the elite squads but weren't so useless that they needed to be babysat.

"How many does that leave us?" Mikito asks.

Lana just listens, looking mostly disinterested in the entire proceedings. I frown slightly at that—Lana used to have a bleeding heart and now… well. Now.

"My squad working the level thirty-plus zone, three more in the level twenty-plus zone. And about six permanent that are being worked up," Jim says, bushy white eyebrows tightening.

"Six? I'm sure I've worked with more," I prod the older First Nation Elder.

"Six permanent. Most of those you've been working with have been, ummm…" Jim pauses, searching for the word.

"Casuals," Amelia says, holding a hand up to cover her mouth as she speaks around her meal. "They're there for the experience, not the hunting."

"Oh…" I frown, shaking my head. Well, that explains the level of stupidity I saw in some of them. But… "Why me?"

"Oooh, oooh. I got this one," Ali says. "You're scary, so the casuals listen to you. You're strong enough that even if they screw up badly, you can save their asses. And you're a horrible teacher. Since they aren't here to learn anyway, that's fine."

"I'm not—" I protest and see nods from all around.

Even Lana joins in, a slight smile crossing her face. I glare at the group, feeling betrayed. I mean, sure, I don't like idiocy and I do shout at them a bit when they make mistakes, but it's for their own good. How the hell are they supposed to learn if no one tells them?

"Sorry, John, but Ali's right," Amelia says. "We want to coach the other groups, not crush them."

I growl softly, crossing my arms, and Ali snickers. "Boy-o's pouting."

"*I am not,*" I snap at Ali, who chuckles out loud.

Lana smiles slightly then glances at the food and the way Amelia and Jim are attacking it before she looks at us. "Are we ready to go?"

I open my mouth to agree, but Mikito cuts in, "How did we lose them?"

The topic brought back to hand, Jim and Amelia share glances.

Jim answers slowly, his deep voice dropping lower. "Not sure. The Kapre let us know they died, and when we got a team to look into it, all we found were signs of a fight. No bodies. The snow overnight hid most of the tracks, so all we know is that the fight was pretty focused."

There were quite a few frowns at that. While monsters do drag away and eat bodies, it was unusual for there to be no bodies at all. Anything that could take out a group quickly and took their bodies was not good.

"Get us the location. We'll swing by that area and see if Ali can see anything else," I say and get a pair of grateful nods.

I ignore Ali's muttering about not being a tracker. I'm sure he'll do the best he can, even if it might not be much. At the very least, we can see if we picked up anything new.

While the System has taken to teleporting in new monster types much less frequently, it still happens. If it's a new monster and one powerful enough to take out a hunting group that quickly, we'll want to squash it before it starts replicating. The last thing we need is to have something truly nasty out here.

Now that we've got this sorted, Mikito stands.

Lana huffs out, "Finally," too loud to have been missed by any of us.

We all ignore the redhead stalking out of the pub, though Amelia shoots a concerned glance her way before looking at us. All I can do is shrug before I hurry after the ladies. With the mood Lana is in, I doubt she'll wait.

***

I snarl, hunkering behind the absurdly strong tree as the barbs from the Ilukin monster tears apart everything else around me. I grip the barb that sticks out of my shoulder and tug it out, feeling the serrated edges tear through my flesh and catch on the metallic edges of Sabre's armor plating. Blood pours out, and I have to mentally command Sabre to not inject me with a healing potion. No point in wasting Credits on that just yet. With a flick of my hand, I toss the barb away and scan the surroundings.

Mikito is crouched in a small depression, barbs flying above her head and forcing her to stay down even as the Ilukin attempts to close on her. To my right, Lana and the puppies are sheltering behind portable force shields and my own Soul Shield, both of which are doing their best to keep them alive. Lana's working on pulling out the barbs in Wynn's flesh. Already, I can tell that the shields are beginning to fail. I swear, recalling how everything went to hell in such a short time.

The Ilukin found us after we'd been to the kill site and found nothing. We'd moved deeper into the zone, hoping to find traces of a monster that could have killed the hunting group. That's when we were ambushed by the Ilukin, crouched at the top of a rise and hidden by the snow. The Ilukin look like the meaner, nastier version of a porcupine with their barbs reversed and all in white. Each time they shift, they shoot and regenerate the barbs in seconds, filling the air with deadly missiles.

In moments, they've denuded the foliage and are in the process of tearing down trees and rock with their barbs. Poking my head around the corner of the tree, I have to pull back quickly as they step up the attack on me, pinning me in place and barely giving me a chance to see.

Shit. Shit. Shit.

"Mikito, they're moving to flank you!" I snarl over our communications channels.

If they keep moving, she won't have the angle left to hide. I focus, slapping a Soul Shield on Mikito just in case and watching my Mana drop. Even as I speak, Mikito's tossing out smoke grenades, providing her further cover. Lana follows her example a second later, the tosses arcing over the shield in front of her. Purple and pink smoke pour out from the grenades within seconds.

The Ilukin are the worst kind of monsters for us to fight. As ranged fighters, the Ilukin are laying down sufficient fire that we have to stay hunkered down. Our group can fight at range, but it's mostly meant to let us cover the ground until we're up close and personal—sort of like the way Romans carried pilum to toss before they engaged. Normally running around in the forest or dungeons makes ranged fighting more difficult, but this time, our reliance on close combat has us stuck with no cover.

"John, the shield's failing!" Lana shouts.

"Cover fire coming." I stick my hand around the tree, firing blind and as fast as I can, dumping the Inlin's full load in seconds.

I track the shots left and right and the slackening of fire gives Lana and the puppies a chance to run. My blind cover fire isn't enough to stop the Ilukin completely and the large dogs are easy targets. Projectiles tear into their furry bodies, ripping skin and tearing muscles even through the light armor the puppies wear.

The Inlin clicking empty, I pull my hand back and listen to the weapon cycle, Sabre loading new ammunition from its stores. No time to wait though, so I stick my head and hand around the tree on the other side, casting Fireball again and again. From the corner of my eyes, I can barely spot the place where Mikito was, purple smoke covering the ground.

"Ali, how many?" I could count the dots on my minimap, but asking him direct is faster and easier as I split my focus between spells and cover.

I snarl, ducking and shrugging as the tree finally falls, catching me on the shoulder on the way down. Physics and Mana-hardened pulp isn't enough to overcome Sabre's armor though, so all I feel is a hard and sharp pressure.

"Seven. Two on the flank, two breaking off to go after Lana, and three here with you. They really don't like the Fireball spell," Ali says helpfully, floating above the trees and watching the group. At this point, the monsters have given up on hurting him and have just concentrated on us, giving us at least one pair of unhindered eyes.

I need to take care of these guys before they get to my friends, but as I open up with another series of Fireballs, I realize the trio has spread out. Fireball's an area effect spell, but spread out as far as they are, I'm just wasting Mana slinging the spell in their general direction.

Ilukin (Level 41)

HP: 1260/1893

MP: 392/577

A quick scan of the other two shows that the first opponent is the most damaged. As I catch another barb in the upper shoulder, pain flashes through my body again. Forced back behind the remnants of my tree trunk, I growl and think quickly about my options. Spells would be great and they certainly seem vulnerable, but my most effective spells are area effect. That leaves the Inlin, whose standard projectiles reflect off the barbs, or my sword, which requires me to get close.

The worse thing is that I'm the best equipped to deal with these suckers. Mikito's entirely reliant on her melee attacks, and while Lana carries a beam rifle, it's not her primary form of attack. I need to get attacking, and I need to do it now.

"*Ali, Blink Step chain to Lana,*" I snap as I poke my head around again.

I focus and Blink the distance to the monster, right above it. Sword in hand, I drop onto the monster, plunging my blade through barbed defenses that react a touch too late. I roll away, dragging the weapon through its body, and come up, triggering a Blade Strike the moment I'm on my feet.

Out in the open as I am, it doesn't take long for his friends to fire on me. That's why I didn't drop straight into the fight immediately. Sabre's shield stops the first few attacks, enough so that I finish off the Ilukin in front of me with a couple more quick strikes. After that, I duck and weave, using the bulk of the new corpse to hide me from attacks as I take on the other two. I work my way forward, always trying to keep the majority of the monsters unable to attack me, though these guys aren't as worried about friendly fire.

By the time I'm done with my pair, a series of barbs stick through my body. I take a few seconds to pull and push them out as needed, groaning in pain and triggering a Healing potion. Cold relief floods through me before I look in the direction Lana and the puppies ran. A Skill activation later, I've ported closer. Ali's already flying ahead of me, and I use his eyesight to bounce me closer to where Lana is, unable to spot her through the heavily forested woods. Being on the run as they are, the damage done by the Ilukin is more spread out, but it's still a good way for me to track the group.

When I finally reach the group, Lana's busy trading fire with one Ilukin while the dogs are attacking another in close combat. Anna has the majority of the monster's attention as she wields whips of flame from her tail, tearing apart barbs that fire at her as she hops in front of it. Howard works the back while Wynn and Shadow rip into the monster from the flanks, ducking in and attacking whenever they see an opening. All the animals are moving slower, barbs tearing wounds wider with each attack, but they refuse to give up.

A split-second decision has me porting over to help Lana, appearing a few feet away from the monster even as my feet hit the ground, propelling me forward. I tuck down low, using the built-up momentum from running to hit it with my shoulder, my sword held out low and parallel to the ground. I hear barbs shatter and I feel the Ilukin's body give way beneath me, but I don't stop, pushing it forward until we smash into a tree. The impact jerks me to a stop, sending a jolt through my spine and making my head hurt before I dig my feet into the ground and twist, pulling the sword free and widening the wound.

Lana ignores us the moment I appear, instead adding her firepower to the puppies, coordinating her attacks with them in an entirely unnatural way. By the time I finish my monster, they barely need any help dispatching theirs, Anna delivering the coup-de-grace by shoving a bar of molten fire down the Ilukin's throat. I Blink forward ahead of the group but stop halfway there when I realize the red dots that make up Mikito's opponents are gone.

We find the samurai seated and leaning against an opponent, naginata laid out next to her, working on pulling a barb from her leg. Mikito's so damaged, I can't even spot a portion of her that's uninjured. Cuts, scrapes, and puncture wounds abound, and the dark red of drying blood covers her completely, pooling around her body and staining the snow, slowly creating a bloody depression that Mikito sinks into. I stare at the young Japanese woman, who gives me a pained half-smile, waiting for her health to rise.

"How…?" I shake my head, wondering how either of the ladies did it.

"Stealth potion," Mikito says.

"Smoke potions for the dogs," Lana adds.

"Smoke?" I blink, and Lana nods.

"Turns them into smoke for a few minutes. Gave it to them to chug. They disappeared and waited while the monsters found me. They hit the trailer while I drew the lead away," Lana finishes the explanation.

"And you?" I ask Mikito.

"Waited till they were next to me, then I attacked," Mikito says, waving around the newly made clearing. "It was… tight."

Tight. That's one way to look at it. Tight. It's a problem with only three of us. Even with Lana's pets, we're often outnumbered and out-leveled. We could really do with a few more party members, but Amelia's too busy to come out often and Aiden refuses. That leaves us with no one else with the appropriate level, not in Whitehorse.

In the end, we have to make do with what we have, and that means some days, sometimes, we end up tight.

Chapter 10

I might have a certain resistance to the cold these days, and certainly within Sabre I'm often nice and toasty. However, that's not true for everyone I hunt with. When the temperature hits -45°C before wind chill, even Lana flat-out refuses to go out, citing the very real possibility of death. It'll be interesting to see how many of the monsters we've been dealing with handle the cold—some of the ones I've seen probably won't survive the winter. Slimy and sticky might be powerful, but it isn't particularly good when snowburn can happen in minutes. The Yukon can be a harsh, unforgiving place, and that's without the rather strange changes the System has created.

Rather than spend my nature-enforced break hunting alone, I've elected to spend the day in Whitehorse. A morning lesson with Aiden has allowed me to understand how Mana can be woven into multiple strands at the same time, the precursor to dual-casting. Understand, if not do. That what he shows me is simple, something most Mages can handle without a problem with the aid of the System, doesn't help when you're actually trying to do it without the System's help. Watching Aiden float five balls in the air and juggle them with ease, I can't help feeling a twinge of envy as I fail to split my concentration even once.

That's the problem with not being specialized, I guess. Never enough time to focus on any one thing. Aiden's morning lesson and my current one are both good reminders of my weakness. Ali and I sit cross-legged on the rooftop of the flat while we slowly "explore" his Elemental Affinity of electromagnetic force. One of the four fundamental forces of the universe, it's a major force that dictate how matter and energy interact. It creates many of the things we feel and see in everyday life—from magnetism to electricity to friction.

Funnily enough, that's about as much as I understand about it—at least on the scientific level. When I tried to purchase further knowledge from the

Shop, Ali bitched me out for hours. The way the Spirit put it, in this case, knowledge is actually a hindrance to using the Affinity. What we're trying to do is perceive and understand the forces around us, then manipulate it directly. All the physics, all the theories are just numbers and figures, data that gets in the way of understanding. It'd be like trying to talk about the colors of a rainbow rather than opening your eyes. Explaining music rather than playing it. Watching a dancer rather than dancing.

In.

Out.

In.

Out.

Seated cross-legged on the rooftop, I breathe slowly with my eyes closed, the cold seeping in through the thermal bodysuit, threatening to rip away my concentration. I ignore it as I try to see the world around me through my Affinity. It would be easier and faster to use a skill like Mana Manipulation, but the point of this training is to bypass the System and its helping hands. And so I breathe.

Each time I catch it, it's as if lines of power in all the colors of the rainbow surround me, shifting as the world shifts. Wind, light, heat, matter, it all shows up. Lines that radiate everywhere from everything at the same time. It's so much that I can never hold the sight for more than a few seconds, the sheer variety staggering my mind and making me lose control.

Each time I fail, I calm my mind and try again. Hours pass, sunlight fading in and out as clouds shift and the world rotates. Each moment passes and each glimpse shows me a little more of the world, of the way Ali naturally sees it. It's breathtaking in its beauty and staggering in its majesty.

And when I have a moment, I try to manipulate it. Just a little. A push here. A shove there. Attempting to alter the flows of force via will and a strange, tertiary muscle I barely understand. I am trying for more than just seeing the forces but understanding what I do when I make these changes, what each line of force means. It's like trying to flex a muscle you've never consciously moved—a failure most of the time, but occasionally, occasionally, you think you might have done something.

You'd think that it would be frustrating. Infuriating. Yet those glimpses, those moments I catch, give me insight into something more, something greater than I've ever sensed before, a connection to the universe that I've never had. For all the mystical crap we talk about, this is the first legitimate example I have that they were right and everything is connected. And so, I find myself reaching, testing, pushing forward without hesitation.

Only Ali playing Ricky Martin's "She Bangs" at full volume next to me pulls me away from training. When I stand, my muscles lock up, making me faceplant into the snow. Hours on a cold, barren rooftop without shelter has pushed even my enhanced body, and I find myself locked up, my body numb. I have to flex my muscles slowly and cast a Healing spell before I can move. As I do so, Ali flicks his fingers and gives me something else to study.

Elemental Affinity Improved

Well. That was nice. I find myself smiling even as my body reminds me of the stupidity of sitting outside in the cold. As my body slowly unlocks and I push past the pain, I find that I've spent more time on this than I meant to. As useful as this exercise was, I have more things to do. Time to get back to work.

***

Down the stairs and out, then back up, I find myself at the Shop. It's been a while since I came here to really shop instead of just selling some loot or pick up pre-decided items. But my last run-in with my mysterious attacker has made it clear—I'm in need of an upgrade. I've been coasting on my previous load-out and Skills, but it's obvious I need to rejigger something.

Not every Shop is the same. In fact, there are thousands, maybe even millions, of them throughout the System. Each Shop caters to different clientele, different funds and needs. Some are exclusive to specific groups or Guilds; others cater to specific tastes like droids, drones, melee weaponry, or more. Of course, I don't know any of that when I first access the System Shop as Ali drags us into his preferred, exclusive shop, this marvel of blue.

The Shop I'm in starts with a simple set of reception counters that greets shoppers before they're guided to their own private viewing rooms. In each viewing room, specialized screens show you the full range of products the Shop holds or has access to on short notice. You can even filter for the full range of items the System can access. Of course, in most cases, those items you have to buy directly from the System Shop are much more expensive—outside of things that only the System can provide, like Class changes or Skills, System information or secrets.

In my private viewing room, a humanoid Fox stands, clad in a purple bodysuit that covers two-thirds of its body and a sash that hangs across its front, covering the rest. It's entirely unpractical, but I guess as a salesman, Foxy-boy isn't particularly in need of practical clothing. Not here in the Shop, at least.

"And how may we help you today, Redeemer?" Foxy-boy asks.

I hesitate, and not just because of the title. I still don't understand why some titles are used more than others. I've almost never heard anyone call me Monster Bane, but almost everyone from the System uses Redeemer of the

Dead. If I had to guess, it's due to rarity, but it's not something I've bothered to dig into. It's not as if it matters, beyond a little embarrassment.

"Can you watch something and give me some advice?" I say, and at his nod, I gesture to Ali.

A moment later, showing on the big screen is the fight between my mysterious attacker and me. While he's busy watching, I take care of the usual housekeeping.

Concussion Grenades (10)

Effects: 50 Base Damage. Damage reduces depending on distance from explosion.
Cost: 100 Credits

Plasma Grenades (10)

Effects: 100 Base Damage. Damage reduces depending on distance from explosion. Chance of on-going fire damage
Cost: 150 Credits

Chaos Grenades (2)

Effects: Variable. Calls up one chaotic event with area of effect up to five meters from explosion point
Cost: 500 Credits

1,000 High-Explosive Rounds for Inlin Type II Projectile Rifle

Effects: 50 Base Damage
Cost: 150 Credits

100 Armor Piercing Rounds (Crafted) for Inlin Type II Projectile Rifle

Effects: 150 Base Damage
Cost: 50 credits

1kg of Assorted Swiss Chocolates (Individually Wrapped)

Effect: Reduces John Lee rage effects. Recommended consumption on regular basis.
Cost: 10 Credits

The last makes my lips twist in a wry smile. Having Ali as my System Companion with full access to my link means that occasionally, the damn Spirit throws in his own little notes. On the other hand, having had Mikito and Lana share some of the data screens they get, I'm more than happy with the trade-off. I wouldn't want to wade through the occasional screens of gibberish they seem to have gotten used to.

Back to work. I keep purchasing, refilling my basic load-out. I rarely need to do this since, unlike most others, I can just dump extras into my Altered Space. By the time I'm done, Foxy-boy has finished reviewing the fight and is ready to talk.

"Suggestions?" I jump right into it, curious to see what he might add.

"Don't fight people who have higher levels than you," Ali says, smirking.

I glare at Ali, hoping to make it clear that this is serious. "Funny."

"Well, Redeemer, if you are looking for certainty in beating your attacker, I fear you might not have the Credits for it," Foxy-boy says before scratching at his hand/paw. "I do believe you are significantly out-classed."

"I got that," I say, tapping the screen. A second later, working to mental prompts, the screen shows the QSM.

Quantum Stealth Manipulator (QSM)

The QSM allows its bearer to phase-shift, placing himself adjacent to the current dimension

Effect: User is rendered invisible and undetectable to normal and magical means as long as the QSM is active. Solid objects may be passed through but will drain charge at a higher rate. Charge lasts 5 minutes under normal conditions.

Cost: 250,000 Credits

I definitely don't have the money to repurchase the QSM. At 200,000 Credits, fixing up the broken QSM itself is cheaper, but it's still not cheap. As much as I want my toy back, that's out of the question.

I state as much before musing out loud, "He's faster than I am. Probably has a Class Skill like Haste or its equivalent. He's also more experienced and has better martial skills. Stronger than I am. If I had to guess, that's his primary attribute. No spells used, but he didn't need any. Might be he doesn't have any. That polearm with his Skills is the killer though."

"So we're looking to either speed you up, slow him down, or keep him at range?" Foxy-boy says, tilting his head,

I nod slowly. "Yeah. Oh, and figuring out how the hell to see him before he hits me first. Or runs away if I'm winning."

Ali snorts at the last. Yeah, fine. The chances of me being in a winning position is low.

"I think I can deal with that. I've got some Advancement Points left from your Level Ups. If we can get a few more Levels, I can focus on upgrading my abilities to scan for others," Ali says.

"Instead of learning to project more music? No. That's tragic," I intone sarcastically.

"The sacrifices I make."

I ignore Ali, turning to Foxy-boy who is staring upward at the ceiling. "Right, so what have we got?"

"May I see your Status Screen? It might help," Foxy says.

"Done." After sending it across, I take a second look at my own screen.

Status Screen			
Name	John Lee	Class	Erethran Honor Guard
Race	Human (Male)	Level	35
Titles			
Monster's Bane, Redeemer of the Dead			
Health	1620	Stamina	1620
Mana	1250	Mana Regeneration	92 / minute
Attributes			
Strength	90	Agility	153
Constitution	162	Perception	55
Intelligence	125	Willpower	127
Charisma	16	Luck	27
Class Skills			
Mana Imbue	1	Blade Strike	2
Thousand Steps	1	Altered Space	2
Two are One	1	The Body's Resolve	3

Greater Detection	1	Instantaneous Inventory*	1
Soul Shield	2	Blink Step	2
Cleave*	2	Frenzy*	1
Elemental Strike*	1 (Ice)	Tech Link*	2
Combat Spells			
Improved Minor Healing (II)		Greater Regeneration	
Greater Healing		Mana Drip	
Improved Mana Dart (IV)		Enhanced Lightning Strike	
Fireball		Polar Zone	

After a while, Foxy-boy states, "You have not designated your last four Class Skills."

"I was kind of holding off on using them till I hit Level 40 and the next tier opened up."

"Mmmm… and you rarely upgrade Skills beyond their first tier."

"Yes. I'm just really liking the versatility." I shrug. "I mean, they're all good."

"True. But at higher levels, each Skill grows in power. Class Skills may also upgrade and achieve a breakthrough—a time when the continual improvement increases significantly," Foxy-boy says and I blink.

I look at Ali, who shrugs. "Yeah, it happens. Except the lowest recorded level for a breakthrough is at ten points. Boy-o here has seventeen Class skill points in total, and with his Class, he ain't ever getting that many," Ali says, and

I growl softly. Ali frowns at me for a time before he straightens up. "Shit. Sorry. Something else I should have told you about to let you decide on, eh?"

"Yes. Just a little," I snap then close my eyes as I try to rein in my temper.

I try to remind myself that Ali has provided more information than he has withheld, that those without a Companion are still struggling to get basic information. This, none of this, is basic. It's complex, detailed data that maybe someone who grew up with the System would know, but us humans don't. It certainly wasn't mentioned in Thrasher's Guide, and I read that one all the way through. I tell myself I'm lucky, and it helps. A little. Mostly, it's the slow breathing.

When I open my eyes, I find the screens filled with information. I take the time to look over the possible options available, starting with the Class Skills.

Class Skill: Haste

Effect: Increases effective movement speed of caster by 20% for duration of Skill use. Costs 1 mana per second.

Cost: 45,000 Credits

Class Skill: Slow Time

Effect: Creates a bubble of slow-time around the Caster, decreasing speed of all objects within the bubble by 10%. Area of effect is 5 feet in radius from caster. Costs 5 mana per second.

Cost: 55,000 Credits

Class Skill: Freezing Strike

Effect: Enchants weapon with a slowing effect. A 5% slowing effect is applied on a successful strike. This effect is cumulative and lasts for 1 minute. Costs 100 Mana to activate. Activation lasts for 1 minute.

Cost: 35,000 Credits

All powerful and they either speed me up or slow down my opponents. Biggest problem of course is the cost—not just in Credits, though that's not cheap either, but in Mana. Theoretically, I could keep Haste up indefinitely with my current Mana regeneration rates, but then I'd be almost entirely reliant on my Mana pool. Not a great place to be, especially when I fight using my Skills and spells as much as I do.

On a whim, based off what I've just learnt, I pull up further information on my Class Skills.

Mana Imbue (Level 2)

Soulbound weapon now permanently imbued with mana to deal more damage on each hit. +20 Base Damage (Mana). Will ignore armor and resistances. Mana regeneration reduced by 10 Mana per minute permanently.
Cost: 25,000 Credits

Blade Strike (Level 3)

By projecting additional mana and stamina into a strike, the Erethran Honor Guard's Soulbound weapon may project a strike up to 30 feet away. Costs 45 Stamina + 45 Mana to activate
Cost: 30,000 Credits

So purchasing the Skills is possible. It even actually adds a significant bonus and doesn't cost me a Class Skill allocation point, which is something I've been trying to avoid wasting on the lower level Skills.

"Purchased Skills don't count toward a breakthrough," Foxy-boy says, cautioning me as I stare at them.

Figures. Still, I twitch my hands and pull up the two other Skills I haven't actually upgraded yet.

A Thousand Blades (Level 1)

Creates two duplicate copies of the user's designated weapon. Duplicate copies deal base damage of copied items. May be combined with Mana Imbue and Shield Transference.
Mana Cost: 3 Mana per second
Cost: 40,000 Credits

Shield Transference (Level 1)

Portion of damage dealt to Soul Shield will be transferred as additional damage to Soulbound weapon. Current rate of transfer is 1 additional point of damage for 20 points received. Additional damage will fade after 1 minute. Mana regeneration is reduced by 5 Mana per minute permanently.
Cost: 85,000 Credits (Discounted to 45,000 Credits with pre-requisites of Thousand Blades)

I read over both and shake my head. As interesting as Shield Transference is, taking another hit to my Mana regeneration would suck. Admittedly, I've increased in Levels enough that my base regeneration rate is quite high, but it's still not great. There's another thing to consider too. I have four Class Skills free right now, but I'm Level 35. That means I've got eleven Class Skills left before I finish my current Class tree and have to advance to Master Class. I definitely want Sanctum, Body Swap, and Portal—Skills that provide me greater mobility and defense in general are powerful. Army of One is also quite interesting, but I'd have to purchase Thousand Blades for that. That means, at the very least, I'd have to spend five Class Skills to get a single point in each of these. That leaves me with six Class Skills free to distribute across all options.

Playing with those numbers, I begin to understand why Ali didn't bother to discuss breakthroughs—it's just too many points to allocate to a single Skill.

I want to upgrade Portal because that'll give me greater range and flexibility with the Skill. And Blink Step has become a go-to Skill, so of course that's a must-buy. Add another point for Soul Shield which is, frankly, amazing at keeping my allies and myself alive and that cuts my "free" options down to three. Assuming I don't want to upgrade Sanctum but I do Army of One because of its ability to dish out the hurt and I'm down to two free Skills. If I really want to make any single Skill more powerful and useful, I'd have to focus on it even further.

And that's not to forget that the third tier opens at Level 40. Which means that if I want to get Sanctum, Body Swap, and Portal immediately, I need to have saved up at least three points. Still, knowing that I'm going to gain at least two more Class Skills between now and Level 40, I should be able to spend three points now. Which probably means that I should be buying A Thousand Blades and the next level of these…

Soul Shield (Level 3)

Effect: Creates a manipulatable shield to cover the caster's or target's body. Shield has 1,500 Hit Points.

Mana Cost: 250 Mana

Cost: 55,000 Credits

Blink Step (Level 3)

Effect: Instantaneous teleportation via line-of-sight. May include Spirit's line of sight.

Maximum range—500 meters.

Mana Cost: 80 Mana

Cost: 55,000 Credits

Both are great upgrades, one increasing the Shield's hit points, the other reducing the cost of Blink Step. Considering I often trigger that Skill multiple times in a fight, the cost reduction is pretty damn useful. I could purchase both, but the penny pincher in me hesitates at the idea of spending all my "free" points. Better to keep at least one point free.

Decisions, decisions, decisions.

"Let's see what else you guys cooked up," I mutter, looking toward the two who have been patiently waiting by the bowl of dip.

Ali doesn't even move, just waving toward the screens.

Type II Webbing Mini-Missile

Base Damage: N/A

Effect: Disperses insta-webbing upon impact or on activation. Dispersal covers 3 cubic feet.

Cost: 500 Credits

"Not much information on that," I say, flashing the screen.

"Can't really go into too much detail. It's a Type II, so it'll hold your opponent for a few seconds at least. If it hits." Ali shrugs. "If he isn't too much stronger than you."

I grunt, acknowledging Ali's point. Damn System will make it so that he can break out eventually, whether or not it'd make logical sense. Still, this definitely has possibilities.

Shinowa Type II Sonic Pulser

Base Damage: 25 per second

Additional Effect: Disrupts auditory sense of balance on opponent during use. Effects have a small chance of continuing after use.
Cost: 25,000 Credits

Nice. Don't have to aim this weapon, except in the general direction, which means if I can catch him before he closes, the son of a bitch will find it hard to escape the effects.

Pinzli Nano Cloud

Base Damage: N/A (Dependent on purchased effects)
Duration: 1 minute
Recharge Rate: 2 hours
Cost: 55,000 Credits

"The nano cloud is a bit different from your other choices here. Think of it as a dispersal and development mechanism. Once purchased, you won't ever have to purchase it again—so long as it doesn't break—as it rebuilds the cloud itself. However, the cloud itself does nothing. You need to purchase the programming to make the nanites act," Foxy-boy says, and I nod slowly. "You can have it dispense toxins, invade and damage individuals and items within the cloud, increase or decrease temperatures, or apply electrical current. The possibilities are endless, if expensive."

I grunt, staring at the cloud with desire. I don't even need to look at the cost of the programmed effects to know this is too expensive for me. Seeing my face, Foxy-boy waves, dispersing the screen before bringing up the next.

Omnitron III Class II Personal Assault Vehicle Lightning Armor Upgrade

Effect: Deals 15 damage per second on contact with armor
Cost: 12,500 Credits

"Cheaper because we've got the Adaptive Upgrades for the armor. We just need to get a small portion of it purchased and Sabre will do the rest," Ali explains. "Figure if you're going to get hit, you might want to hurt back."

"Not bad…" I say.

There are a few other tech options available, mostly variations on the theme—stand-alone or integrated weaponry to slow down opponents or damage them at range or hurt them when they're close. Costs range from the cheap but barely effective at 10,000 Credits to the 90,000-plus Credit options which would nearly wipe me out. I flick through them for a time before I turn to our last category. Spells.

Spell: Haste

Effect: Increases effective movement speed of caster by 10% for duration of Spell.
Mana Cost: 100
Spell Duration: 1 minute
Cost: 35,000 Credits

Spell: Slow Time Bubble

Effect: Creates a bubble of slow-time decreasing speed of all objects within the bubble by 10%. Casting range of 50 feet.
Mana Cost: 500
Spell Duration: 1 minute
Area of effect: 12 feet
Cost: 50,000 Credits

"Hey, that Slow Time spell. It's not centered?" I say.

"Nope. It's more flexible, but it's a lot more expensive and you aren't automatically excluded from the Class Skill. You can also miss since the bubble doesn't move once cast," Ali explains.

"Still, that's pretty sweet." It's a powerful spell, but the Mana cost is tremendous.

Scanning down the list of spells, I find the usual variants. After a few seconds, I can tell that most are just variations of the Class Skills we've already considered. The tradeoff is often in terms of higher Mana cost and casting time, but the spells are often cheaper to buy and more flexible to use. The Haste spell, for example, can be cast on others, a Web spell could be dispersed at a caster's command, and on.

I don't know how long I spend reading over Spells, which trigger ideas for Skills, which are then countered by potential technological options. Hours going over data. And that's the reason why I try to avoid coming in here too often. You could spend days, weeks even, trying to figure out the best option, the best "build" as Jason would say.

There's only one problem. There's a saying that an army is always getting ready to fight the last war. As much as I've prepared, I wonder what the next fight will bring. And what he might have up his sleeve.

In the end, worrying won't get me anywhere. The future is uncertainty. Better to make a decision and go with it. Turning to Foxy-boy, I start talking and pointing.

Chapter 11

There was a book once that said that to become a master at any one thing, you needed ten thousand hours of practice. Not just any kind of practice, mind you, but concentrated, focused practice. Practice where you focused on learning, rather than just doing the same thing again and again. Ten thousand hours. That's a lot of time—years, decades even—of pure, focused concentration.

Imagine this, if you can. You are on the roof of your apartment, practicing in the dark with only the light of the moon above and reflected light from pristine snow below, cold air biting at your lungs with every breath. You swing your hand from the right and summon your Soulbound weapon into your hand two-thirds of the way to the target as you've practiced hundreds, even thousands of times. The weapon appears and alongside it are two identical swords, trailing the first weapon's path by about a foot, like after-images of a strike.

You hit the target and follow-through all the way before you unsummon the weapon so that you can call it to your other hand, which is already striking to the top of the head. Except you now have to make sure you only banish the original weapon, otherwise the duplicates never finish their strikes. Of course, that means you should remember to banish those other two when they've finished their first strike so they may follow up with the second cut you throw.

Oh, and don't forget that the floating weapons are moving on predetermined paths that you have no ability to alter. Take a step too far, twist your body the wrong way, be a touch too slow when you banish a weapon or be too fast and you're now inflicting damage on yourself.

Now try to focus on all these things and ignore the giggling of a highly amused petite Japanese woman and an olive-skinned, shoulder-padded Spirit.

"Enough already!" I snap at Mikito, banishing all three weapons and releasing A Thousand Blades, letting my Mana regeneration refill my pool. I growl, rubbing the latest cut to my knee, my workout clothes stained with blood. "You were supposed to be helping."

"Sorry!" Mikito says and bobs a short bow. By the time she comes up, she's smoothed out her face at least. If you weren't Asian and used to reading repressed emotions, you probably wouldn't catch the tightness in her eyes or the humor lurking in their depths. "It just—"

"It looked like a three-day-dead Goblin attempting to dance on an electric wire," Ali supplies.

I growl but have to admit, even if only privately, that the last half hour has been less than impressive. I can get the first and second strikes in about fifty percent of the time, but after that, everything becomes a flurry of swinging iron and blood. Keeping track of all the different blades, what's called forth and what's not is nearly impossible, even if all I'm trying to do is forms.

"Too much," Mikito says, waving toward where I am.

"I know," I say.

She shakes her head, pausing to find the words. "You're doing too much. The Skill is new. When I learned Haste, I focused on just moving, not fighting. Once I knew how to move, I added turning it on and off in bursts. Only later did I add fighting."

"But—"

"Mikito's right, boy-o. Stop using the Honor Guard sword technique. Keep the sword summoned, focus on getting used to having the blades trail along. Maybe even get used to using the summoned blades as additional weapons," Ali says.

"I don't have time..." I snap my mouth shut. Right. I asked Mikito to come out into the cold for her suggestions. Arguing with her after I asked her for her advice is stupid. It's just that I can feel the pressure, the need to get my Skills working fully. And that's not her. That's all me.

"We good?" Mikito asks.

I nod slowly. I rub my neck for a second then pull out a piece of chocolate, popping it into my mouth as I walk back to my training spot. The smooth, silky feel of melting chocolate and the rush of sugar perks me up a bit, reminding me that not everything has to be solved immediately.

The next hour plays out better. In the corner of my mind, I note that Mikito has started training herself, only partly paying attention to my progress. I know that she feels the cold, that it's hurting her and damaging her body with each second. She doesn't have the resistances I do. Yet Mikito is ignoring it, letting the System regenerate the damage while she trains. It's a level of dedication I find intimidating and drives me to push myself.

Wielding three blades that aren't connected to one another is strange, but now that I'm not making them appear or disappear, it's easier. I don't run into them as much. I just need to change the timing of my strokes and attacks and occasionally my positioning. Follow-throughs that would work before don't, but the addition of the other blades open up more possibilities.

It's a fascinating hour that's interrupted by the increasingly loud voices from below. Something in the tone, in the phrasing twigs a corner of my mind and I find myself walking to the edge of the roof. I'm soon joined by the short Japanese woman, her naginata held casually by her side.

Beneath us, one of Roxley's guards is speaking to a human couple. He's turned away from us, so I can't read his lips and he's not shouting, so we can only catch occasional words.

"… speak to… our fault. Can't… we are…"

"FUCK you. You bought the city, you should fix it," the woman of the pair shouts. The man has a hand on her arm, but his bladed stance to Roxley's guard is not exactly defensive. Whatever his reply, it's drowned out by more cursing from the woman, her wide gesticulations throwing off the man's arm.

"It nearly ate me. How the hell are you keeping us safe? The children were *playing* with that rat yesterday. It was the size of the toddler!"

"… bought a …"

"We bought a house. Our house is right over there!" the woman screams, pointing in the direction of the river. "You couldn't defend it. You just ran like cowards. Now it's gone and I'm living with a damn Indian! He smells even worse than the cows do."

My lips twist and I almost step forward to drop down and have words with her. It's only Mikito's hand on my arm that stops me.

"We aren't going to be of help here," Mikito says. "She'd just scream about us foreigners butting in."

I grunt but step back, forcing myself to walk away. The guard can handle it—it is, after all, what they're paid to do. Stepping in now will just make the woman think she's getting ganged up on, which will raise the stakes for her. Sometimes, the best thing you can do is nothing.

"You done?" I say, seeing Mikito walk to the roof exit.

She nods, and as the voices from below continue to bombard the roof with colorful and highly anatomically impossible language, I find myself following the short Adventurer.

"You're nearly Level 50," I state as we take the stairs.

Mikito bobs her head slightly.

"Do you know what Advanced Class you're going to get?"

"Chukanbushi," Mikito says. "Middle Samurai. It is an Advancement on my Aonisaibushi Class."

"I thought your Class was Samurai," I said, frowning.

"No. It is Aonisaibushi. Do you see it as Samurai?"

"Yes. I thought…" Well, actually, I never did mention it. I mean, why would I? It'd be like telling Mikito her hair was black. Superfluous.

"Sorry, boy-o. Translation error. I'm pulling up the Class data that Mikito provided and well, yeah. I see what I did wrong here," Ali says, and in a moment, Mikito's data changes.

"This happen a lot?" I ask Ali, who spins around in a circle while still seated and floating.

"Yes? Remember how I said I'm translating things from the System or Galactic? Well, don't forget I've got to filter that through the information I inherited from you and what little data I've garnered since then. And the language downloads of course," Ali says. "It's not going to be one hundred percent accurate all the time."

"No harm done, I guess." I'm not even sure that the difference between each Class is as it stands, so having this information doesn't really help. Looking back at Mikito, who has walked over to the kitchen to begin dinner preparation, I ask, "You happy with that?"

"Yes. It is suitable," Mikito says, washing the rice.

"What kind of Class skills are you going to get?"

"Uncertain. It would either be a continual increase in my current abilities or an enhancement on other Skills that aren't present now."

"So your current Aoni… Aino… Junior Samurai Class gives you physical Skills like Haste, your weapon Skills like Cleave or Counter-Strike, and the physical enhancement Skills, right?" As I speak, I pull some chicken from my Altered Space storage and lay it out on the oven rack before grabbing paprika, pepper, and salt. I lean over to start the oven while I say, "So what's not covered?"

"Armor and protection skills. Mental training and resistances. Riding skills. Archery." Mikito puts the pot on the counter and sets up the cooker before she pulls meat out of her inventory and marinates it. "All those were traditional. If the System is calling from our history, even corrupted, it could be any of those."

I grunt in acknowledgement, tossing the chicken a bit and dusting everything with a little bit of flour. I wonder, if the System is calling forth or adjusting some existing Classes to fit our history, is there a Eunuch class out there? Does it have specific requirements? And more importantly, why am I asking such questions?

"You okay with either of those options? Ali mentioned you can get some better specialized Classes if you worked for it."

"This is a better Class," Mikito points out. "I used the Basic Perk we received to upgrade it. And I looked into it—most of the other requirements are too difficult or impossible on Earth. Not as if I'm going to participate in killing a Dragon. Or visit all fourteen moons of Ryunii. Wherever that is."

"It's in…" Ali stops. "Right, rhetorical question."

Vegetables next. It looks like a pink banana, tastes like a mixture of broccoli and chocolate, and is, most importantly, easy to prepare. I snap and toss the pieces into the bowl that Mikito has kindly laid out while we continue to speak.

"Any idea what Lana's going to get? She's a few levels below you, but…"

"We've talked actually. Lana has some interesting options. She can either become a Beast Master (Advanced) or a Beast Lord. It seems to be a question of ownership versus partnership," Ali pipes up this time. "The first option gives her more skills to expand her pets and control them. The second limits the number, but she can upgrade her pets more directly and make each puppy more powerful."

"Any idea which way she's going?" I ask, and Ali falls silent. "Ali?"

"I would have said Beast Lord before… but… Lana's gotten cold, boy-o. Like, she-bitch level cold. I'm not sure anymore."

"So I've noticed. Where is she anyway?"

They shrug. She hasn't bothered to contact us since our initial discussion this morning, so we're kind of working in the dark. Hopefully she's resting. She certainly needed it. On the other hand...

On the other hand, there's something there that will need to be dealt with. Soon. Just not today.

***

"How long can this weather last?" I mutter as we stomp through the snow.

It has been a week and a half of -30°C and lower temperatures and it shows no sign of letting up. After the third day and having fought off a Swarm attack, Lana decided that she'd done enough waiting around. So out we went. It only took a few more days before the rest of the advanced and elite hunting teams decided that she was right. The cold isn't going anywhere and the larder needs to be filled.

"A month maybe?" Lana says. She'd know, as the only native Yukoner in the party.

In fact, for Mikito and me, this is our first Yukon winter, and so far, I can safely say that it's every bit as cold and dark as you could imagine. Sun's up at nine and sets around five, leaving most of the day shrouded in darkness.

"Got another," I say, walking over to the frozen ground squirrel.

I loot it before dropping the corpse into my Altered Space. Evolved as it was, the ground squirrel had gained a good three feet in height, but obviously the System hadn't compensated for the additional heat-loss. Or at least, not enough, not with the temperature staying this low all day long.

"Not good," Ali mutters, staring at his screens.

"Credits without fighting? How is that bad?" Lana says as we troop up the mountain.

Wynn bounds over, a corpse dragged along behind it, which is promptly looted by Lana before I store the corpse.

"The monsters keep the Mana flows balanced, just like the buildings do. Too many of them dying means Mana absorption is down. The System will adjust for that by adding more monsters, probably teleporting them right in. Or just forcing further evolutions of the ones already present," Ali explains. "By now, most other areas would have found a decent balance to the kinds of monsters around. Sure, there might be Swarms hitting one place or another, but not that much."

"So we're going to see monsters that can handle the cold now? Ice Elementals and that kind of thing?" I ask.

"Maybe, but probably not. The System doesn't care that much, but it's not completely stupid. It'll probably try to find close-enough analogues from other worlds. Farther North though, up in some of your mountains? Pretty sure you have them there already," Ali answers.

Fun. As I reach out to touch the dead-looking fir to see if it's lootable, I find myself slipping sideways from an unexpected impact. The damage is negligible, though I'm unable to see for a second as I push myself out of the white blankness covering me.

By the time I get out, Mikito is crouched behind another tree and the puppies have spread out, with Anna the center of attention as more balance-ball-sized snowballs come crashing down around us. Anna's blazing red, flames flickering around the fox's body and melting any snowball well before it hits her. She's so hot, the ground beneath her furry feet has turned to glass.

Our attackers are a strange sight—so white they blend right into the snow-covered backdrop, barely four feet tall, and with scoops for arms. Round, tubby, and humanoid, their faces host only a single glowing crystal. Snowballs form above their hands before they cast them toward us with a swing of their arms. All in all, it's like being attacked by a bunch of demented snow-children.

It takes me a moment to realize that Lana, having been attacked by multiple snow-children, has been buried in the snow. They keep piling on the snowballs so that she can't get out. My own attackers have started in on me again, though with my foot braced against the tree, I weather the impacts much better. Of course, it doesn't help with the snow piling up on top of me. Before I'm completely buried, I trigger Blink Step to flank our attackers. The dip in my Mana pool is less thanks to the recent upgrade, which is nice, though unnecessary right now.

On the other hand, since these guys are annoying but not immediately dangerous, this is a great time to test out some of my other new toys. I start with the sonic pulser, angled as I am so that I catch most of the snow-children in its area effect. When I raise my left hand, the pulser pops out of its recessed guard and lets loose a thrumming screech that sets my teeth on edge. And I'm behind the damn thing.

The snow-children scream, some falling to their knees, others clutching their heads. Only one manages to throw its ball at Mikito, who neatly dodges the attack. The Samurai darts up the hill in a Haste-assisted sprint that brings her up against the last few unstunned monsters and goes to work. I keep the pulser going, carefully keeping an eye on the over-use indicators, and thank the System that it actually worked. It's only when I triggered it that I thought to consider if the lack of ears on the monsters would make this less useful.

"John. Stop!" Lana shouts through the coms.

That's when I realize one of the negatives of this weapon. The pets are on the ground, paws held over their ears as they howl in pain. Even outside of the direct influence of the pulser, they are entirely unhappy.

Whoops.

Time to try something new. I skip using the rather expensive and new missiles, instead Blinking over behind the still-recovering monsters and triggering A Thousand Blades. I cut and move, leaving the duplicates to finish the job, the weapons trailing along as I disembowel, decapitate, and otherwise slaughter the monsters. Even as I move, I can't help but note the more powerful glow around my sword as Mana Imbue's second purchased level piles on the damage. It's over in an artic breeze, such that by the time Lana finally frees herself fully and has calmed her pets down, we've already started looting.

"So. Cold," Lana says through chattering teeth. She's so close to Anna, I'd be scared of her burning up if I was her. Still…

Lana Pearson (Beastmaster Level 46)

HP: 183/350

MP: 476/590

Conditions: Frozen (-5 HP per second)

"You know, Lana, I know you got a bit cold recently, but this might have gone too far," Ali says, floating next to her. Teasing aside, I see concern in his eyes.

A series of Heal spells helps slow down the damage, and the warmth from Anna brings Lana back to normal. Certain that she's taken care of now, I glance at Mikito, who is staring into space. Even as I open my mouth to say something to her, the information above her head shifts.

Mikito Sato (Middle Samurai Level 1)

HP: 710/710

MP: 370/370

Conditions: Cold (-1 HP per minute)

"Congratulations," I say as I pocket the last of the loot. Crystal Eyes. Kind of morbid if you think about it. Which I don't. And won't. Learning to compartmentalize things like that is the only way to stay sane in this crazy world.

"Thank you," Mikito says, walking down to join us. At Lana's puzzled glance, she explains. "I got my Advanced Class."

"Good on you!" Lana smiles, flashing a much-missed grin as she walks over, her body only shuddering once in a while now, and gives Mikito a hug.

Mikito returns it awkwardly, before Lana steps away and gives Mikito another smile.

"That was new," I say to fill in the silence after a while. I get rapid nods, the puppies moving around us to paw at the shattered remains while Anna curls up on bare earth, flames banked to nearly nothing. "You good to go, Lana?"

The redhead doesn't even pause before she nods and gestures for us to continue. Right, more corpse looting and trouble hunting. Not as if we could be sitting in the Nugget around a warm cup of mulled wine or whisky.

***

Nine hours later, we're finally tramping back into Whitehorse. Other than three quick stops for food, we've been pounding the snow, looting corpses and dumping them into my Altered Space. Sometimes I really hate having that extra space—if we were any other team, we'd have called it a day hours earlier.

Nine hours of tramping through the snow in freezing weather has shown the breadth of the damage the arctic chill has done. Monsters the size of a house, creatures made of stone, and furry lizards litter the frozen landscape, most not even touched by scavengers. Unsurprisingly, we find ourselves fighting a lot less, which disappoints Mikito, who wants to test out her new Skill. I have to say, I'm impressed. Each time she activates it, ghostly Samurai armor shimmers into being around her, adding a layer of protection. Unfortunately, it's not particularly strong just yet—though Mikito says she intends to upgrade it with further Skill points. Which also explains her desire to fight.

Lana, on the other hand, doesn't seem to care as much. If anything, I'd call her happy—happy to see the monsters dead, happy to loot them for their belongings, and happy to wander through the sub-alpine forests relatively unharassed. It's why I don't complain about how long our hunting trip has taken and am just grateful when we finally see the walls.

"Lana. Good to see you back," one of the guards calls as they open the gates and drop the shields for us. The relief on the guards' faces is palpable.

"What's up?" Ali says, flying right up to one guy, who shrinks back.

"Bill's team is still missing. He should have been back already," the original guard replies, brows furrowing. "Did you see them?"

"No. We were out pretty far to the north," I say, turning unconsciously toward the way we came. "Which direction?"

"What are you thinking, boy-o?" Ali says, floating down beside me.

I purse my lips, debating. I don't like Bill, but his people make up a core number of our hunting group. If they need help…

"Sorry, sir, they didn't tell us," the guard replies.

I grunt, knowing that once they hit the road, they could have spread out anywhere. And the Yukon is big. Even with our abilities to sense others, there's no way for us to cover enough ground. Not and have a realistic chance of finding them. And it's not as if I ever learnt to track.

Still…

"Here we go again," Ali mutters.

Mikito says nothing while Lana sighs overly loudly before clicking her tongue, signaling the puppies to turn around.

***

Green eyes that once sparkled with humor lie flat and lifeless, staring at the sky. Blonde hair spills artlessly around her body, uncovering pointed ears. The hole through her chest is neat, almost surgical in its precision. I find myself brushing the hair away before I close her eyes and put Luthien's body in my Altered Space.

"John?" Lana says, a hand on my shoulder.

I look up, blinking at tears that threaten my eyes. Stupid. She cheated on me. Dragged me up north. Dumped me. And yet I'm feeling a sense of loss that threatens to spill out in tears. I draw a deep breath, forcing it away. Stupid. Lana's hand squeezes my shoulder, offering comfort.

"I'm fine. I'll get Bill." I stand to walk over to his body, and Lana lets her hand fall away as I do so.

Unlike Luthien's, his death was more violent. Much more violent, his body missing an arm and a leg, his chest caved in and his face crushed and missing its lower jaw.

All around us, the signs of a massive fight are clear. The clearing around us for hundreds of meters is torn and destroyed, trees holed, undergrowth burnt away and snow melted. Yet for all of that, we're missing two bodies. Around us, the puppies sniff and paw at the ground, searching out clues.

"This looks like your attacker's work," Lana says, gesturing around us.

I have to agree. We're no forensic scientists, but we've seen enough combat to be able to read the clearing. The marks and attacks from a long-bladed weapon are clear. It's no monster, that's for sure, and that doesn't leave us much. While the puppies and Ali scan for signs of the rest of Bill's team, Mikito keeps watch.

"Yeah. I wonder…" I fall silent, not wanting to voice my suspicions.

"If he took out the other party?" Lana's lips twist. "Once is chance, twice is coincidence, three times…"

"Pretty sure once was enemy action already," I say, my voice hard. Not hard to guess who either. A newcomer since this just started happening recently. Someone with an extremely high level and immensely skilled to be able to kill this quickly.

A bark from Wynn has me looking at Lana, who nods. Right, best to find the other two. Even if all we can do is return their bodies to Whitehorse.

***

"You're late," Ingrid says as she fades in behind us.

Mikito snarls, her naginata stopping its swing inches from decapitating Ingrid. Not that the raven-haired First Nation woman looks excited.

"Sneaking up on friends isn't nice," I say, looking at the cave. "Luke in there?"

"I wasn't expecting friends. Luke's pretty cut up. Lost both his feet," Ingrid says.

I grimace. "Well, we'll put him on one of the puppies and we'll head back."

I take a closer look at Ingrid. Other than some torn-up armor and dried blood, she looks to be well. Which doesn't mean much with our regeneration.

"What happened?" Lana asks as she climbs down Howard. Her hand comes up, the old caring redhead back for a second. The tightness in Ingrid's face makes Lana's harden too and she turns away, heading into the cave with Howard trailing.

"We were ambushed. Tall, lean bastard wielding a sword on a stick. A bit like yours, Mikito," Ingrid says, answering the question even if Lana's not here. "Appeared out of nowhere and killed Luthien first. One attack, right into her chest. We couldn't hit him, not at first. He was too fast, too good. Bill… he let him cut him. Took the cut to his chest and hugged him close, let us get in our attacks. We hurt the bastard, hurt him good. Made him run off."

Ingrid pauses, her breathing having grown hoarse. She starts up again soon after. "Couldn't take their bodies. I took their equipment, then I took Luke with me. Thought he might be back after he healed, but I used my Skills. Hid us. Came here. I thought… I thought he would come back."

Ingrid's voice breaks and tears stream from her eyes. She's hugging herself, the tension from the hours alone, waiting for an unstoppable attacker, finally breaking through her control. Ingrid sobs, dark hair spilling over her tanned skin. Then Mikito is there, holding the taller woman to her slight frame, patting her back. I watch for a second more before I turn away, the naked emotion too much for me.

"Can we track that son of a bitch now?" I say, finding refuge in my rage.

"Possibly. I'm dumping what I can into it, but there ain't no way of telling till we run into him again," Ali says.

"I want his head."

"I know."

Lana leads Howard out, Luke strapped to his back like a pack. The slightly portly hunter waves to me, his face grim as he dangles from the back, legless.

"Luke."

"John," Luke replies, his Quebecois accent strong and clear. "Thank you for coming for us."

"Always." I glance at the women.

He follows my gaze to where Lana has joined the other two before we both look away. From the tracks on his face, it's clear Luke's been doing some crying of his own. Not that I blame him but…

"I'm going to scout," I say to no one before walking into the woods.

Better to let them have the moment to calm down, gather themselves. We're quite a distance from safety and Ingrid was right—we could still be attacked on the way back.

***

Hours later, we're finally back in Whitehorse. Mikito and Lana have taken the remainder of Bill's group back to his place with indications that they might stay the night. That leaves me with the joyous duty of reporting to Roxley. Enhanced Constitution or not, I've been up for over twenty-five hours by this point, most of it tramping through the wilderness in temperatures cold enough to freeze a penguin, and I'm exhausted. Yet this needs doing, which is why I'm riding the too-fast elevator to Roxley's offices.

Well, I see someone sleeps in the nude. My mind comes to a crashing stop as the doors slide open, the brief sight of a mostly naked dark Elf stuttering my brain. He's busy belting the robe when the doors open, and for a moment, I regret the fact that the elevator wasn't faster.

"John. What's so urgent you needed to wake me?"

Roxley's voice brings me back to my senses, and I answer. "Bill's dead. So's Luthien. My attacker—the halberd-wielder—found and killed them. Pretty sure he's targeting the hunting groups now. I'm going to go and fuck them up now."

"You cannot," Roxley says, his voice filled with urgency and concern. "We don't have proof."

"We could buy it from the Shop. Hell, we don't even need to. You know it's them. I know it's them. They know it's them."

"It would cost too much. And even if we did, what happens then?" Roxley says, putting a hand on my shoulder. "We can't beat them. You can't even beat the Weaponmaster. And if you attack them now, Labashi will step in. And that's just the two of them. They've got an army waiting in the wings."

"So we do what? Just wait for them to get around to killing us?"

He doesn't respond.

"Roxley?" I ask, looking at the Tuinnar. Really looking at him, at the lines on his face and the worry that creases it.

"I don't know. I don't know," Roxley says, his shoulders slumping.

"My lord?" Vir says, coming out of the elevator behind me.

I jump a bit, not having realized he'd arrived.

Vir's fully dressed and looks disapprovingly at the two of us. "I believe the Redeemer has provided you the basics. I will debrief him further. You should rest."

"Vir…"

"My lord. You should rest," Vir's voice grows stern, like a teacher to a child.

Roxley twitches at the tone, yet he drops his hand from my shoulder and nods numbly, walking back to his room.

Vir turns to me. "Come, Redeemer. It seems we have much to speak of."

"Vir—"

"Lord Roxley is under a great deal of stress. He needs his rest," Vir says.

I nod slowly, taking the hint and not pushing it any further. Not that I need to. It's clear enough, even to me, that Roxley doesn't have a plan.

Chapter 12

Even on the short walk to the Nugget from my flat, I can tell that the news of our most recent losses have spread. The few people who move through the twilight-lit streets move with hesitation, their shoulders drawn in and eyes flicking from side to side, trying to see all the threats that aren't there. Those who are on the streets move fast, a shuffle-walk that would make a speedwalker envious.

The pub is filled, people huddled around and speaking in hushed tones over pitchers of Apocalypse Ale. The Yukon Brewing's own hand-crafted beer would put down an elephant and is just about strong enough to give a System-registered human a buzz. My entrance to the pub elicits more than a few stares, side conversations, and in a few cases, accusatory glares.

I grab a seat where I can find one, ending up nearly smack-dab in the middle and alone. No idea if my team will be making their way here, but until they do, I get to weather the stares and disapproving looks. The stares I'm used to; the disapproving looks are a bit more of a puzzle. It's not as if I could have done anything to save them—not more than I did anyway. Long-range communication continues to elude us. Our current technology isn't good or powerful enough to cut through the woods, the hills, and the snow. The closest thing readily available would be a Skill, but even that is limited by range and the requirement that everyone connected has it. Eventually we'll be able to add repeating towers and maybe even System-registered satellites, but that's well in the future and a lot of Credits that we don't have.

I'm just starting on breakfast when someone finally gets the courage to say something to me directly. The self-elected troublemaker is short, with buzzcut hair and an aggressive stance. "What are you doing about this?"

"Hmmm…" I frown, putting my utensils down and looking at the man. A quick glance gives me his name, which I promptly forget, and his level, which I do remember. 28. Not horrible, but not great. "Do about what?"

"They're killing us. I heard it's the Elves killing us, hunting us down and killing us! What are you going to do about it?" He jerks his head forward as he speaks.

I mentally sigh, staring at the man. I know what he's really asking, why he's asking. Even someone as emotionally stunted as I am can tell—he's scared and he wants someone, anyone to fix it. The fact that I'm one of the leading, if not the leading, human combatant means it's up to me. For all my understanding, I want to tell him to bugger off—that the problem is as much his as mine. That no solution I come up with would be possible without further help. That they need to keep going out, training and fighting and leveling. I could, I want, to say all that and more. But it wouldn't help him. Or anyone else who is staring at me, listening in.

So I finally say, "I'm working on it."

"You're working on it! Working on it!?!" Crewcut splutters, rage suffusing his face.

"Yes. It's complicated—"

"Doesn't seem complicated to me." This time, it's a larger man, somehow managing to keep the chub on his body even after the System. "They're killing us because we ain't kicked out that Tuinnar. We kick him out, they leave us alone."

"Then what?" I ask, staring at Chubster. "They come in and take over, right? Is that what you want?"

"Does it matter? They ain't human anyway," Crewcut says.

"Roxley has been fair to us. Hell, he barely even taxes us beyond the Shop. You sure you want to trade the devil you know for one that's willing to kill to get their way?" I watch the rustle my words generate. If they want to assume the Truinnar are doing the killing –and I don't blame them, I'm assuming that too– then I might as well ask the hard question.

"We can't fight them, and they're just going to keep killing us. Better to be alive than dead," Chubster says.

"Really? I think you're being a bit unimaginative there," Ali pipes up, shaking his head. "Torture, slavery, serfdom, being a second-class citizen."

As Ali speaks, I stand and raise my hand, forestalling any further words from the Spirit. I let my gaze travel around the area, meeting various eyes, and pitch my voice to carry. "Look, I'm going to tell you this straight. Things are bad and it'll likely get worse before it's over. I'm doing what I can and I will continue doing so. But all of you are going to have to decide what you want.

"Roxley's given us free rein to chart our own lives, to grow and level at our own speed and pace. He's let us buy our own houses, make the city our own as best we can in this System-ridden world. You can choose to support him. Or you can roll the dice and hope the Duchess is better. She sure hasn't promised anything better from what I hear.

"Decide whichever you want. You're all grown-ups. Just realize you're going to have live with them."

I shut up and sit down, turning back to my meal. When Crewcut opens his mouth to say something else, Sarah cuts him off with a hand to his arm and a smile. The pretty and visibly pregnant young waitress pushes him back to his seat, eyes glinting with malice. Crewcut only needs one look at her eyes to decide that he'd rather not engage with her.

Just like that, the confrontation is over and I return to my meal and my thoughts. One thing they have right—we don't seem to have a solution, a way out of this. Neither Roxley, the council, nor myself see a way that doesn't involve losing. I chew on my meal, the taste ashen as I try to piece together a real plan, something, anything to break this Gordian Knot.

***

I'm nearly done with breakfast when Minion comes walking into the Nugget, his entrance letting in some of the cold winter air. The suited politician stumps over to where I polish off the last of my bread, and he glares down at me. I take my time, swallowing my latest mouthful and draining my cup of coffee before I look at him.

Surprisingly, Minion doesn't look annoyed. Eric just stares at me, perfectly serene and patient before he speaks. "We'd like some of your time, Mr. Lee."

"Well, if you asked so nicely," I say.

Ali, floating beside me, twitches a hand and pays for our food, sending the Credits to the Nugget's account. Extremely convenient.

Minion leads the way to a boardroom in the old city hall where a group of worried human counselors sit, speaking in hushed tones that stop the moment we walk in. All the usual suspects are there, from the matronly Miranda to silver-haired Norman, as well as some of the more prominent members of our business and hunting groups. Jim offers me a quick nod as I step in, and I return it before facing Miranda.

"John, we heard about Bill and his group. However, we'd like to hear about it directly from you," Miranda says.

I nod. Fair enough that they'd want it from the horse's mouth. I quickly give them a summary of what we found and discerned, along with the good news that at least two of his party survived. When I finally wind down, the silence in the room is heavy.

"Those son of a—" Jim breaks the silence, fist clenched.

"Jim," Miranda says, cutting off the old hunter.

He growls, and she meets his eyes. There's an exchange of information there, one that I'm not privy to, but it is enough to make Jim slump backward into his chair, arms crossed. Miranda turns to me when she's sure Jim is done.

"You said there were no signs of who did this?" Miranda says, and there's an intensity to her words and gaze.

I weigh the unspoken command in my mind, balancing what Roxley said as well, and finally answer. "None."

"That is unfortunate," Miranda says, sharing a glance with Jim and Eric.

"We will need to take additional precautions when sending out hunting groups," Eric says, rubbing his chin.

A mental snort from Ali echoes my own thought on this.

"*What can they do? That Weaponmaster can kick any of the other hunting groups' asses without breaking stride,*" I send to Ali.

"*Well, if it's the Weaponmaster, they can tie him and the Envoy down with events. So long as the teams don't go too far, they can still be contacted too, so if something goes wrong, we can pull them back,*" Ali sends.

I find myself nodding, which gets more than a few curious glances shot my way.

"Very well, Eric, I'll leave you and Jim to deal with that." Miranda turns to me, fixing me with a straight look. "What has Lord Roxley said of this?"

"Vir debriefed me, and I'm sure Roxley's getting briefed in detail too," I say. "I'm sure he'll look into it."

"His enemies are targeting us, and you think he'll look into it?" Eric's voice drips with derision.

"Yes, I do." I let my gaze wander over the angry and scared group and wonder if a variation of my previous speech would work. I don't think so though—this group, emotional as they may be, has it under control. So time to roll the dice. Even a little bit. "But that's the wrong question you're asking."

"Oh? And what would the right question be?" Norman says, fingers steepled in front of him.

I flash the silver-haired boomer a smile. "What happens when Roxley isn't our lord anymore."

"Well, the attacks stop for a start," Norman says.

"That's nice. Though when the bully takes his foot off your throat, you don't normally thank him. What else?"

"Well, they'll upgrade the city to a Town of course," Eric answers, waving. "The city is no use to them as a Village."

"Which we're about to do by ourselves anyway."

"John, if you have something to say, say it," Miranda says, irritation clouding her voice.

"Nothing much. Just the fact that if you intend to do what I figure you're thinking of, perhaps you should take some time and think about what will happen," I say.

"Maybe spend some Credits, find out what's happening in other cities," Ali adds.

Miranda nods calmly while Eric sneers at Ali. I let my gaze roam around the room, gauging the mood and seeing that while the people might still be quiet and terrified, they look more thoughtful now too. Maybe, just maybe, what I've said has done some good. After confirming there's nothing more they want with me, I leave on that thought.

That, and the knowledge that unless we figure out an actual, workable plan, we're arsed anyway. It's one thing to say we shouldn't give in, and another to watch your friends die one by one.

***

Two days later, I'm finishing up my breakfast when a knock resounds off my door. Standing in the doorway is Vir, trying to look stern and implacable as always. However, I've spent enough time around him and his kind to read the lines of tension in his body and the wrinkles near his eyes.

"John, your presence is required." Vir says.

I nod. I glance around the room, noting that there's nothing for me to grab, and follow him out. In short order, he's led me up Main St. to the City Center. Interestingly enough, Lana's pets are seated outside the City Center, giving hint of what is to come.

Lana and Mikito are with Roxley in his offices, tension radiating from everyone. Behind the seated Lana is Amelia, one arm casually resting on the butt of her gun and looking thoroughly displeased.

"*What's going on?*" I send to Ali, who grunts.

"*I'm asking,*" Ali says. "*Doesn't look good, does it?*"

I repeat the question aloud while waiting for Ali's answer.

Roxley's face grows tighter for a moment before he replies. "Ms. Pearson has betrayed us." He continues, cutting me off before I can. "As you know, she is a major landowner in town. As I got ready this morning, I was alerted to a sudden drop in the stability of the city's Mana flows. It seems Ms. Pearson sold her buildings back to the System."

"Lana?" I ask her, shocked by the news. "Why?"

"I needed the Credits," Lana says, not daring to meet my eyes.

"So she has stated. However, the sale of System-owned lands back to the System is significantly lower than a resale to another individual," Roxley says.

I remember that now, having sold the Key to Haines Junction to the System myself. It was a cents-on-the-dollar kind of thing.

"What do you have to say for yourself?" I look at Lana, hoping she has an explanation.

Lana sits there in silence before she looks up, defiance in her eyes. "I had a contract with the Envoy. If I sold my land to the System, they would give me the full purchase price for it and twenty percent of its worth and I got to keep what I received from the System too."

I closed my eyes. So. She did betray us. *"What percentage are we at?"*

"66%"

"And before?"

"We lost 7% through her sale. We lost another 6% from others."

"She's not the only one," I state, meeting Roxley's eyes, and he slowly nods.

"They approached most others who had residences in Riverdale and made the same offer," Vir explains.

"So why is Lana being singled out here?" I ask pointedly.

"Ms. Pearson was the single largest landowner who took advantage of the offer. And through her control of your foundation, she might be able to affect us by another eleven percent," Vir says.

I frown, staring at Lana before I speak slowly. "Are you Contracted to sell the foundation assets?"

"No!" Lana snaps. Amelia behind her stirs a bit then stills when Lana doesn't make any threatening moves. "I wouldn't do that to you."

"But you would sell your land, knowing what it means for the city," Roxley says, his voice filled with disapproval.

"It's my land," Lana states again.

"You could have sold it to me. Or anyone else," Roxley said. "Instead, you destroyed our ability to become a Town."

"Lana, why did you need the Credits?" Mikito asks.

Roxley stays silent, his jaw flexing as he works through his emotions. Lana shuts her mouth, refusing to say.

"Ms. Pearson, your reluctance to answer is not helping your case," Vir grates out while Lana's lips tighten.

"*I think I can help…*" Ali sends to me. I'm surprised. He normally just jumps in, but for once, he's hesitant.

"*Go ahead. Can't make it worse.*"

"*Har!*" Ali floats down to her. "Lana. I know what you're trying to buy. I can say it or you can. Truthfully, it'll sound less crazy coming from you."

Okay. Maybe I was wrong. Lana stares at Ali, her lip curling upward in disdain, but she stays silent.

"Lana was looking over the details for resurrection in the Shop, searching for a way to bring Richard back. She hit upon the Frinkzin Replicas," Ali says.

His words draw indrawn breaths from Vir and Roxley.

"Can the System bring people back to life?" I frown, not entirely sure how I feel about that idea. It seems impossible, but so much of our lives are impossible that I can't discount it entirely. For a moment, hope blossoms in my heart and I move to squelch it—there's always a price for things like that.

"Sorry, boy-o. Dead is dead," Ali says. "Frinkzin Replicas are one of many attempts to get around that. Not the worst, since Richard's rotten enough that I guess Lana decided against the reanimation option. The Replicas pull data from the System and upload it to an artificially created body."

"Oh my God, Lana!" Amelia gasps while Mikito looks ashen, staring at Lana in horror.

"You don't…"

"Don't you dare. This, this will bring him back." Lana's voice grows shrill as her nose flares. "I'll bring him back and we'll be… we'll be fine."

"Not so much, toots. Frinkzin Replicas aren't the people who left. Even individuals who lived their whole lives in the System aren't made properly. Aren't made right. The System can only register actions. Words. Events. It doesn't understand, doesn't record motivations, reasons, choices," Ali says. "The monsters that came out of the Replica creation—and they were almost all monsters—were what got it banned."

"Richard's no monster!" Lana snaps, her fist closing.

"No. But his Replica would be. Think, Lana. What does the System know? That he owned pets. That he used them to kill monsters. That he hunted and let the pets eat their kills. That he chose to fight instead of running," Ali states. "Our lives, your lives, in the System, it's all about death and fighting and leveling. The monsters that come out of the process—that's all they do. They can't, won't, care. They just kill and level and often don't make a distinction."

Lana shakes her head, refusing to listen to Ali. He growls, floating upward while Roxley and Vir trade glances again.

Finally Roxley steps forward and squats next to Lana. "The Tuinnar have many experiences with the resurrected. With those who would bring back the dead. We live for hundreds of years with the System, but that is often not enough." Roxley pauses, his hand opening and closing unconsciously. "Four hundred fifteen years ago, we fought a war across all our holdings because a son could not give up his mother. The Tuinnar no longer allow the dead to be raised, in any form or visage. Only grief comes with their resurrection."

"I don't care. I just want him back," Lana says, fingers digging into her arms. The sharp smell of blood cuts through the air, bitter iron on our tongues.

"Perhaps, but who will you sacrifice for that?" Unlike the rest of us, Vir's voice is hard, caustic. "Will you let him kill Mikito? Andrea? The children? Who are you willing to sacrifice for your selfish desires?"

"I won't let him do that," Lana says bitingly.

"Will you kill him then? Frinkzin Replicas are notorious for lacking a sense of self-preservation. Once they begin, they will not retreat," Vir says. "You will have to choose: an innocent or your 'brother.'"

"Stop it!" Lana shouts at Vir, standing up swiftly and glaring at the Tuinnar. "Just stop it."

"Or will you let us kill him? Because I guarantee you, Lord Roxley and I will not see such a creature in our city."

"I won't let you kill it. Him," Lana says, correcting herself almost immediately. Yet I can see the way her eyes dart from side to side, the increased respiration and the white-knuckled grip as her careful control gets pushed further.

"You were right the first time," Ali says. "We Spirits don't really get into this entire soul business, but calling a replica soulless would be pretty damn accurate."

Again, silence. I gritted my teeth, before I spoke again. "Lana, think of Richard. Do you really think he'd want you to bring him back and hurt those he loved. You? Mikito? His children? Think about how much damage you've done already, doing this."

"Enough!" Lana says, her voice breaking. "I just… I just want my brother back. I don't want to be alone anymore." The last is said barely above a whisper.

Mikito pushes forward until she's in front of Lana, then she enfolds the larger woman in her embrace. The tiny Asian murmurs something in Japanese, words that no one else understands, but it doesn't matter. It doesn't matter because it's her tones, her presence that makes the difference. Lana finally breaks down, harsh sobs erupting from her throat as she holds on to Mikito.

I watch this, a lump in my throat, and I curse myself. I missed it, missed the depth of Lana's pain, of her need. I missed it not because I wasn't looking but because I wasn't willing to confront her about it. To push it. And now, we're here. All I can do is watch, unshed tears burning my eyes as I wait.

In time, Lana stops crying and pulls herself together. Mikito pushes away, and Amelia hands them tissues. There are a few quick, slightly embarrassed smiles before I find myself fixed with glares by all three women.

"What?" I say, blinking.

"Idiot."

"Baka."

"Oh, John…"

"What?" I state again.

"Redeemer, you are hopeless. Handsome, but hopeless." Roxley sighs, coming back from the corner where he and Vir have been working quietly while waiting for the group to get themselves sorted.

"That's my boy-o."

"Ms. Pearson, am I to believe that you have given up on your plans?" Roxley says.

Lana slowly nods. I stare at her, wondering if we can believe her. It's strange—I've never asked her what she believes in for the afterlife. Yet her choices here are insane, more so when you consider the fact that she might have believed in souls. Grief makes us do stupid things, and from experience, it takes more than just a single crying session to get over it. It's unlikely she'll do it and I hate to doubt her, but…

"*Ali…*"

"*I know. I'll keep an eye out for purchases.*"

"Good. I must admit, I would feel more comfortable if you did not have access to the foundation and its resources," Roxley says before his shoulders slump. "It does not matter that much, I guess. We will not be able to meet the requirement in time. Not now."

Lana winces, opens her mouth, then shuts it before she adds, softly, "I'm sorry. I'll give up control of the foundation if you want. I can't even buy any more land, not in Whitehorse. It was one of the stipulations."

"That's it then? They've won?" Amelia cuts in, glaring at all of us.

"What can we do?" Roxley says, shaking his head. "The taxes on my lands are coming due and I have not the funds for them. Even if I sold all my gear and released my guard, I cannot cover both the taxes and the shortfall in land. And if we somehow miraculously managed to become a Town, we would have no defense against Labashi and his people."

Of course, that elicits a quick discussion of people asking what taxes and lands he's talking about. It doesn't take long, but at the end, everyone is depressed with the realization that they're coming for us every way they can.

"And you're going to give up?" Amelia says, leaning forward and glaring at us with fists on ample hips. For a moment, I'm back in grade school, being told off by Ms. France for sticking another eraser up my nose.

"We are not giving up. We will do our best, but we cannot win on this path," Vir says, a hand held out placatingly to Amelia.

"Then change the path!" Amelia says.

"We're trying. Lord Roxley and I have attempted to contact our allies for aid and Credits to no avail. We have begun to speak to less savory organizations as well. We are trying," Vir states while Roxley's lips twist.

Mikito is crouched next to Lana, who has retaken her seat, a hand on her knee while the redhead looks guilty.

"Your liege, he raised your taxes knowing you could not pay it?" Mikito says slowly, searching out Roxley's eyes. Black eyes meet, and on the confirming nod, Mikito continues. "A liege who does not reward the loyalty of his citizens has no honor. In turn, he is owed none any further."

Roxley frowns, meeting and weighing something in Mikito's eyes.

It's Lana who asks the question we humans all carry. "Aren't you samurai all about, you know, following your lord till death?"

"And where did that lead us?" Mikito shakes her head. "The samurai aren't, weren't, as… Hollywood as you believe. The code of Bushido that is in the movies, it was not as universally accepted as they would have you think. Loyalty is important, but it is only one aspect of the code. And Lord Roxley has obligations to his people too."

I shut my mouth, clamping it tight. Right. I kind of feel like an ass for forgetting that stereotypes are just that—generalizations that might hold some truth, but lie just as often. I should know better—not every Chinese man knows martial arts and can't roll their Rs.

"Ms. Sato, you have given me much to think about." Lord Roxley executes a formal bow to her, which has me raising an eyebrow.

Mikito nods back to Roxley.

Ignoring the byplay, Amelia snaps, "It still hasn't fixed our problem— we've got a bunch of murderous assholes coming to take over our city. I'd almost rather see the city burn than let them take it."

"That's helpful." Ali snorts, spinning upside down. "Let's just burn the town, salt the earth, and invite a bunch of Goblins to stay too. That'll stop them. Not."

"Ali, stop flying. And we're not burning the town…" A nagging thought pushes against my mind, forcing me to trail off. Something. Something… flying. Burning…

"Redeemer…"

"Shh…." Lana shushes Roxley as she stares at my face. "He's thinking."

"Oh, hell. Not again," Ali says.

But I barely hear them as I try to find what it was that was niggling the back of my mind. Something…

Oh.

"I think I've got a plan. Well, sort of. Maybe."

Chapter 13

Completing the basics preparations takes two days. Two days of scrambling and sneaking around, of putting plans into play and talking to the right people. Two days of cajoling, threatening, and otherwise speaking with old friends and new enemies.

I find the mage late at night, looking tired and grumpy after he finished another private lesson. His long hair looks a touch greasy and unkempt, released from its manbun as he shook it out while the student ambled out. I don't think I improved his mood.

"What are you doing here?" Aiden says.

"Looking for the best mage in the city."

"Nope. I'm not going out. I can't. Not again," Aiden says, and even at the mention of it, I see a slight tremor in his hands.

"I know." I wish I could ask him to come, but he's made his views clear. And even if the mage shows a level of unexpected bravery at times, what we're about to do is something I want only volunteers for. "Wasn't here for that. But the city's going to need you, need your gifts and Skills while we're gone. The Swarms won't stop coming, the Bosses are still growing. The System is popping monsters in. None of that is going to stop, and the city needs to be ready for it."

"You make it sound like you'll be gone for a bit."

"For a bit. Maybe a long while."

"John…"

I shake my head, clapping the mage on his shoulder. "Don't worry about it. You just take care of our city."

After that, the rest of the preparations are simple enough. More gear to buy, more Contracts to write, more instructions to give. All the while trying to keep the damn Envoy and her people ignorant. Thankfully, everyone is willing to accept the fact that we want to take the time to shore up our equipment before heading out again as a good enough excuse for our continued and unusual presence. All of it is simple enough to do without arousing suspicion, till we leave one morning before the sun crests the horizon.

Which is why I'm surprised to see someone waiting for us on the Robert Pearson road, seated on her bike.

"What are you doing here?" I ask Ingrid, noting how she's cut her hair short and increased the armor and insulation she's wearing.

"You guys suck at this entire sneaking around town thing," Ingrid explains. "So where we headed?"

"None of your business. We got this," I say.

"Not a chance. I'm coming and you aren't stopping me," Ingrid retorts.

"This…" I open my mouth and shut it, glaring at the three who aren't backing me up. "You know we're going to do something really stupid, right? Possibly fatal?"

"It's your team," Ingrid says, shaking her head. "Of course it's stupid and dangerous. But it's effective and it'll screw with them if you get it right, right?"

"Yes."

"Then I'm in," Ingrid says. "So where are we going?"

"Carcross."

***

The ride to Carcross is fast and easy. While the roads might not have been cleared, they're still mostly level, which lets the pets keep a good pace. Anna, strapped in her usual place on Howard with Lana, cracks a yawn and sleeps through even the short fights on the way in. Unlike what her brother would have done, Lana has left Elsa in the city, having decided that a pet turtle—even one that breathes fire—isn't particularly useful for what we're about to do.

When we get through the gates, which are higher and stronger than they've ever been, we're greeted by Jason and Elder Badger. I grin, waving as Ingrid stares around the changed town with wide eyes, taking in the sights. I admit, I find some joy in her expressions, knowing we probably looked the same when we first arrived ages ago.

"Andrea. Jason." I get off Sabre, sending a command for it to follow as I shake their hands. "Didn't expect you to meet us."

"Our sensors told us you were coming. Figured we'd say hi," Jason said, smiling and glancing over at Ingrid. "You recruiting?"

"Of sorts. There's a lot we need to talk about," I say. "Can you invite whoever is appropriate from the Guild?"

"Very well," Andrea says, bobbing her white hair before she stomps away.

I frown, noticing the cane she's acquired, and raise an eyebrow at Jason.

"She's tired. Complaining about her arthritis," Jason says.

I blink, staring at him as I parse that together with my own experience of having my tendinitis disappear on the System's appearance.

"*Probably psychosomatic. Her mind's way of establishing control,*" Ali sends to me.

I grunt, deciding not to pass on that information. Whatever gets us through the day, I guess. Still, I make a note to have a word with Andrea later on.

Since Lana and Mikito know the rough outlines of the plan, they split off, leaving me to explain to the group that gathers in their city center. I quickly go through the pressures Whitehorse is facing, outlining some of the things the Envoy and her people have done.

I end with, "And that's why we'd like your help. If Whitehorse falls, it won't be long before they come for Carcross."

Flanked by Eilon and Ixlimin, the Guildmaster has stayed quiet through the entire explanation. Seated on a child's booster seat, the four-foot-tall pixie stares at me with multi-colored eyes, absorbing every word I said. When I'm done, he speaks. "This is dire news. We, of course, knew the Duchess had targeted Whitehorse but did not realize matters were this grave. Thank you for the information.

"But I am unsure what, if any, aid we may offer. Angering the Duchess of the Pourquoi States is dangerous, especially for a Guild of our size."

"You know we'll help you, John, but what do you need?" Andrea says. "We can't afford to give you much Credits. We're on a tight budget here too. And you know we're low on fighters…"

I shake my head, dismissing her words. "The Credits might be useful, but it's something you should speak with Roxley about directly. As for fighters, I think we've got that covered. I have a plan."

I'm really beginning to get a complex from the way every time I use that word, people wince. At least the humans do.

"What is it?" Jason asks, his head tilted.

"Well, there's this Dragon, you see…" I savor the wide-eyed expressions as I explain the plan. Or at least, as much as I can tell them.

***

"You know, you're absolutely insane," the Guildmaster says.

"I've been told that, Jin," I say, glancing at him before smiling. "So you guys going to help?"

"It is a risky plan. Too risky for the Guild to take part in." Jin turns those multi-colored eyes on me. Green, red, and pink swirl as they lock on me with a mischievous glint. "However, I cannot stop my adventurous colleagues from taking on a legitimate Quest if one were to be offered to the Guild."

I grunt, already wincing internally. "And how expensive a Quest would this be?"

"Expensive. We are talking about tracking a Dragon to its home and leading a group of under-leveled Adventurers there," Jin says, tapping his lip. "I could not, in good conscience, offer such a Quest without suitable reward."

Andrea cuts in, her voice curt. "Jin, we will speak of this Quest together. We've got to discuss your people's most recent incident anyway. Partying with the Dwarves after shift and leaving our pub wrecked is not acceptable."

Jin's mischievous look falls away and he leans forward slightly, his wings fanning out behind him before they retract behind his back. For a moment, I get a chance to view them fully in all their splendid, multi-hued glory. At Andrea's gesture, I walk out of the room with Ingrid following me, hands on her hips. It's only when we're most of the way out that she breaks the silence.

"So. A Dragon," Ingrid says leadingly.

"Yeah…" I glance at her from the corner of my eyes. "You know, I'm kind of glad you're here. Your Skills…"

"Yup." Ingrid shakes her head. "And you didn't want me to come."

"Insanely dangerous, remember?" I point out.

"Luthien was right. You're a damn softie," Ingrid says, smirking. "I'm a big girl. And this world isn't safe."

I nod, falling silent while I figure out where the girls are. It takes a few seconds to guide the pair of us to them. At some point, I'll have to brief Ingrid a bit more. I told the Carcross council part of the plan, enough to convince them. But with the way the System works, I need to keep most of it close to my chest. Either way, it's time to get Lana for the next step.

***

"Shaft Leader?" I inquire, staring at the four-and-a-half-foot tall Dwarf who has his greying hair in dreads.

He's got his feet up on the table, relaxing after a hard day's work, with a big pint of beer in his hands. Light gray eyes stare at us inquiringly, weighing and assessing with practiced ease.

"We understand you're part of a larger clan?" Lana asks, flashing him one of her patented dazzling smiles.

The dwarf blinks, sitting up as she hits him with the charm offensive. It's unlikely that anyone of his rank can't shake off the effects of a charm spell, but having a beautiful woman talk to you still wakes up any red-blooded male.

"That I am, and that we are. The Stonebottom Clan." The dwarf grins, offering his hands to Lana. When she takes them, he pulls her to him, knocking heads with her gently and sneaking a look down her blouse. "Romi Graniteknee. What can I do for you?"

"Well, we've got a little business proposition for your clan, if you're willing to listen," Lana murmurs, still bent over until Romi nods. Then she straightens up and takes a seat. "Now, we were thinking…"

I lean against the wall, watching her work the poor dwarf over. Not that she has her way completely, but Lana's experience at negotiating deals shines here. It's a delicate task and one that I'm glad she's heading, even if Romi drives a hard bargain. Still, at the end of the conversation, we have what we need, if not what we want.

***

The evening before we embark on the most dangerous thing we've ever done, we spend our time doing something entirely pedestrian. Perhaps it's by choice, perhaps it's just the way people deal with mounting pressure, but we spend the evening hanging out with Jason, Mike, and Rachel over good food and alcohol. No hunting, no fighting, just tall tales and ribbing. Unsurprisingly, we shoot down Jason's offer of coming along—something that Rachel looks entirely grateful for. Mike's offer is harder to turn down.

"Seriously, Mike, we don't need you," I explain, waving and trying to settle down the ex-Constable. "We're getting the Guild to help, so that'll boost our numbers. And we aren't exactly intending to fight our way in. Kluane's well outside our Levels, so stealth is the watchword."

He grunts, rubbing at his cyberarm unconsciously while we talk.

"And Carcross needs you," Lana adds, prodding the big man. "It might be a lull now, but the Swarms are going to keep coming and there's no guarantee the System won't drop something new. Best thing you can do is keep leveling out here."

"Doesn't sit right with me." Mike chugs his beer. "But you're right. Just seems like I'm always being excluded from all the fun things."

"Eh, it's a good thing. Merrow won't bitch to me about you being gone," Jason says.

The girls, as one, turn to stare at Mike.

"Merrow? Wait, the Cat-girl?" Rachel asks, her eyes wide.

"Yup."

"A Cat-girl?" I ask, my voice rising slightly.

"That's not their—" Ali says and gets popcorn thrown at him.

The women lean forward, fixing their gaze on the large and suddenly shy constable.

"So, Mike, this Merrow…"

As the girls prod the poor man for more information, I sit back and enjoy the show. For all his grumbling, Mike doesn't actually mind speaking about his new girlfriend once he gets rolling. Who'd ever thought he was that open-minded?

***

"Eilon. Ixlimin," I greet the pair as we meet up with them the next morning. A quick glance at their Status Bars is all it takes to get information from them. Not a huge change in their stats, to tell the truth, which works for me.

I let my gaze wander to the other three in their party. One's a wolf-human hybrid, a staff in her hand; another is a blue-skinned humanoid with four hands; and the last is a Yerick. All are clad in high-tech skinsuits, thin armor plates lining their bodies, and both melee and ranged weapons are slung across their bodies. Interestingly enough, the Yerick has a bow across his body, though I see no arrows.

Jakrim Lurra (Level 3 Axe Warrior)

HP: 1020/1020

MP: 530/530

Condition: None

Valeria Iillora (Level 42 Elementalist)

HP: 230/230

MP: 1430/1430

Condition: None

Jazae Lamarr (Level 4 Scout Leader)

HP: 840/840

MP: 790/790

Condition: None

"Nice team," Ali says, his eyes roaming over the group. "But are you guys going to be enough?"

"Ixlimin can run interference for the System while Jazae will scout ahead and swing us around as many monsters as we can. When we can't, Valeria has a number of concealment spells," Eilon says. "We're also the only team that volunteered."

"Beggars can't be choosers," Lana says and nods to them. "Day's not getting any younger."

Rolling out, our newly enlarged group reaches the woods within minutes with Jazae leading the way. We could use the roads and go faster, but the plan is to do this quietly, which means we skip the roads and go cross-country.

Watching the Galactic team in action and the various options they've chosen to navigate the wilderness is interesting. Mikito and Lana ride the huskies, of course, and Ingrid's bike, like Sabre, has been outfitted with anti-gravity plates that keep it off the ground and handle the terrain easily. Like us, Jakrim uses a bike, somewhat more rugged and post-apocalyptic but still very much a bike. Valeria and Ixlimin both fly on their own power, using Magic and integrated technology in equal order. Interestingly enough, Eilon and the Scout are on foot. Jazae walks but somehow still covers more ground than a flat-out run, while Eilon's just freaky. The Eldritch Knight floats alongside us, never seeming to strain no matter how fast we're going. I guess being partially incorporeal has some benefits.

Since we don't need to hide till we're at the icefields, Jazae leads us on as straight a course as the terrain allows. Of course, that means we end up meeting more than one group of monsters. For the first fight, we step back and watch the Galactics go to work. Even as Jakrim, Ixlimin, and Valeria attack from a distance, pounding the unfortunate slimes, Eilon floats right into the center of the group and attacks with his sword, slicing and dicing without care. Attacks mostly pass through him, doing damage but not displacing his body. In short order, the slimes are dead and we're moving.

The Galactics take the lead on the next encounter as well, before we start working on figuring out how to fight together as a group. Jazae never makes an appearance at this or the other fights, always staying a step ahead of the main group as she trailblazes for us.

After a bit of a rough start, we start gelling. It's a not difficult transition—most of us melee fighters just have to remember to hold back and let the ranged attackers pound our enemies a bit till they arrive. After that, we're normally too tightly packed for ranged attacks, but with the monsters we face, that's rarely a problem. While they aren't under-levelled, there're just too many of us to make most groups a credible threat. Sadly, that also means we aren't getting much in terms of experience.

By the time we call it a night, we've covered about two-thirds of the distance to Kluane. We could have traveled faster, but toward the end, we started running into Level 70 monsters. Still not impossible, but the fights are tougher and require us to rest and wait for Mana and health to regenerate. We start being more cautious as well, because as we get closer, the zones will get higher and higher.

Setting up camp is quick, with a series of portable force fields linked to keep out potential trouble and a quick clearing of snow by Anna. Tents are pitched, additional security measures like automated gun turrets are added, and a fire is started within minutes. Watches are divided based off rest requirements, and the mages and Ingrid crash out after a warm meal. The melee fighters stay up later, our enhanced Constitution ensuring that we handle the trip better.

Having volunteered for first watch, I'm surprised when Lana sits down beside me, Anna flopping her head on Lana's legs for a good scratching the moment she does. Red fur is combed and ears are gently scratched as Lana stays silent. I look at the redhead, noting that helmet hair or not, she looks ravishing. Not knowing what she wants to say or why she's here, I find myself speechless as always. This is the first time we've had a chance to really talk since the meeting with Roxley. Ali floats away from us, engaging Eilon in conversation.

"I'm sorry," Lana says after the silence has stretched on too long.

"There's no need," I say automatically. Even as I say it, I realize it's the truth. She might have betrayed us in a way—but she was right, the land was hers to do with as she desired. We might have wanted a say, but we didn't have a right to it. And… "You were hurt. In pain. I'm sorry. I should have talked to you more. Helped more."

"I didn't want any."

"Doesn't matter," I say, shaking my head. "I should have been a better friend. I'm just not very good at this. At that."

"Being a friend?"

"No. About, well, talking about you know." I grimace as I struggle against my old training, my old social conditioning.

"Opening up? Showing people you care?" Lana says, and I nod. "It's not easy for anyone."

"It seemed easy for you," I retort.

"Seemed. It's never easy. Caring for others, empathizing, you just get better at it with practice."

"Yeah…" I fall silent, staring into the darkness. I glance at my minimap, seeing nothing new of note, before turning back to Lana. "So how are you doing?"

"It hurts when I think of him. Hurts worse when I realize I've forgotten about him, that I stopped hurting. I know it's stupid. I even know what my old therapist would say. It's not as if I didn't experience this when our parents died. I know I shouldn't feel guilty for living, but it still feels wrong."

"I know…" I say, rubbing my face. Gods, do I know. "Emotions never do want to listen to logic."

"I wanted him back so much, even when I knew it was wrong, I ignored it. Knew that it wouldn't be him, couldn't be him. But I thought maybe if it was even mostly like him, it'd be okay. Enough to make it stop hurting," Lana confesses.

I almost say something about how it doesn't make sense, what she said. But then again, pain and grief don't make sense. It just is.

"I used to love the Yukon. Couldn't imagine living anywhere else. The woods, the winter, the weather. Now, every place I look, every person I meet reminds me of him. And I hate it. Hate that Richard gave his life up for this, for us, just because he couldn't look away. I wish…" Lana stutters to a stop and shakes her head. "I should have burnt all his comics."

"All?"

"Yeah. We got into a fight once when we were kids. Stupid sibling stuff— I can't even remember what about. I was so angry with him, I walked into his room and grabbed some of his comics and threw them into the stove with the firewood," Lana says, and I look at her in horror. She ducks her head slightly, the blush setting off her freckles for a moment. "I know. But I was only ten. Our parents took away my allowance for weeks till I paid him back."

"Huh. Spiderman, right?" I say, and she nods. "He told me about it. I don't think burning them would have mattered. He'd have found another reason to be out there."

"Yes. The idiot always wanted to be a hero." Lana bends down, burying her face in Anna's fur.

I shake my head, looking away, then grunt reflexively as Howard drops his head onto my lap, looking for a scratch too. I peel off my gauntlets before I comply with his furry demand, digging my flesh into silky fur while I check my map again.

We fall silent for a time, scratching the fox and puppy in silence. It's a companionable silence, a mutual moment of peace in an otherwise deadly and dangerous world. We're silent for so long, even the animals trade places.

Lana finally speaks. "John."

"Hmmm…?"

"Do you…?" Lana blushes slightly before catching my eye and tilting her head toward her tent.

"Uhh…"

"I'm not emotional. Well, I am but not, you know," Lana says. "No promises. Nothing more than friends."

"I'm on watch."

"Ali?" Lana calls, and the Spirit, who has returned to floating above us, comes down.

"Got it, toots. Go clean your tubes, boy-o."

I growl at the Spirit, then turn to look at Lana, really look at her. I take in her pale, freckled skin and the disarrayed red hair. The all-too-serious expression that's contradicted by the rising blush. The straight back that reminds me of the strength she carries, and the smiling violet eyes.

I've said no before. I get the feeling if I say no now, it'll likely be the last time she would ever ask. And for good reason. There are a million and one reasons to say no. The fact that I don't know where this is going. That she's still vulnerable. That I'm still vulnerable. In the end though, the only real question is—do I want this?

***

Five hours later, we're on the road again. Everyone but us has gotten some rest. I'll admit, I'm grateful that the high-tech Galactic-made tents are soundproof. Otherwise, we would not have created a restful environment for anyone else. Or at least the humans—the gods know what the Galactics might think of sex. Perhaps it would have been restful for some of them.

We've only been moving for a short period before Eilon comes floating back to where I ride Sabre.

"Among my party, when someone is skipping his—or her—watch rotation for any reason, we generally inform the next on the list," Eilon says as he floats next to me.

"Sorry. My Spirit was watching," I mutter, looking down as I throw out my feeble excuse. It's not as if I had much longer on my watch—we'd split it such that there were only two watchers a night.

"Yes, well, Spirits generally aren't considered substitutes. Same with drones or AIs. Too easy for the System or monsters to fool. They're also often not effective as first responders," Eilon says, chiding me.

I take it with stride, nodding.

When the Eldritch Knight feels the rebuke has sunk in properly, he adds, "I'll admit, your Spirit is different from most. His scanning abilities are impressive."

I grunt, not caring to let him know that Ali's Linked to me. While not unique, it is rare since the Mana cost of having a Linked Spirit is high. In my case, I don't have to pay for it since it's being paid for by the System, but for most, it would be another drain on their Mana regeneration rates and thus too expensive.

Having done his duty as the leader of the group, Eilon moves back to his place in line. Once again, I let my eyes rove over the group. Jazae's out of sight as always, while Eilon and Jakrim play point man. Mikito and Ingrid bring up the rear, while the mage, Ixlimin, Lana, and myself are in the center of the group with the puppies. We're in a tighter formation than yesterday, the puppies not as spread out since the terrain we traverse forces us to stay close.

We're passing through a small gulley into a clearing, exiting from trees that have gained a metallic sheen and sap that dribbles silver, when they hit us. Eilon and Jakrim are out of cover when our attackers open fire, bolts of blue and red tearing through the air. At the same time, additional energy beams strike at us within the trees, Hakarta appearing in shimmers of light as their shielding falls. Attacks flash forward, converging on us from all directions in an attempt to surprise us.

All to be met with layers of shields and Mana. I almost wish I could see their faces when their ambush fails. Already Valeria is casting a Wall spell, sealing off one side of the battlefield for a few moments while the rest of us focus on the other side. Most of my Mana is gone, having used it to layer Soul Shield on my teammates, but I've got enough to spare for a Blink Step. When Sabre completes its change, I trigger the Skill, putting me behind the Hakarta team.

The Hakarta are smooth, trained. A pair spin around, searching for me, while the others focus fire on the rest of the team. Unfortunately for them, the pair who spin around aren't the ones I picked to attack. My sword cuts into the black armor-plated back of the Hakarta, duplicate blades trailing along behind my initial strike and cutting again into our ambusher.

Out of the corner of my eye, I glimpse the rest of the team at work. Ingrid and Ixlimin are gone, disappeared completely from sight. Mikito takes a more direct route, charging the group that hit us from behind. On top of Wynn, the Samurai and puppy cover the ground in fractions of a second. Ghostly armor surrounds both of them, beams of energy impacting and creating a scatter of rainbow light as it washes backward. Anna, released from Howard, is bathing one side of our line with flames, the same side that Valeria is busy throwing up reinforced earthen walls to provide cover against. Howard drops to the ground and slinks forward to the untouched side as best as he can, lowering the bulk of his body out of the range of fire. Shadow takes a more direct approach since he was closer, attacking the closest Hakarta, shadowy and real teeth closing on different limbs. Lana's hiding behind a tree, tossing out smoke grenades to give us additional cover while the occasional beam bounces off the remains of my Soul Shield. In the vanguard, Eilon separates into four copies, each of them charging a different Hakarta. Jakrim, on the other hand, just guns his bike, letting loose with his own integrated beam weaponry as he closes in on his attackers.

That's about all I see before I'm caught up in my own fight. Damage readouts flare as beams dig into Sabre's armor, its shield finally failing. I kick away the son of a bitch that's trying to gut me, then turn fully down the line to make sure it's clear of friendlies. Once I confirm that, I trigger a barrage of missiles that coat and lock the Hakarta in place. Lana and the puppies take full advantage of the break in fire, tearing forward to close in on the trapped soldiers.

Two more directly behind me are still free, so I focus on them, running and dodging as I close in on them. Ali floats down to the injured Hakarta that

I kicked away and plunges tiny hands through his armor before doing something that elicits a bone-chilling scream.

I watch the damage readouts flare in my HUD even as I close in on the shooter, duplicate blades flickering to life. The rifle comes up, blocking the cut, and I let my sword disappear while I stab outward with my other hand even as I quickly step sideways to cover the ground. The Hakarta jumps back as he's forced to dodge the two duplicates that I haven't dismissed, but it does mean that my thrust catches him straight on, Mana-infused blade cutting through armor as though it's not there.

"Walls failing, boy-o. The mage is good, but earth walls can only take so much," Ali sends, urging me on.

No time. Mana's nearly out, so I raise my right hand while dismissing the duplicate blades and trigger the Inlin, letting projectiles rip into the Hakarta's body on full auto. Seconds pass and the bullets tear a hole all the way through the Hakarta, his armor unable to withstand the assault. I'm on to the next attacker, forced to duck and dodge as the Hakarta fires.

Hakarta Private (Level 35)

HP: 450/450

MP: 153/240

Condition: Afraid (Reduced Reaction Time)

Not strong individually. But they've got good gear, good tactics, and the numbers. When Ali first noticed them, we did a count and worked out the plan. Unfortunately, because they were shadowing us, we couldn't break anyone else off and had to literally walk into their trap. Good news, we were able to quietly put together a retaliatory plan of attack.

I make my way to the last free private on this side, grab him by his neck, and throw him with all the strength I have through the trees and into the crumbling earth wall. Sabre's Shield flickers on as I bounce forward, taking the rocket that the private launches as he scrambles to his feet. My newly reformed Shield crumbles under the force, but the explosion isn't enough to throw me back. Powered armor and System-enhanced strength power me through the explosion to plunge my blades into the body. Dust and rocks explode around us, and I'm glad I don't breathe the air directly.

In the midst of the new group, I open up with the sonic pulser for a few seconds. Not long, not with the pets here, but long enough to hurt the privates and disorient them while the team regroups. Inlin reloaded, I open fire, projectiles ripping through metallic foliage and striking flesh. I rake my gun over the group, not trying to kill but rattle. They fire at me, and I focus for a second, dropping Sabre into my inventory and taking the shots directly. Pain rips through me as beams burn and cauterize flesh. The minimal armor of my armored skinsuit shreds.

Even through my Greater Regeneration, I can see my health drop, but it's better than letting Sabre get ripped apart. I hunker down, hiding as best I can amongst the churned earthen remnants of the wall and hope that my team can get here before I have to run. The sudden slacking of fire makes me look up to see that the rest of the Hakarta are engaged with the team and getting torn apart. A quick glance at the minimap shows that Jazae's already sneaked back, and together, the three Galactics have dealt with the attack from the front and are returning to help. I'd been slightly worried about that, since the Hakarta had concentrated their forces on the front, but it seems I shouldn't have bothered. Their initial assault blunted, the Hakarta never stood a chance.

"What was that about?" Jakrim asks later on, when we've healed, looted, and dispensed the goodies.

Dimensional grenades, beam rifles, and badly mangled armor suits are the loot we acquired—that, and a small portion of their Credits. Still, it's a better haul than some monster fights we've had.

"Ambush," Ali says, smirking.

"Seems like they could have hit us harder," Eilon says, shaking his head. "Twenty-one privates, two sergeants, and a lieutenant don't seem to be enough."

"Probably didn't expect to have to deal with your team," Lana says as she casts a Heal spell on Shadow. As we watch, the Husky's broken leg slowly regenerates under the focus of her spell.

"Too bad our mysterious attacker wasn't here," I say, staring at the bodies. I'd hoped, but I think if he had come out, he probably would have left when he spotted Eilon's team. The Weaponmaster might be tough, but he's not that tough. I think.

"So you were expecting to be attacked," Eilon snaps, floating closer suddenly. "You put us in danger without warning us?"

"We told you the ambush was coming when Ali picked up the group. You didn't seem that bothered," I state.

"That you expected an ambush before we left would have affected the Quest," Jakrim growls. "Is there anything else you are not telling us?"

"A ton," I say. "But nothing that changes the Quest. Nothing that will affect you guys. Unless we do get hit again by the guy we expected."

"Your mysterious attacker," Eilon says, and I nod. "Any thoughts on why these fellows and not him?"

Ali floats down and flickers through a series of his clothing to draw attention to himself. "Best guess? They weren't sure exactly where John and his team were going. We left enough breadcrumbs to make sure they knew we expected to be gone for a while. Since our mysterious attacker can't leave the city for too long, they must have decided to use the B-team."

"Twenty-three Hakarta." I stare around at the corpses, doing the math. Yeah, that'd make sense. Good as we are, twenty-three of them with the benefit of surprise against the three of us? That would do it.

"Deep waters," Eilon mutters, and I shrug.

"You were there when we talked about this," I say.

Eilon grimaces, nodding slowly. Politics are politics. After all, it wasn't as if he didn't know what he was getting into when he signed on.

"So we going to go or we going to just hang out here, talking about our feelings?" Ali says.

He might be blunt, but he's right. Within minutes, we're on the move again for our main objective. The icefields.

Chapter 14

The start of the Kluane National Park is only a two-and-a-half-hour drive from Whitehorse. It's a gorgeous, sprawling wilderness that covers over twenty thousand square kilometers of space, and the icefields comprise about eighty percent of the land area. And somewhere in those icefields that constantly tick upward in zone levels, a Dragon lives.

Now entering the Kluane National Park zone (Level 100+)
Note: Zone levels are currently in flux during transition period.

We're hunkered down just inside the zone level, Jazae taking the time to scout our approach a bit more carefully now. Ali's had to limit his scans significantly since some of the monsters at this level might be able to pick up a broader, less guarded scan. Luckily, my own Skill is significantly more short-ranged and passive, so it acts as a good secondary safeguard.

"John?"

Lana's voice cuts through my reverie as I stare at the notification. I dismiss it with a thought, looking at the redhead who has ridden her puppy close. Now that we're in, we won't be fighting as much as hiding. While there are monsters within our level here, any fight increases the likelihood that someone, something at a much higher level will find us. Better for us to stay hidden.

"This is where it all started, you know. For me," I say, pointing farther north. We'd adjusted our angle of approach a bit since we want the icefields and not the lake, so we never saw Haines Junction or the lake. "Kathleen Lake."

"Ah." Lana slips her hand into mine and gives it a squeeze. "You don't talk about it much. Or your past."

I nod. Compartmentalizing my life, pushing aside the past so that I can live in the present. Dwelling about what was lost, who was lost is not my way.

Can't be. Because if I did, I don't think I could keep going. Still… "Not much to say. Spent only a few days here, running from one monster to the next, desperate to get out of the zone before the really nasty monsters came into play. I started at Level 1."

"Boy-o had to be forced to fight a damn ant," Ali says, chuckling.

"Do you remember the hare?" I laugh silently. "You thought it was a rabbit."

"I figured you wouldn't make it past a week," Ali adds while Lana and the rest of the team watch us reminiscence.

"Nearly died probably a dozen times. That giant almost got me."

"I remember you staring at his dong," Ali says.

I snort. Yes, that was one memory I wish I could forget. "Gods. Was it, like, eleven months ago?" I shake my head, realizing how much and how little time has passed. So much has happened since then.

"What was your first day like?" Ali says, turning to Lana.

"Terrifying. Richard…" Her voice breaks for a moment. "Richard and I, we accepted the System's 'suggestion' for the Class right away. It seemed right, you know? We had the ranch to watch out for and the animals. When we tried the truck, it didn't start. So we waited. Our first kill was this segmented, caterpillar-like thing. Richard used the axe while the dogs tore into it. We didn't dare leave, not the first day. Just stayed home, killing the things that came for us.

"Sometimes… sometimes I think we should have gone out. Found some of our neighbors. Maybe we could have helped them survive."

I give Lana's hand, which I haven't relinquished, a squeeze, the pressure more a sign of comfort than physical reassurance—not with the gauntleted gloves we both have on. When she looks at my face, I shake my head. "Don't.

You did what you had to do. Maybe you could have helped them. Maybe you would have died. There's no way of knowing. So don't kick yourself over it."

Lana nods slightly, giving me a wan smile.

Ingrid turns her head toward Mikito. "How about you?"

Shit. Lana and I wince, knowing this story.

"I… my husband and I were at the hot springs. At one of the cabins. He died," Mikito says flatly then clamps her mouth shut.

Ingrid rolls with the answer with equanimity as she adds her own story. "Yes. My husband and my sister-in-law too. They were visiting us, in our apartment. Dawson. There weren't many of us. But the monsters that came, they were big. Nasty. There was this slug-like thing that crashed through houses and attacked those hiding inside. Killed dozens before it finally died. Then there was this raven—it'd evolved. Burnt down the houses on the other side of the river. We couldn't hurt it—but we didn't need to. It flew over the river and a tentacle snatched it out of the air. That was on the third day though. I think. It kind of blurred together."

The Galactics listen but say nothing, watching the trees while we wait. I wonder how they feel about this, about our stories. The little I've gleaned, their lives varied as much as, if not more than, humanity's existences on Earth did before the System. Some might grow up in large, settled, stable zones while others grow up in small, impoverished towns where the monsters are just a step away. No different really than a first world or a failed state denizen. Whatever else the System brings, it surely doesn't bring equality.

"Time to go," Eilon breaks in, nodding toward the treeline ahead.

We stow the bikes except for Sabre, which I keep in mecha mode, and take to the mountains on foot. A few additional bags of easily disposable equipment is grabbed, though we carry the vast majority of what we need in my Altered

Space and our inventories. From now on, we're going on foot. It's easier to hide when we're walking.

***

We walk up and up, hiking through the mountains with ice and snow beneath our feet. Wind howls, sending loose snow skirting around our bodies and chilling exposed skin, senses stretched to their utmost as we search for trouble. Snow-capped peaks with granite peeking around the edges greet our vision, dark clouds gathered above us as we climb ever higher.

We've dodged a series of issues already, most notably a clan of Snow Giants and a pair of Ice Elementals, but we haven't been able to skip everything. A Snow Leopard with an extra pair of tentacles on its back pounced on Ingrid, taking her down and savaging her before we managed to kill it. We had to rest and hide while Valeria manipulated the snow, clearing the blood from the ground, and Ingrid regenerated the lost limb.

The climb is nothing for us, enhanced Constitutions and occasional spells of regeneration keeping us on our feet. We cover good ground even if we spend large portions of it hiding, backtracking, or skirting around potential problems. Thankfully, the monsters that pick up our presence are often too smart to take on such a large group without backup—another change from lower-level monsters. These ones have some level of basic sentience and control over the stupid aggression the System instills in them.

Two days of this and we finally make the icefields. In just over two days, we've covered more than seventy kilometers, walking for over twenty hours a day. Pristine white snow covers the ground, occasionally broken up by dips where packed, blue-white glacial walls show up. It's a barren land, much more than anything else we've seen before.

Now entering the Kluane Icefields zone (Level 130+)

Note: Zone levels are currently in flux during transition period.

The zone notification makes us all draw a deep breath, the unspoken tension ratcheting up further. But finally, we're getting closer.

The cave Jazae finds for us to rest in is small, cramped, and cold. However, a simple portable shield keeps the wind out, and a secondary exit gives us a quick escape if something big and nasty finds us. It's good enough for the few hours of rest we need before we continue.

Two weeks of trekking through the icefields. Late-February and the weather is utterly atrocious. We're constantly fighting through snow and freezing winds, backtracking and hiding in the snow while we wait for predators bigger and nastier than us to leave the region. Pushed, battered, and frozen, we struggle on every day, some days barely covering a few kilometers. In one particularly unlucky day, we lose nearly ten kilometers as we backtracked. Temperatures range from a balmy -10°C to a lung-hurting -40°C. And that's all before we add on the wind chill.

We lose Wynn first. An Ice Worm—Level 137—comes out of the ground, teeth snapping closed around the puppy. Mikito barely rolls out of her seat in time, Haste and enhanced reflexes throwing her out of suddenly unsteady seat. She lashes out with her weapon as she falls, scoring the only attack. The Ice Worm comes up and goes down, still holding Wynn in its mouth, and never returns, the puppy's surprised yelp the last noise we hear. Lana screams and scrabbles, trying to go after it but it's useless. Lana spends the next little while sobbing into Mikito's back but we can't stop. Not now.

Jakrim dies next. A clan of Ice Yetis evades Jazae's recon and spots us. Together with their tamed Snow Leopards, they hound us for hours while we attempt to lose them and fail. We end up having to make a stand, fighting the score of Level 90+ monsters against a giant snowdrift. A spell pulls more snow from the ground, creating a magical blizzard that hampers the effectiveness of our beam weaponry. No one dares to use projectiles—the loud noises would likely bring something even worse. The fight devolves into a close combat melee, with Eilon, Mikito, Jakrim, and me on the front lines. Jazae and Ingrid fade in and out behind enemy lines, striking and disappearing before they can be injured, while Ixlimin, Lana, and Valeria take them on at range with spells and beam weaponry. Anna and the pets fill in when they can, striking and backing off from the frontlines.

When he dies, it happens fast. We're all bleeding, all damaged, life sapped as environmental cold damage slows our regeneration. A missed parry, a cut that disarms the Yerick, then the blade slides in. It injects a poison that starts freezing his blood, and while Jakrim is scrambling for a potion, an Ice Spike rips out from the ground. It catches him in the stomach, punching through armor already weakened by the cold and battle, and hangs him in the air. By the time we can get to him, the Yerick is dead.

The Galactics grow grim at his death. It's one thing to know that this was a dangerous, probably even suicidal, mission. It's another to lose a friend, a party member.

Luckily for us, as we get closer to the Dragon's lair, the fewer monsters there are. Not even the stupidly aggressive creatures of the System want to annoy a Dragon. When we reach the base of the giant mountain, we've barely seen a monster in hours.

"This is as far as we go," Eilon says after we hit the base of Mount Logan.

Jazae has returned to the group, and we're hunkered down on a small overhang in the rock, one made of equal parts snow and stone.

"Fair enough," I say and glance at the shared map. Another five kilometers from here—though it's mostly up—before we're there. A cave in the side of Mount Logan, one that the Dragon has made its own. I wonder if it carved it itself or if the cave was always there, waiting to be used. I look up, staring at the stars that blink in all their glory out here, and make the decision. "We'll hit it tomorrow."

At my word, we break for the day rather than just take a quick rest stop. We've gotten so used to doing this that the shield and the reflective camouflage wall go up in minutes while Valeria weaves additional spells of concealment around the camp. Everyone settles in quickly, pulling out food and resting mats in quick order. Even if today—really, tonight since we've been traveling at night mostly—was shorter than normal, we've still been moving for eight hours.

I don't sleep, instead standing against the edge of the camouflage wall. There's a stark beauty to the icefields, white snow that dances with the colors of the Northern lights. I look up, seeing the purple, green, blue, and yellow shift as the bands of color illuminate the sky. Stars, so many damn stars, the band of the Milky Way clear to the naked eye. Not a single human, monster, or spirit in sight. Just nature in all its scary glory.

"Beautiful, isn't it?" Lana says as she comes up to my side.

"Yes," I reply softly. "One of the most beautiful things I've ever seen."

"John. Tomorrow…" Lana stops, seemingly unsure of what more to say. "Come back safe."

"Repetitive," I mutter, and she shoves me in the shoulder with her own. I flash her a quick grin before I grow serious. "I'll do my best."

Lana falls silent, snaking gloved fingers into mine. We watch the icefields for a while, just enjoying the sight. If I'm going to die tomorrow, this isn't a bad last night.

It's later that evening, when everyone but Ixlimin, who is on watch, has gone to sleep that I call Ali over. We've not had much time or space to do this, but with a few hours left and a mind that threatens to overcome itself with jitters and concerns, I need to take my mind off the upcoming day. Elemental Affinity training works as well as anything else. Eyes closed, legs crossed, I reach out once again to sense the world.

You'd think, being in the barren edges of the world, it would be easier. There's only ice and snow covering hard granite out here. You'd be wrong— since every molecule, every single inch glows with power. But this time round, I'm not looking at the whole rainbow. I'm searching for individual lines of power, ones I can play with and adjust. Some are wider and stronger than others—though that doesn't say much, since we're talking in terms of millimeters at best—and those are the ones I focus on.

It's a long, tedious, and often frustrating process. And it's just what I need as I work to calm my mind.

Chapter 15

"All right, you all know the plan. Ingrid and I will sneak in. You hold and stay here for a day. If we don't get back by then, we've failed. Get out, get home, and do your best," I say, meeting my team's eyes.

Lana refuses to meet mine, but Mikito nods quietly while Ingrid yawns, looking bored. A part of me wonders how I ended up with three women on my team, but another can see how everything happened, step by bloody step.

"Any questions?" I ask.

"Who gets your PAV?" Jazae asks, pointing at Sabre, which I've left on the ground in its bike form. As much as I'd like to bring the mecha, we're going for stealth. She just won't be of any use if we get found out.

"Mikito. Ali's added her to the software. She won't be able to control it as well as I can, but it'll do," I answer.

Mikito nods again, shooting me a grateful smile. The choice wasn't hard, not really. I still recall Mikito's excitement at seeing Sabre the first time. Sometimes I'm surprised she hasn't bought her own yet—but I guess none of us have had Credits to spare. Not yet at least.

"Anything else?"

Receiving no other questions, I jerk my head toward the door. Within seconds, Ingrid and I are out, tramping through the snow. It's surprisingly warm today, barely -10°C, so under our high-tech layers, it could have been a balmy 25°C. Ali floats next to us, keeping an eye on his screens as we tramp on in silence. There's nothing to say, not yet at least. Both of us know the plan.

The decision to enter during the day was hotly debated during the last two weeks. Dragons have a tendency to sleep a lot, resting for days between meals. Ice Dragons in particular are well known for their long periods of inactivity— days, sometimes weeks, might go by before they decide to stir themselves. Laziness, or perhaps a lack of immediacy from being effectively immortal, characterized Dragons. What that meant was that we could hole up for days or perhaps weeks before we could find a time when the Dragon wasn't in its lair. Sneaking in while it was there was always an expectation.

That left the question of night or day. Since there was no way of telling if the Dragon was awake or not, it seemed to me that the most logical choice was to sneak in when it most benefited us. No point in worrying if it was asleep if it slept for days. Going in during the day also had the added benefit that if the Dragon did wake and get itself a Giant snack, we'd have a chance to exploit it.

Unsurprisingly, none of our plans involved fighting it face to face.

***

The cave entrance is surprisingly smaller than I expected, just over twenty feet tall and half again as wide. While I've never seen the Dragon up close, it looked huge, but somehow, the entrance isn't as big as I thought it'd be. I guess the fact that the Dragon's thin and long rather than fat and bulbous like a Western Dragon accounts for the difference. Or you know, the monster might just be cheating and using a Class Skill or something.

"*Ali?*"

The Spirit floats forward, shrunk down to only a couple of inches tall as he scouts ahead. Ingrid and I squat a short distance away, camouflage clothing keeping us from being spotted while we wait.

"*First cavern is clear. Waiting at the entrance to the second,*" Ali sends.

We climb up, our bodies tight to the ground and sneaking forward as quietly and quickly as we can. Ingrid's Class Skills make her invisible to my naked eye, but as we're partied, I can watch her dot on my minimap. As planned, she stays ten feet behind me, just in case. Really, with her Skills, it'd make more sense if she was the one leading, but I'm the one with the link to

Ali. If any one of us has a chance of getting an early warning, it'd be me. Anyway, she isn't the one who came up with this stupid plan—Ingrid's not even supposed to be here.

Light, coming from the sun outside, glints off ice crystals. Curls and whorls of frozen water that illuminate green and blue walls of dihydrogen monoxide. Black granite peeks out from underneath the snow where claws the size of my torso have dug into the earth. The only sound I can hear is the howling wind, bringing ever more snow and cold. Even through the filtered air of my helmet, the chill cuts into my lungs, waking me.

"*Here,*" I say, spotting Ali as I creep forward. I crouch low, not in the entrance but near it, and wait.

"*Have I told you how much I hate being bait?*" Ali grumbles as he floats forward.

"*Not bait. Scout.*"

"*Doesn't feel like that to me,*" Ali shoots back. Still, for all his complaining, he goes in.

There are stories about Dragons. Stories about their strength, their power, their wisdom. There are millions of tales carried through the Galaxy via Mana to at least give us a little bit of a heads-up, a minor chance of surviving. Splintered, shattered into a million different versions. But some things are so strong, so powerfully key to their narrative, that they carry through. Their strength. Their power. Their wisdom. And their love of their hoard.

When Ali gives me the all-clear, I slide into the next cavern, keeping to the shadows. What I see next takes my breath away. Crystals and gems of all shapes and sizes are piled high and glowing ever so gently. Tiny ones barely the size of a dime, some the size of a human torso, and everything in between. Red, green, blue, yellow, all of them burning with a familiar blue light. They're piled high, but not carelessly like in the movies. Small forcefields all around the treasure keep the crystals and gems neatly contained. Behind me, I hear a soft, quickly muted gasp as Ingrid spots the treasure trove as well.

At Ali's prompting, I head left, carefully edging up a staircase of frozen water. It takes me above the cavern floor, curling around and over the force fields that hold the crystals together. Up here, the subtle glow is almost painful to look at, the accumulated intensity reflecting off frozen walls. For all their brilliance, all the wealth, my attention is taken by the Dragon.

Ice Dragon (Level ????)

HP: ???/???

MP: ???/???

Condition: Sleeping

Long and sinuous like a snake, flared crests all along its back. Not pure white, but a white streaked with the green and blue of glacial waters. Lanky, scaled legs—six that I can count easily—and a pair of small, almost dainty hands near its front. Each pair of legs contains claws that could rip apart a school bus. Wings, folded up against its body, rise and fall as the Dragon breathes.

"*The light…*" I send to my Spirit, who sends back a sense of affirmation.

The light from the crystals is rising and falling with the Dragon's breathing. As it sleeps, the Dragon is channeling Mana unconsciously through the crystals, turning them into Mana batteries. The action is so subtle, I probably wouldn't have noticed it months ago. As it stands, I can't tell if the Dragon is adding to or taking power from the hoard. A creature of legendary power unconsciously manipulating Mana even as it sleeps.

Quest Update: the System

The Dragon's secret

Exp +5,000 XP

"That's it?" I send to Ali, staring at the brief Quest update.

"That's it, boy-o. Nothing else. Just that."

I hear the confusion in his thoughts, and I don't blame him. 5,000 XP is an amazing haul. And for what? For watching a Dragon sleep? I don't understand, I don't get it. It's obviously an important piece of the puzzle, but I don't understand where it fits.

Damn it, not now. I bite my lip, the pain forcing my mind back to the task at hand. Questions or not, I have something more important to do.

Right. I'm in, staring at the Dragon and its hoard. The easy part is done. Now comes the real challenge.

***

"Can we still do this?" I stare at the Spirit then again at the flux of Mana, the way the crystals charge and disperse. They seem to be fully connected to the Dragon sleeping on them.

"I don't know. Shifting the crystals right now might wake it," Ali sends back, obviously mulling over this new development as much as I am.

"That's what I was scared of."

If we can't even touch the crystals without waking the Dragon, then we're in trouble. Not completely screwed, since we could potentially hide till it leaves, but we don't know how long that would be. And the longer we wait, the higher the chance something else will go wrong or some other monster will find us. Add in the fact that we're on a deadline of sorts, and I'm not sure we can wait long enough for it to awaken naturally. Still, I have a little time, so I spend it watching the flow of Mana, trying to understand the connection.

Wind flows, snow gusting in a bit from the outside, depositing snowflakes on the crystals. The Dragon breathes and crystals shift, seconds turning to minutes to hours. Inside the cave, nothing much changes and I gain no enlightenment.

In the end, I make a decision. A hand twists, slowly packing a small snowball before I take aim farther down the cavern. A gentle toss and I watch as the snowball arcs, splattering against the ground and breaking apart. It's only slight, but a crystal moves, shifting in position.

A snort and a rumble as the Dragon turns uneasily in its sleep. Claws knead the crystals beneath its talons, its tail shifts, then slowly, slowly it settles. I find myself exhaling slowly, not realizing I'd held my breath.

Another snowball, this time a little larger, a little more compact. I choose another spot, a distance away from the first, and toss it before shrinking back against the wall. A futile effort if the monster wakes. The Dragon shifts again, obviously cognizant of the changes in its hoard. Twenty minutes later, when the Dragon has settled, we pull out, making sure to leave as little disturbed as possible.

Well, time to scrub that plan and come up with a new one.

***

"John!" Lana calls a relieved greeting as we arrive back at our resting spot finally. "Did it work?"

"There are complications," I reply while shaking my head.

Unsurprisingly, that comment makes everyone perk up and gather around. When everyone is there, I quickly explain what we found. Interestingly, everyone gets a quest update too for the information on the Dragon and its hoard. It's not just seeing it that matters, it seems, but actually knowing about the Dragon's mana manipulation.

"So we need the Dragon to not be there when we do this, eh?" Lana says, and I nod.

"Guess we're going to be waiting a bit." Eilon rubs his chin as he stares outward.

I know his feeling. We're safe here, mostly, from random monsters. Too close to the lair for random monsters to stumble on us. But…

"The longer we stay here, the more chances the Envoy has of causing trouble. And the year will be up soon," Mikito says.

Unconsciously, we all look it up, checking the countdown. Two and a half weeks. That doesn't leave us a lot of time at all.

"Not it," Ali says immediately.

"What?" Eilon looks at the Spirit while Lana snorts.

"He's not volunteering to be bait," I explain.

"Not it," Valeria adds, and I mentally groan.

"Why do we need bait?" Jazae asks.

"Well, duh. We need it out, so we should make it come out. That means someone has to be bait," Ali explains.

That a number of the group are nodding is not good, especially since the plan was never to interact with the Dragon.

"I should point out that our quest was to bring you here and back. This portion of your journey is entirely up to you," Eilon adds. "In fact, if you intend to do this, I'm requesting that you give my team a chance to move to a safer location."

I stare at the Eldritch Knight, pale white flames dancing in his eyes, and I try not to feel betrayed. He's doing the right thing by keeping his team away from this insanity. Mentally, I understand. Emotionally, I want to scream and shout at him. The simple fact is that we've been at this for ages and tensions are high. I force myself to breathe deeply instead of replying.

"That's fair, Eilon," Lana says. "And fighting the Dragon is still not the plan. We just need it out of its lair."

"When we hunt moose, it is easier to call them to you rather than search for them. Can we not do the same with the Dragon?" Ingrid asks. "There is so much land out here…"

"We set up the bait beforehand then attract its attention. Draw it to the location we want while a second team sneaks in and completes the mission," I finish, nodding. "That can work. So we split three ways. Eilon and his group head off, escorting the bait team till they break away. We give them time to get away and have the bait team set up. And the third team waits here for their chance."

I get nods all around, then we get digging. The rough plan is there, but the details still need fleshing out.

***

Two days later, we're finally ready to do this. Here I am, all by myself on the frozen plains, corpses all around me. We discussed and planned this every way, and in the end, even if the original plan was mine, the best place for me is right here. Playing bait. Of course, Ali bitched and moaned about it, but he's here too, floating alongside me, listening to his latest singing reality TV show. For all his bitching, the Spirit is a good friend.

I walk in a spiral, dumping corpse after corpse from my Altered Space, their bodies cooling immediately. Steam comes off some. Others are already so close to frozen they just land with a thud. A feast for our Dragon. This is all or nothing, so I'm getting rid of it all.

Other than Ali, I'm the only one here. Mikito, Lana, and her puppies are with Eilon and his group, farther down the icefields. Ingrid is at the cave, waiting for me to make this work. When I'm finally done, the bodies artfully displayed, I draw a deep breath and work up my courage to take the next step.

Drop the bodies, move away, and hide a distance. Remotely trigger the explosives I've set up in the center of the spiral. Sit back and wait and hope that the explosion and resultant spray of blood and bone will be enough to awaken the Dragon. A simple plan that should be easy enough to do.

What I didn't expect was that by the time I'm done, I've attracted quite a bit of attention. Most of the monsters involved ignore me as I run away, the feast in front of them too damn attractive. Unfortunately, most does not mean all. I get a half kilometer away before I get pounced.

Even when it hits me, I can't really see it. Sabre's shield takes the brunt of the damage while I spin, the sword I conjure cutting lightly into a paw. A spray of blood as I hit, then it's gone, the monster's invisibility exerting itself fully. Just a second and all I saw were claws, scales, and a hissing visage that looked like a cross between a tiger and a dinosaur. That, and it's information.

Zainuk Stalker (Level 121)

HP: 4338/4538

MP: 1529/1787

Conditions: Invisible

I throw up a Soul Shield, crouching low and edging to the side as I search for the monster. Ali's got nothing and neither do I, so I can only wait. I spin around slowly, hands held wide and to the side, almost taunting it to strike at them. When the next blow comes, I'm two thirds turned away from it. Claws strike my arm, the shield surrounding it sparking. By the time I recover to swing at it with my sword, the Stalker is gone.

Again and again, it taunts me with strikes even as I back away. When I draw my hands back, making it have to come a little closer to attack me, I can never hit it. Attacks come quickly and from my blind spots, striking at my legs, my shoulders, draining the shields at an alarming rate. Frustration mounts as fast as my shields fall, each blow by the monster dropping ten to twenty percent of my shields. First, Sabre's goes and then Soul Shield.

"Help?"

"Sorry, boy-o. Can't see anything. Also… ummm… you guys are attracting more attention," Ali sends back.

I take a quick glance and realize that the monsters attracted to my meal are tearing through it pretty fast. And some on the edges have decided that it might be better to find food outside of the main pack.

If they finish everything before the Dragon comes, we might not be able to keep it here for long. Hell, it might go looking for what woke it up. Neither of which is optimal. We want it annoyed, with an easy target, and well fed.

The next attack by the Stalker tears through my armor and claws open my leg, flesh parting like plastic wrap under the assault. I stumble a little and the monster jumps on me, throwing its weight against my body, claws punching through armor. I fall and roll around, landing on my back as a great weight lands on me. It pins my arm and chest, a scaly, long-nosed snout rearing back to finish the job.

"Do it."

At the same time as I send the thought to Ali, I trigger the sonic pulser. The explosion and the sonic attack distract the monster on top of me, giving me time to buck off the creature. I roll and twist, triggering the mini-missiles that splash and solidify, trapping the monster. For a second, I think it'll work, the monster outlined as it struggles around the fast-set concrete. Then it surges forward, shattering its encasing, hissing through rows of needle teeth.

Not fast enough to avoid the Blade Strike I send crashing into the charging monster, tearing apart scales and flesh. The blow rocks it, and it darts sideways, dodging the follow-up attack, then it's gone again.

I snarl, edging away and eyeing Mount Logan, wondering when we'll see a reaction. Where the bodies were, a small distance away, the planted explosives have left a giant crater, flames from the white phosphorous still burning through the snow. Some of the smarter monsters have fled, others have fallen to preying on injured brethren, while some of the greediest have just returned to eating.

The next attack rips armor along my chest plates, opening up my chest and armor. Stumbling back, I know the follow-up attack is coming, my sword held in front of me as I get ready to fight back. I'm trying to figure out another way of dealing with my attacker and wishing I had the QSM. I keep backpedaling, waiting for the next attack. It never comes.

Fear Effect Resisted

The roar that emanates from the lair shakes the ground, even kilometers away. Snow ripples, an avalanche begins on a distant mountain, and the monsters stop their current activities, turn tail, and run. Emerging from its lair, the winged Dragon soars into the sky and circles as it gains altitude.

"Move, boy-o!"

Realizing I'm just standing there, not moving, I boot it as well, going from standstill to a full sprint. Once I'm certain the Stalker is doing the smart thing, I trigger the switch, Sabre transforming into its bike mode. Wheels inflate, sliding down from the back, armor pulling away from my extremities and back even as the gravity plates trigger, keeping me afloat as the transformation occurs. The transformation is smooth, and within seconds, I'm riding the gravity bike and beating a hasty retreat.

As I gun the bike and let her rip—metaphorically, since the bike is entirely silent—my mind is rolling over my options. Me being delayed near the food was considered and planned for, but not as thoroughly as we could have. Adding the fact that I'm injured and bleeding alters the equation further.

So long as we're on level ground, Sabre's faster than the Dragon. Probably. Problem is, pushing her at any serious speed will drain her Mana battery, and while the recharge rate in the higher-level zone is amazing, it might not be enough. The fight and the use of Sabre's shield earlier means I start running away with the battery at 86% charge. Worse, while the fields are mostly flat, there are a number of mountains, hills, and ridges that jut out. I'll have to curve around them and avoid other known dangers, all of which the Dragon can ignore. In the long run, even with my initial head start, things could be dicey. Really dicey.

Right now, the goal is to put as much distance as possible between myself and the other monsters. The more we spread out, the easier it'll be to tell who the Dragon is going after. After all, there's no guarantee that I'll be picked on. Until we split apart enough, it's all guesswork. If the Dragon decides to go after other prey, I just need to find a spot and hide, making sure I don't attract any further attention. So long as the Dragon isn't too annoyed, it shouldn't be willing to waste its time hunting me down.

As I gun the bike and hunker down low, willing every ounce of speed possible from the bike and my Skill, I pray the Dragon isn't chasing me. If it is, my options are significantly less attractive.

Chapter 16

There is a statistic, an attribute in our status screen, titled Luck. For most games, the Luck attribute is broken. It either does very little or it does too much. There's no real middle ground—and really, for such an obscure-sounding attribute, that's no surprise. Defining the attribute and how it works guarantees that someone will try to exploit it. It's why good game developers keep the information hidden.

Call it luck. Call it fortune. Call it random chance. We humans have a tendency to blame our misfortunes on a higher power, on things we cannot control. Or at least that we don't believe we can control. I'll admit, I did—I do—the same. I dumped points into Luck, thinking I could tilt the odds in my favor. A lifetime of bad fortune and bad breaks, now regulated by an impartial System.

It's a sweet lie that a few points here and there can change your life. It's the same lie that faith healers, homeopaths, and diet plans peddle—that with just a few easy steps, you too can change your life. No mess, no exertion, no pain.

I moved north and my girlfriend broke up with me. But I should have paid attention, noted the long calls and the long trips up here, the way she avoided my touch when she came back. I lost a job, but I could have put in more effort rather than coasting by, doing the minimum amount of work necessary to avoid being the first person on the chopping block. I could have saved more, eaten out less, canceled the cable TV I barely used.

That's the thing—past choices impact our future, sometimes in ways we can never foresee. All the choices I made before led me to this park when the System came into play. That gave me a slew of powerful Perks, granted me a chance to survive and thrive. Gave me something to do that truly mattered.

Not just another client's shitty corporate website, but something meaningful. Something important.

We make our own luck, and whether good or bad, we'll never know.

Which is a long way of saying that I've got a Dragon on my tail, annoyed and probably going to rip my head off when it finally catches me.

***

About ten minutes into my ride, we'd plotted the Dragon's path and knew it was coming toward me. There were still a few other monsters it could have been chasing, so I kept low and pushed Sabre even more. Five minutes after that, it was pretty clear the Dragon had decided that the unnatural, technological marvel was the cause of its premature awakening.

In the corner of my eye, I see the power bar. 78%. *"How long?"*

"Well, if Ugly doesn't pick up speed again and you don't have to curve around another mountain or the wind doesn't…"

"How. Long," I snap at Ali, knowing he can plot the go-point better than I can.

"Six minutes. Give or take."

Mostly take. I look at the map again, wishing there was something, anything I could use to hide. Unfortunately, on top of the mountain range as we are, on snow-packed glaciers, there are no forests to hide in or caves to duck into. That means all I can do is run until it's time to kick off the next part of the contingency plan.

We're moving at around 210 kilometers an hour, faster than I've ever pushed Sabre. Yes, yes, I know that F1 racing cars can go faster, and hell, some car racing enthusiasts have done more—but they don't have to worry about monsters and traps trying to kill them.

I have to admit, there's a shot of adrenaline to this, a thrill I never felt in my pre-System life. I never drove a car anywhere as fast—and I don't think I'd be able to do this with Sabre without my enhanced attributes. As it stands, my arms are twinging from the exertion of holding my body down as winds buffet it.

There's a fine line to this. The faster I go, the higher the drain on the Mana battery. Do that too long, and Sabre stops and I get eaten. Go too slow and the Dragon catches me and eats me sooner rather than later. Either way, at this point, I'm about to get eaten.

Of course, there's no subtlety, no stealth to this. Which means sooner or later, I'm likely to run into trouble. Even as I think that, an Ice Worm breaches the ground ahead of me. I swerve, the link sending my mental commands to the PAV even before my body can react. I curl around it, missing its mouth by inches.

"Time?" I send to Ali, breathing deeply as I try to get myself to calm down.

"Two minutes."

Ahead of me, a herd of brown-furred, six-legged wannabe wooly mammoths in a circular, defensive formation. They have tusks and horns and are about twice the size of an elephant. They are at the minimum Level 105, their fur so strong that my guns won't penetrate to do any real damage. The only mercy is that they're placid creatures. For System animals.

That means that instead of charging me, they only lash out when I'm close, heads dipping to wave ice-covered tusks and horns at me or to whip trunks at my speeding form, their actions generating waves of spiked ice. Can't afford to stick around, so when I close in on them, I gun the engine and whip past them. The sudden burst of speed throws off their aim and the Soul Shield takes the few attacks that manage to hit, dropping ever lower.

I still lose a bit of time, swerving around the group and ducking between waves of ice, draining the battery further as I push the gravitics and engine. I watch as the battery drops by another five percent and I grit my teeth.

"Time."

Almost at the same time that Ali sends that thought, I hear the explosions. Each set is another twenty kilometers from the initial explosion, on opposite sides of each other, creating a simple triangle. Explosives dug into the ground, encased with ice and System-generated meat.

I risk a glance back, seeing the Dragon stop its direct pursuit, banking to the side to consider my distractions. I turn back to the road, listening to Ali's report.

"He's circling and rising. Higher. Higher. Oh crap… yeah, he's got enough height to call the bluff, boy-o. Sorry. He's straightening out and coming for us."

The explosions were meant to draw the Dragon's attention. They were kind of a last resort, never meant to be set off. A way of giving me a chance to get away while it flew off to investigate. It didn't work. That's it. No more tricks, no more plans. All I can do is hunker down and trust in Sabre. Run and hope.

71%.

***

"Persistent little lizard, isn't he?" I growl. I'm long past where I should have met Lana and Eilon and the rest of the team. I've blown past them and numerous other monsters in my headlong rush out of the icefields.

47%.

I smile grimly, watching the numbers flicker again. Even as I weigh the new numbers in my mind, another imperious roar erupts behind me, a reminder of my pursuer.

Fear Effect Resisted

Shuddering, I push aside the effects and correct Sabre's course. I force myself to breathe properly, to even out and calm down. I might resist the effects, but that just means I still have conscious control. It does nothing for the gnawing pit in my stomach, the adrenaline surge, or the slight tic in my eye. Or perhaps the fear effect is so great that this is the result even after being resisted. I no longer have the adrenaline or the distraction of a fight, so I can only hunker down and push past it.

The only good news is that the Dragon's occasional roar of irritation has ensured that my way forward is cleared. I'm making great time, mostly because anything and everything with half a brain has gone into hiding or otherwise taken a defensive posture.

46%.

Minutes seems like hours, the bike speed having dropped to a sedate 90 kilometers per hour. I peer ahead, my eyes peeled for the slightest motion that might indicate a dumber monster than usual. Searching for potential exits, maybe a cave or two I could slide into and eventually lose the Dragon. But the terrain is barren, beautiful, and absolutely boring. There's only so much white you can see before your brain just stops registering it. Within minutes of the roar, my mind drops back into the meditative state it has acquired from driving through the icefields.

Behind my visor, my eyes narrow as my vision shifts, the flow of Mana and energy becoming clear to me again. I see the currents of Mana, the ripples of energy that powers everything in the System and beyond. A slightest twitch of my hand and I guide Sabre into the deepest currents, the Mana engine pulling deeper and recharging the battery faster. It's a miniscule improvement—the sheer depth of Mana in this zone is staggering as it stands. But every little bit helps, every iota of power we can draw forth gives me a few more seconds as the kilometers flash past.

45%.

The state I'm in, the mindset that allows me to tap into my Mana Manipulation skill, is the same one I use for exploring my Elemental Affinity. Manipulating both is not physically hard. It's not even mentally difficult to see the lines of power, not right now when the pressure is on, when every movement, every thought, every second matters. The only problems are the occasional roars, the screams that make my body shudder and twitch even as I force myself past it.

Lines of energy, waves of forces, shifting all around me. There's so much, I still can't grasp it all. In some ways, I find it easier to focus as the shifting flows of Mana overlay everything, hiding some of the interactions from view. Yet the more I watch, the clearer the interactions between the two forces are. Mana is the air, the substance that everything, even the Elemental Forces, resides in. And yet when manipulated, it can affect the forces directly, increasing, decreasing, loosening, or tightening bonds.

We've crossed the Kluane Glacier, all 160 kilometers of it. The zone notification tells me as much, if not the change in the scenery. Barren, snow-swept glacial lands lead to frozen rivers that I glide down, taking the twists and turns as fast and tightly as I can. Each time I do so, I lose ground to the monster above me, the thread of worry gnawing at my gut.

"*Boy-o*," Ali sends, pulling me from my thoughts, "*he just picked up speed.*"

I blink, the vision falling away, the memory of what I grasped disappearing. The minimap tells the story as the monster closes in. It's only a few kilometers away now, each flap of its wings bringing the Dragon closer. Fast. Too fast.

29%.

That's it. That's all there is. I have no choice but to push Sabre, even if it means the battery drains faster. On the other hand…

10%. That's when I'll stop and turn around. Because if we hit 10%, I'd rather fight and die than get caught running.

"So… I've been thinking."

"What is it?" I send back.

Before he can reply, I shudder, my hands clenching the handlebars as the roar comes, shaking its frame and creating spidery cracks in the snow. Echoes of its roar cascade back, but the initial effects die away, resisted once more.

"I might be able to adjust our speed a little. Reduce the air resistance of us moving by manipulating the molecules ahead."

"Sounds good to me."

"Yeah, about that. I've never done it before, not in this state."

"What's the worst that could happen?"

"Boom."

"Still better than chomp," I point out wryly.

"On it." Ali floats down, his body just above the front of Sabre.

For a moment, nothing seems to happen. Then I notice it. The slightest shift, a minor alteration in the air resistance. Our speed ticks up slowly for a moment, then I drop the power usage. Our speed drops again, but it's easier to breathe, to hold my position. We creep back up as Ali gets better at it.

Through our connection, I can feel some of the concentration Ali is exerting, the focus that is required to do all this. It's like a diamond edge of pure concentration that cuts into my mind unknowingly, a shared pain that the Spirit forgets to block.

Curiosity tugs at me and I open myself up to see what he's doing. Colors flow, forces shift and swirl under my eyes, and I see the little Spirit, hands splayed outward, surrounded by tendrils of golden force. Those tendrils flow outward, wrapping the bike and the air ahead of us in a cone of power. Lines of force between molecules dance as electrons and protons, hundreds, thousands of them are manipulated. The sheer complexity is breathtaking, something I can't even presume to grasp. So I don't.

I watch, and eventually, I reach out, taking a bit of the burden off the Spirit. I join him, focusing on Sabre and myself. I have no chance of matching his ability, of touching and adjusting millions of air particles before they hit us, but the PAV and myself? That, I can handle.

Pain comes with this. My body feels as if it's being pulled apart, nerves on my skin on fire. Worse is the mental strain, a pounding headache growing in intensity with each second. Pain that leaches through my mind, and in a corner of my mind, I feel the strain on Ali increasing as well.

Above, in my display, I see my hit points drop. The System might compensate for some damage, but what I'm doing to Sabre, to myself, is too great for it to handle. I don't have the expertise, the skill that Ali has.

But it's working. Even as I've dropped power on the bike, we've sped up. At first, keeping pace, then slowly out-distancing the Dragon. I hear a roar, but I'm so focused, so wrapped up in the pain that surrounds me that the fear effect doesn't even affect me.

My world narrows further to my Affinity, the bike, and the terrain before me. It narrows till all I know is that. And nothing else.

***

A shift in the flows in front of me finally draws me out. Something has changed. Something significant. Only when I realize that Sabre is beeping and slowing, the Mana Battery drained, do I understand what happened. The change is due to how much slower we're going, the bike no longer able to sustain forward momentum. It's only good programming that shuts down the engine before the anti-gravity plates, ensuring we don't just crash.

I lick my lips, tasting blood from my nose. My head throbs, my eyes are sandpaper dry, my mind muddier than the edges of a leech-filled lake. We're stopping… something important about that. Something to do with movement and speed. Something…

My mind snaps awake, understanding flooding through me. Perhaps the System heals me sufficiently or perhaps I just needed time, but I remember why. I look at the minimap, searching for the tell-tale deep black of the Dragon. Nothing.

"*Ali!*"

"*Flurgle-wurk .*"

"ALI!" I shout as I twist around the bike, searching the skies. Nothing. Nothing at all.

"What? I'll be right there, Heidi," Ali mutters. "Just got to get the chocolate…"

"Ali. DRAGON! Where is it?" I snap, craning all around.

"…shĭ." Ali finally pulls himself together enough to pay attention.

Silence, but I keep my temper intact now that I've got a semi-coherent answer from the Spirit. I can tell, through the connection that is slowly fading into the corners of my mind again, that he's mostly back to normal. Interesting that I could sense him like that. I've never before, but then again, he's never been that distracted either.

"Nothing, boy-o. Well, okay. No Dragon," Ali says, frowning. "Pulling up historical data…"

I ignore his mutterings as I guide Sabre to a nearby clearing before it finally comes to a full stop. I get off the bike as it drops like a stone, my feet sinking into the ground and compacting snow and earth as the vehicle shifts into battery-saving mode. Walking away from the bike for a bit, I eye the surrounding trees and skies, searching for trouble. Nothing.

"What happened?" I whisper, my memory foggy. All I remember are the streams of power, of riding and riding. Around me, I notice the snow-covered trees, a feature that was missing from the icefields. How long were we driving? How far did we go?

"Right. So the Dragon dropped off about twenty minutes ago. Turned around about a good forty kilometers back, twenty kilometers after we exited the last zone change," Ali says. "We must have gotten far enough away from its lair that it decided it'd had enough."

I nod slowly. That was our only hope really, that we moved far enough away from its lair that the Dragon would decide to return. It wasn't as if we had actually damaged its lair or even attacked it. All we did was disturb its sleep.

A small, niggling part of me wonders if the team might have done something else to draw it back. Another explosion, another attack. It's a niggling worry, one that I can't shake. Especially since being out here, wherever here is, means I can't head straight back to Whitehorse or contact them. On the off-chance the Dragon just got distracted, I need to make sure it's not about to hunt me down. The last thing I want to do is lead it to Whitehorse.

For now, all I can do is wait while Sabre slowly recharges and I figure out where I am.

Chapter 17

Where I am is about a hundred kilometers or so north of Haines Junction. Following the Kluane Glacier and the river that led out of it meant I swung much farther north than I had planned. It puts me a good hour's drive from Haines Junction and another three or so—on the highway—from Whitehorse. Hundreds of kilometers away in the best of conditions.

It also puts me smack dab in the middle of a Level 80+ zone. Not completely insane, considering Sabre gives me a bit of a boost, but not ideal either. In fact, standing around quietly while I wait for the bike to refill its battery to a useful level leaves me feeling pretty exposed.

"I'm really getting a feeling of déjà vu here," I think to Ali.

"Under-leveled, all alone, and with some big nasty potentially about to eat you?"

"Yup."

"Yeah, it's real nostalgic. I was kind of hoping we'd given up on this part of the insanity," Ali sends back, a wry tone in the thought.

I smile, slowly stretching and reveling in the lack of pain. There're a lot of things I hate about the System—the way it forces us to join it, the constant shifting evolution of monsters, and the need to kill and fight constantly—but its ability to heal damage quickly and constantly is a blessing. Having lived with the on-going pain of tendinitis, I can't help but revel at the lack of pain most of my life now involves.

"So, boy-o, figured you'd want to see this," Ali says and twitches his hand.

A few seconds later, data pops up in windows.

Mana Manipulation Increased to Level 28

Elemental Affinity Increased to Low

System Quest Update (+500 XP)

As you increase your understanding of how to manipulate Mana, so does your understanding of how the System influences Mana.

"A few other updates on skills too, but nothing particularly important," Ali adds as I finish reading.

I grunt, considering the new information. One of these days, I really should take a look at my skills list—but as Ali pointed out a long time ago, what's the point? I can either do it or not—it doesn't matter if I have points in a skill or not. That and staring at numbers, watching them go up just for the sake of the increase, seems a touch narcissistic. I've got better things to do than stroke my ego.

"Four hours," I mutter, staring at Sabre.

You know, this is the first time in a while that I've actually been in a zone that would be a challenge. Lips pursed, I stare into the forest, my hands flexing unconsciously. I have four hours…

"Oh hell, here we go again…"

***

Sneaking through the snow-covered forest without the backup of the QSM or Sabre is probably not the smartest thing I've ever done. On the other hand, I kind of justify it as not wanting to be near the mecha if the Dragon decides to come back. If it does return for some reason, the chances are it'll be within the first twenty-four hours. After that, if it doesn't hunt me down in a week or so, I figure it isn't that interested and I'm in the clear. I'm probably being a bit paranoid to wait that long, but in this case, paranoid works.

What it does mean is that over the next little bit, I've got nothing better to do than go hunting. Luckily, I've got all the gear I need to live out here by myself, and with my Altered Space, I've got the space to store any corpses I come across, so I won't even be losing out that much.

Of course, first I have to find monsters. Even the low-level critters that would make up the ecosystem of a high-level zone are scarce. Mostly, I ignore them—there's little point in killing oversized rats or lightning squirrels. Not only will it not give me much experience, it'll mark my location to some of the predators. While I'm not opposed to the fight, I'd rather be the one doing the stalking than the other way around.

An hour and change of me slowly wandering through the forest finally finds me some proper trouble. Peeking around the edge of the tree, I stare at a group of long-limbed, humanoid monsters with grotesquely long noses and oversized fingernails. Pale white with grimy black hair, the creatures huddle around a brazier for warmth.

Huldrekall (Level 78)

HP: 470/470

MP: 1030/1030

Conditions: None

A quick count brings the total on hand to eight monsters. With the hit points they have, they won't be particularly hard to kill. Hard-earned experience tells me that if they don't have significant levels of hit points, that generally means they hit hard. Truthfully, I'd prefer the other way around since I'm not running Sabre right now.

Based off pure levels, I'm approximately Level 70 right now, give or take a few levels due to my unique situation. However, the numbers by themselves don't tell the full story. Within each Class Level, there are variations in the strength of Classes. These are generally categorized as Basic, Standard, or Prestige Classes, with each level indicating the differences in both attributes gained and Class Skills available. Of course, it isn't exactly clear-cut—with so many variations, it's inevitable that there are Classes that provide Standard increases to attributes but have horrible Class Skills or vice versa. Still, it's generally believed that monster levels are rated for Standard Classes.

That means that an equivalent Basic Class would be seriously underpowered facing the monsters ahead of me, while a Prestige Class of the same level would be roughly twenty percent more powerful. Of course, that assumes the individual has a Prestige Class through both Beginner and Advanced progression, which is not a guarantee.

Add weapons, training, and the unfair advantage of access to the Shop and a large Credit pool and you begin to realize why levels are, at best, a bad approximation and, at worst, a misleading statistic. Taking all that into account, I shouldn't have a problem with just one of the Huldrekalls. There are, however, eight of them, which means I have to be smart about this fight.

I guess it says something about me that I don't ever consider not fighting them.

***

Twenty minutes later, my preparations are complete. Nothing too elaborate this time, since they do say that surprise triples your force. I figure surprise and a bag of high-tech weapons puts us just about equal. About 30° away from me on either side, a pair of automated beam-rifles sit on their mounts. The targeting mechanism on the rifles isn't particularly sophisticated, but attacking from surprise, they should do their jobs. Beneath our feet and facing outward,

I've got a series of explosives set to go off once the rifles and I are charged. As a fallback position, I've linked a pair of Chaos grenades and smoke grenades.

In an ideal world, I'd have set up another surprise or some explosives on the other side of the clearing as an additional distraction mid-fight. Unfortunately, the trees over that way are pretty sparse, and even working slowly, I've probably taken more risks than I should have setting up the weapons. Making my way all the way over there and back might be pushing my luck too far.

I'm ready, so in the end, there's nothing to do but kick it off with a bang. Or in my case, a slowly and carefully built-up Fireball that takes a few seconds to cast. I toss it overhand toward the center of the group. Three of the eight are staring roughly in my direction and look up at the movement, the fastest already standing as the Fireball arcs toward them. The other five are clustered around the brazier, alternately rubbing their bodies or holding their hands toward it in an attempt to get warm.

What looks to be lousy security practices are shown to be extreme confidence in their shielding. The Fireball splashes against an invisible barrier and explodes, flames washing over the group and outward in a truncated sphere of flame and smoke. Even as the fire dies down, I've triggered the guns, whose beams do just as little.

Three of the Huldrekalls stay crouched, hands held toward the brazier. The other five twist toward the threats, raising their own hands. In seconds, the clearing is filled with magic—shards of ice, swirling green balls of power, and cyan rays of light slamming into my pair of portable shields and my Soul Shield. I twist and duck, scrambling away even as the portable shields fail within seconds.

Oh shit. Mages were not what I expected. I recall the Mana portion of their attribute and kick myself mentally. I should have guessed—but actual monsters with the ability to cast spells is just new. Ali, hovering low to the ground, is waving in concentration as he remotely works one of the beam rifles, taking over from the automated targeting software. Assuming those three who didn't rise are supporting the shield, I can't win this fight. By the time I chip away at their shield, mine will have failed.

So I call a strategic withdrawal, scrambling away as fast as I can. Howls erupt from behind me, the noise so alien I can't tell if it's rage or excitement. Alongside the cries is a sudden explosion, then silence as my rifles are destroyed. Within moments, Ali is darting alongside me, flying backward and fading through shrubbery as he keeps an eye on the monsters.

I zig-zag as I retreat, trying to throw off their aim. My Soul Shield fails a few seconds later, a cyan ray of power tearing through my torso and cooking flesh beneath it. A stone dart clips an elbow and tears a chunk out of my thigh before I finally scramble over a nearby rise, disappearing from view. In my haste to get over, I flop flat and slide down on my back, leaving a wide and clear trail of blood as I dig snow into my open wound. A hand twists and turns, pulling forth a health regeneration potion that I drain. My sword in my other hand digs into the snow to help guide my descent.

"*Gotcha,*" comes Ali's triumphant cry, a cry punctuated by a series of explosions and a sudden in-rush of air. Inrush?

Huldrekall Slain +784 XP

(Out of level and Dungeon World resolution bonuses applied)

"*What the hell?*" I send to the Spirit even as I leg it further.

Ali rarely bothers to show me this information, though in this case, the knowledge is useful. From my minimap, I can tell the Spirit is on his way to me, having stopped briefly, but the addition of a glowing red dot is troubling.

"Chaos grenade opened up a rift, sucked in one of the Huldrekalls before it closed. The other Chaos grenade joined two of the Huldrekalls together. That's the new dot," Ali sends back.

The Chaos grenades look to be buying me time, even if the smoke grenades were drawn into the rift. As I run away, I can't help but glance at the small rearview window that my helmet overlays, hoping to see something. Which is why I catch the glimpse of the column of white light that slams into the hilltop behind me a few seconds after I've left it.

"Satyr's hairy butt," Ali swears. *"That would have hurt!"*

"That was for you?" I send back, feeling irrationally cheated. They didn't throw anything that nasty at me.

"Yeah. So that Chaos grenade? It kind boosted mashy-boy."

"Thousands hells."

That piece of information is enough to make me pick up speed. Not that it helps. When the combined monster crosses the ridge, my mirror treats me to a firsthand view of the spell it's casting. The only good thing is that the spell has a bit of a lag-time in forming, so I manage to get partially out of the way. Even then, the light sears away my armor and cooks my flesh, my hair sizzling beneath the strike. My legs are the worst damaged, being the longest in there, nerves on fire as I bite back my scream.

I land on the ground and roll, the cold snow a relief along cooked flesh. Powerful regeneration or not, the bubbled flesh and stripped bare muscles will take a while to heal. Pain pounds me. A bare few months ago, it would have been enough to put me down, leaving me curled up in a corner and whimpering. Long days and hundreds, maybe thousands, of battles have seen me cut, stabbed, impaled, burned, and torn. I've been injured again and again and had to fight through it. This? This is bad, but it's not the worst I've had. A glance at my hit points shows I'm down to half, most of it from that single hit.

First things first—I throw up a Soul Shield. Second, I cast Greater Regeneration, layering the heal-over-time effect on the potion. Thirdly, I trigger Blink Step, getting away from the lights forming above me as Ugly casts his spell again. Should have done that earlier, but that's the thing about fights—you do the best you can, and sometimes, you forget to do the right thing. I Blink above Ugly, calling my sword into hand and triggering Thousand Blades a micro-second later.

I drop, falling like a stone, ready to cut apart the combined Huldrekall. It's an ugly sight, the Huldrekalls that made up this creature having been smushed together like an angry toddler with new plasticine. It's a monster, a Frankenstein creature with oversized heads and multiple limbs, screaming in pain through one distorted mouth while its health slowly see-saws as the System alternately punishes and rewards it.

It doesn't see me until my blade cuts into the top of its left shoulder, tearing through skin and bone. My angle of descent changes with the attack, and I end up falling sideways a bit more than I'd like, so I twist, shifting my trajectory. That pulls out my sword, but the creature is already turning toward me, a hand waving through the air. Bad for it, good for me as the follow-up blades cut into its newly exposed body.

I make my sword disappear a second before I fall, my extended hand hitting the ground first, then my elbow, absorbing a little of the impact with each second. I twist and roll, pain flaring through my arm and shoulder and back before flaring into aching agony when my legs hit the ground as it reminds me that I'm still not healed. Above me, the monster roars as my blades take their tribute of muscle and bone.

Just like I knew it would, his life points drop like a stone. No defense, all attack. Unfortunately, while I'm rolling to get back up, it's his turn. A pair of raised hands, separate spells forming. Then Ali is in front of its face, distracting it with music. It's loud and brassy, screaming guttural heavy metal of some form. The distraction works for one hand, but the other stays pointed, Ice Darts pinging off the Soul Shield. Funny that the Soul Shield didn't react to my drop when I reappeared

Sword reappearing, I lash out diagonally, calling forth a Blade Strike. Once. Twice. Thrice in quick order. Blades of projected power impact the monster, ripping skin and breaking bone. Injuries pile one on another as it staggers backward, an arm flying off from the final attack.

Before I can throw a fourth attack, a beam of power hammers into the side of my Soul Shield and cuts right through. Flesh sizzles and my reflexive flinch sends me twisting away and off the crest of the hill, rolling down the packed snow. I dig fingers into the snow, pulling myself to a stop while Ali jinks above me, drawing fire and dodging as best he can.

A Fireball spell thrown above to explode near the combined Huldrekalla. The creature attempts to dodge, but the Fireball is an area-of-effect attack. No dodging a giant sphere of flame, especially when it curls and reflects around the hill. Finally, finally, it dies and Ali, dodging back to me, flicks up damage reports for the two Huldrekall on the other side of the hill that got caught in the blast radius. It's mostly incidental, but it's better than nothing.

I have a few seconds before they cross the ridge, so I take it to cast a Greater Healing. Between the regeneration effects and the spell, I'm back up to half my health again, which isn't great, but I can survive. If I can avoid getting hit, I can win this. I don't know why they split up, but without their shield, it's now just a question of who can hit harder and more often. As I pull myself up and crouch low, I can't help but grin widely. My turn.

***

Never split the party. Even a non-gamer like me knows that rule. Every time you do, bad things happen to you. In this case, the bad thing is a pissed-off Chinese man with a grudge. Blink Step takes me in close. My sword, my fist, and a few spells do the rest. By the time they get a bead on me, their health is already a sliver of what they started with.

The trio at the base camp who keep up the shield are the only ones who survive. I can't take down their protection, not with all three of them supporting it, and an attempt at Blinking in results in me bouncing off the shield itself, my body shuddering with shock as an overdose of Mana runs through my body. Luckily, they don't drop the shield, just staring at me with disapproving and angry eyes.

The loot from the System from these guys is weird. I don't even know where to start with the crystal skulls I'm given. Like most things with the System, you just have to shrug and move on. That being said, there's something strange about looting and storing dead humanoid corpses. Even if I don't see them, I can't help but feel that it's a bit morbid to carry around humanoid corpses in my Altered Space. Perhaps it's because with a good squint, you might even call them human.

After I give up on killing the remainder of the Huldrekall, I make my way back to Sabre. By the time I get back—after swinging wide and hiding my tracks as best I can—she's charged enough to be useful again. After tossing the remnants of my skinsuit armor and dressing in another one, I'm pretty much good to go again.

I've got a week till I'll consider it safe to head back. Add another week or so for the rest of the team to make it back to Whitehorse. That gives me two weeks and change to train out here by myself, and now that I've got an idea of the actual degree of difficulty, I can truly begin. I learned something while running away, tapped into something new. I've got two weeks to figure out if it's real or just another pipe dream.

A mental command has Sabre wrap itself around me before I stride forward. Time to get to work.

***

Two weeks. Two levels in that time. The out-of-zone bonuses and the Dungeon World resolution bonus both helped in the experience gain, along with the fact that I'd been most of the way to my last level before I started. Having nothing better to do but hunt and fight for two weeks has been very good for the experience gain, even if I took the last day off to relax and meditate. For what's coming, I want a clear mind.

The hunting and fighting wasn't just for the levels. I'd picked up some new abilities and toys a while ago, and fighting alone, I have a chance to really test them out. The Freezing Blade spell is interesting, if not as useful as I'd hoped. It's cumulative but not directly—it seems to be somewhat multiplicative. So the monster kept getting five percent slower than before, which meant after four hits, they might be only twenty percent or so slower than they started. Still pretty good, but not groundbreaking. On top of that, the duration isn't a guaranteed minute since resistances can reduce the duration by varying amounts. Sometimes on the same monster type.

Since I have a very limited supply of webbing missiles, I declined to test them further. I know how they worked and I've tested them enough. The sonic pulser is probably my favorite toy of the lot, since its attack often gives me a brief opening to lay down the hurt. Polar Zone sort of helped but wasn't powerful enough in its current level to add more than a minor slowing effect.

It was nice if I needed to muddy up the fight or slow down a group, but the mana cost made it less useful than Freezing Blade for single attackers. Of course, I had to hit with Freezing Blade first, while it's hard to escape a damn blizzard.

Once my prey was slowed or otherwise disabled, Fireball became the go-to spell, especially against the cold-resistant monsters that run around out here. Lightning Strike did the same damage as usual, but it didn't have the benefit of Elemental Weaknesses being applied to these monsters and it's more dependent on the situation. Fireball throws up a giant sphere of damage; Lightning Strike hammers attackers that are close to each other.

I also realized I was beginning to have problems with having too many choices. Sure, a bunch of my Skills are passive, but between my weapons, my Skills, and my spells, I have a plethora of options for any fight. Having to balance Mana usage among Skills and spells and decide which option is best became a headache. One that, on a few occasions, had seen me get hurt while I decided on the optimal choice.

All things considered, I'd probably be best limiting anything else I bought for a little bit until I got used to using what I have. Or perhaps just focusing on upgrading each Skill, spell, and weapon. It'll keep decisions in battle easier.

Two weeks of grinding has definitely helped smooth out my fight style and gained me the pair of levels. Before I finally take my leave, I take one last look at my status screen.

Status Screen			
Name	John Lee	Class	Erethran Honor Guard

Race	Human (Male)	Level	37
Titles			
Monster's Bane, Redeemer of the Dead			
Health	1700	Stamina	1700
Mana	1310	Mana Regeneration	98 / minute
Attributes			
Strength	94	Agility	161
Constitution	170	Perception	58
Intelligence	131	Willpower	133
Charisma	16	Luck	30
Class Skills			
Mana Imbue	2	Blade Strike	2
Thousand Steps	1	Altered Space	2
Two are One	1	The Body's Resolve	3
Greater Detection	1	A Thousand blades	1
Soul Shield	2	Blink Step	2
Tech Link*	2	Instantaneous Inventory*	1
Cleave*	2	Frenzy*	1
Elemental Strike*	1 (Ice)		
Combat Spells			

Improved Minor Healing (II)	Greater Regeneration
Greater Healing	Mana Drip
Improved Mana Dart (IV)	Enhanced Lightning Strike
Fireball	Polar Zone
Freezing Blade	

It's a pity I never hit Level 40, and one of the reasons I've been pushing so hard. But my leveling has slowed down ever since I hit Level 30, and gaining two levels in two weeks is amazing. My System inventory is full, my Altered Space is full, and I've used up the vast majority of projectiles and missiles. It's time to go back and get this done.

Chapter 18

Before the System, it would have taken me four hours or so to drive back to Whitehorse. Roughly four hundred kilometers. A tiny road trip by Canadian standards. Except that was before the System, before the winter and a highway that hasn't been cared for in nearly a year. Now there are monsters and snowbanks and a smorgasbord of dangers in the way.

The choice is always to go fast or slow. And when you put it that way, of course I'm going fast. Gunning down the road at just over a hundred kilometers an hour, the sounds of the wilderness drowned out by the wind screaming around me, I shoot past groups of monsters before they can react, before they can hope to launch more than a few attacks. The few attacks that hit bounce off.

Ali is flying ahead of me, scouting for potential problems. And there are some. Trees that have fallen, creating impromptu barricades. Snowbanks that have accumulated to the point that Sabre couldn't take them straight-on. Ambushes laid by monsters—spells to slow or capture prey, ropes and vines to block off escape, once even the corpse of a previously slain giant.

I have a day and advance warning, so I take the threats straight-on for the most part. Most ambush creatures just don't have the ability to take a punch, and when counter-ambushed, they end up slain easily enough. Four times, I avoid the fight. The first is the shifting, amorphous humanoid figure that had slain the giant. That Ali couldn't read his Level was warning enough.

The second is another group of Huldrekalls crouched above a brazier near the road. Memories of their powerful shield spell are enough for me to avoid that fight. I don't have time to draw them away, and running into a prepared position against those guys is a bad idea.

The third happens at a river, a group of water elementals crouched under the tottering bridge. No way was I going to start a fight with a bunch of elementals standing in their element. The last group is a bunch of tiny humanoids that looked like children. Their levels were extremely low, but I draw the line at some things and killing creatures that look like human children is one of them. I still have nightmares and flashbacks to the Goblin dungeon, tight corridors and small bodies clutching each other as we did what needed to be done.

A day and a bit to get back to Whitehorse. I admit, I take great pleasure in sneaking into the city, bypassing the walls. Of course, I couldn't bypass the shields if I hadn't had them keyed to me already, but coming down the cliffs from the airport keeps things quiet. Sneaking in while its dark, I take the time to make sure no one sees me as I enter the City Center and sell my stuff at the Shop. Refueled and rearmed, I exit the Shop to find Vir waiting for me.

"Adventurer Lee," Vir says, inclining his head.

"Vir." I look around, noting that he's the only one here. "Roxley not back yet?"

"There was a slight delay. He will be here in two days," Vir says.

"The others?"

"Not here. Did you fail?" Vir asks, his eyes tightening in concern.

"Depends on what the others say. We were separated," I answer, my lips flattening. "Plans changed."

Vir's face twists as conflicting emotions war for control. In the end, he nods resignedly. "They always do. It will be less than optimal if your team failed."

Less than optimal. The euphemisms that we use. "Will Roxley be able to handle his end?"

"My last communique with him indicated his side of the plan is progressing well," Vir replies. "We will be able to trigger the first part of the plan."

Unsaid is the truth that the first part of the plan doesn't matter if part two isn't ready. Unfortunately, we don't have much of a choice—each part had nearly as much lead time as the other. All we can do now is wait.

"Should I?" I incline my head toward the door.

Vir stays silent, considering the question. I can understand that. I was never supposed to be back here alone. My presence could throw things off. But on the other hand, you don't have so many people disappear and not raise a few suspicions. Having me here alone could buy a little more time. Time that we need for my team to show up. On that note...

"Should we?" A thumb jerks backward toward the floating silver sphere, the connection to the Shop.

"Trust in your friends, Adventurer," Vir says, shaking his head. "Best make yourself known. Might make them ask a few more questions."

"And if I'm asked?"

"Be your usual friendly self," Vir states flatly, getting a choked laughter from me.

Right. Rude works. Rude definitely works.

***

Breakfast the next morning in the Nugget is an affair. I get more than a few looks, but no one is willing to talk to me, to be the first to breach the cone of silence I sit in. Food arrives, hot and delicious, and I eat and eat.

"Labashi," I greet the Major when he arrives, my message having finally gotten to him.

"Adventurer Lee." Labashi drops his big, bulky, green ass in a chair. He glances around, eyes roving over the plates of food and drinks and my sole presence.

"Got something for you." I nod to Ali, who floats over, a hand hovering over the table for a few seconds before the tinkle of fallen electronics and metal resounds through the room. Scraps and dogtags taken from the fallen Hakarta that ambushed us rain down

"Ah…" Labashi stares at the pile, running his fingers over the scrap. Tusked lips twist before he takes them into his inventory. "My thanks."

"How much did they pay you?"

"Enough."

"You know, I'm less than impressed with this. I understand why, but still, less than impressed. So you'll do anything for the right amount, eh?"

"Not anything. We will not destroy the Corp—whether it be physical or with acts that would be anathema to the acquirement of future contracts," Labashi says. "What we can and will do is covered in our contracts."

"Good to know. Now, about our Contract." I lean forward, fixing him in the eye. "I figure trying to kill me pretty much invalidates any previous relationship or contract."

"And if I disagree?"

"Then we're going to have a spirited discussion, right here and right now." I open the gates and let my anger out, let him see it. My hands clench, my breathing tightens, and unconsciously, I shift forward in the seat slightly as I ready myself for battle.

The Hakarta doesn't flinch. He doesn't even seem particularly worried. No big surprise. He's got a ton of levels on me and probably more combat experience than I'd care to guess at. My threat to him, personally, is less than spectacular. Then again, that isn't the point.

"Very well," Labashi says as he reads the determination in my eyes. "A pity, but understandable."

Contract with Labashi Ruka Voided

"Well played, boy-o. You were right that he wouldn't want to keep the contract if you pushed it. Not anymore," Ali sends. *"Still, did you have to threaten him?"*

"Have to? No. Want to? Yes." I nod at Labashi, letting him know I've received the notification. I sit back, breathing slowly as I put a lid on the anger.

"John…" Labashi stops, frowning before he continues slowly. "You do understand that we know of your plans. Yours and Roxley's?" I grunt while Labashi continues, his voice low. "Standing up to me, while foolish, is courageous. Doing so with the Marquisse is foolhardy. She knows Roxley has secured additional loans. They have already taken steps to backdate the taxes owed.

"Your own attempt at the icefields has obviously not worked the way you wished it to. It would be a waste for a promising warrior like you to throw away your life in a futile battle."

I keep my face utterly still while he speaks. I'm not good enough to fake a reaction, so I go with the non-reaction route. It's not great, but it's better than nothing. Growing up in my family, keeping my feelings and reactions muted became almost second nature. I let Labashi stare at me, dark green eyes searching my brown ones for a reaction.

The Major sighs, shaking his head. "Adventurer Lee, it was interesting meeting you. And I hope you understand that none of this is personal."

"No. Not personal," I murmur, watching him leave. Just cataclysmic.

Watching the Major leave, I know I'll have to stick around and keep their attention for the next few days. Have to be prominent enough without being too interesting. The last thing we want is for them to really dig.

***

The ship drops out of the atmosphere to land at the airport with nary a noise. It's enormous, three times the size of a 747, wide and bulbous. The ship, shiny green steel, is bulbous and twisted, using force fields rather than physical structures to streamline the body while descending. It's a transport ship, big and blocky and perfect for traveling between the stars and occasional landings. For a transport ship, it has quite a few guns sticking out at all angles. Makes you wonder if Roxley chose the ship because of the additional weaponry or if interstellar travel is just that dangerous.

Anyone who is anyone is here, waiting on the ship to dock. Capstan, Vir, Amelia, most of the hunter teams, and a bunch of curious lookie-loos. And of course Labashi, his people, the Envoy, the Weaponmaster and his guards, looking as if they're just here because they're curious and not because a giant transport ship wasn't part of their plans.

When the ramp drops and the doors open, Roxley walks out, dark green hair framing pointed ears on dark skin, clad in a new left-button tunic in silver and gold. What's missing on the tunic is his house's crest, the small embroidery of crossed sword and rifle worked into Tuinnar words. I never did ask what they meant. Roxley's lips are twisted in a mocking half-smile as he walks down the ramp, a small distance between him and the other Tuinnar, who follow hesitantly. Those behind him span a wide range of body types, from short and stubby to tall and elegant, old to young. They all carry some form of weaponry, but their clothing is informal, relaxed, and lacking the armor plates of hunters or adventurers.

As interesting as Roxley always is, I'm more curious about the Envoy's reaction. Her eyes narrow as Roxley comes down, taking in the change of appearance and the growing stream of Tuinnar citizens, who are met by Vir and Minion in all their officious capacity. Within seconds, the newly arrived

Tuinnar are escorted to the back of the ship where their belongings are being unloaded under the watchful eyes of an ex-baggage handler. The corralled help are efficient, if unskilled.

"Lord Roxley," Lady Priya the Envoy says as she walks up. Her eyes rake his trim form, stopping for a brief moment on the missing crest. "What is the meaning of this?"

"A minor correction. I am no longer Lord of the Seven Seas, Lady Priya," Roxley says, eyes glinting in humor. Not that she wouldn't know that if she didn't look carefully.

"So it is true then. You have given up your claim on the Seven Seas." Lady Priya stares behind him at the people exiting the freighter. "And those behind you? Traitors the same?"

Flanking her, the Weaponmaster clenches his fist slightly, while Labashi looks bored.

"No traitors. Just citizens invoking their right of free movement afforded to all," Roxley says.

"You emptied the barony of your people," the Envoy hisses. "You took them all out and hid that fact from watchers. The barony is nearly empty, devoid of citizens. You have weakened your House."

"Not my House, as I have stated." Roxley steps forward, lowering his volume even as he raises his intensity. "You, your Duchess, and the Duke gave me no choice. You gave my people no succor, no help when we needed it. When we sought to better ourselves, you raised our taxes and forced me to choose—to wallow in our poverty or to strive for something more. Are you surprised that we chose not to lie down and die?"

"And so you took the Credits you borrowed from the disreputable and dishonest and decided instead of paying your taxes to hire the freighter," Lady Priya says, dark eyes glinting. After a moment, she laughs, peals of laughter that ring out through the tarmac. "Well done. Very well done. You have dealt with one of our plans.

"Now what?"

"Now my people go to the City Center and purchase places to stay, stores, and land throughout Whitehorse. And with their help, their funds, we should meet our target. In time to ensure that my Contract is fulfilled," Roxley answers, hands behind his back.

"Ah, of course. And with that, our legal leverage," Lady Priya says, continuing to smile. "Except, well, Ms. Lafollet?"

Miranda walks forward, the matronly lady bundled up in layers of sweaters, jackets, and a toque against the cold. "Lady Priya?"

"I believe it is time for us to complete our transaction," Priya says imperiously, turning to stare at the cold-looking older woman.

"You asked me to come out here to do this? I could have done this at home. Inside," Miranda says, hunched around the cold. "Some of us didn't put points into Constitution you know. It's -40°C right now with wind chill at least."

"Ms. Lafollet, the deal," the Envoy says, her voice making the air even chillier.

"Fine. Fine." Lafollet raises a hand. After a few quick stabs at an interface only she can see, she adds, "Done."

Priya turns to Roxley, looking to gloat before she pauses, her lips tightening as she reads over a screen only she can see. "What is this?"

"All the lands owned by the City Council, as agreed upon," Miranda says. "The city building and the dayhome."

"Where are the parks? The butchering yards?" Priya snaps. "If you haven't completed your end of the contract—"

"The System would know and have registered it," Miranda says, shaking her head. "If you look, you'll see the contract is complete. We did what was agreed upon. Now, I'm going home where it's warm."

"How…?" the Envoy begins, her eyes narrowed.

Capstan, who has been quiet thus far, rumbles a reply, "You spoke with the City Council, but never the General Council. All those lands you are looking for, they are held in trust by the General Council. City lands, city property."

"You sold them…" Priya shakes her head. "No. Impossible. I have notifications with the Shop. You could not have outbid me."

"We didn't. Those lands were transferred long before you came," Capstan says. "We had certain… problems with the City Council before you arrived. Much has changed, and while the human council stands, the General Council is what makes the decisions and owns most of what you seek."

I swear, I can almost see the Envoy's desire to growl or stamp her feet. Instead, she twists her fingers as she manipulates the System notifications. After a moment, she turns away from the screens to stare at Roxley, her voice calm once more. "It certainly seems you have won this round. You will have your town upgrade. Congratulations."

At those words, she stalks off, trailed by the Weaponmaster and Labashi. Roxley watches her go for a moment, lips thinned.

"Well, that went well," Ali says, drawing a slight smile from Capstan.

"It is but the beginning, Spirit."

"Duh," Ali says.

Roxley walks up to me, lowering his voice as he nears. "John, good to see you."

"And you." I glance at his hair. "Changed it again?"

"Yes. Like it?" The Tuinnar flips his head, sending his hair billowing around him. I grunt at the display, even if I do enjoy it. "I thought it appropriate, considering my new status."

"About that…" I place a hand on his arm. "Are you okay with this?"

Roxley's face flashes with anger before he smooths it out, his voice calm and controlled. "Of course. As I mentioned, they gave me no choice. At least here, my people have an opportunity to improve."

"I'm sorry…" I begin, unsure of what else to say. Roxley just gave up his birthright, his peerage for his people and this city. I have no idea what that's like—I'm just a pitiful commoner after all. Still, no matter what kind of brave face he puts on, it couldn't have been easy.

"Nonsense. This was the least of my duties." Roxley turns, letting his eyes rake over his people, who are already tramping down the staircase toward the city that's set at the back of the cliffs.

I grunt, falling silent. Fine. If he doesn't want me to say things like that, I won't.

Still, as I turn away, I catch his last whispered words. "And thank you."

Since the Envoy hasn't decided to kick things off yet, there's nothing more for me to do. Not yet. Now all we can do is wait for the other shoe to drop.

***

"Mikito." I exhale, spotting the young lady at our shared apartment.

She lowers the naginata, looking drawn and tired before nodding in greeting. A hand moves up, twitching, and I exhale as I see the notification.

"You did it," I say, relieved.

"We did," Amelia answers, making me jump and spin.

I dismiss my half-conjured weapon, growling at the black-haired First Nations woman as she smirks at me. "Lana?"

"She's alive. Out of town," Mikito answers, waving outside. "Her pets aren't particularly sneaky. She's at the Cutoff."

My chest releases, a tension in my shoulders and back that I hadn't realized I had been carrying finally relaxing. "Any casualties?"

"No more. The dragon stuck around for a few days, so we had to go slower than we liked. After it went hunting and finished eating, we were able to get back without running into much trouble. Now if that's it, we're going to sleep."

The pair walks to the bedroom, long weeks on the road obviously having taken a toll on them. When the door closes, I find myself slumping against a nearby wall, knees suddenly weak. This might just work.

Chapter 19

Another three days pass without incident. The newcomers are welcomed into the city, nearly doubling the city's population with their presence. As expected, their Credits and land purchases are sufficient that we finally cross the eighty percent threshold, triggering the transformation of the city from Village to Town and stabilizing the Mana flow all around. I think it's the fact that people can now walk the city without looking over their shoulders that helps with the integration of the newcomers. At least the number of incidents Amelia has to deal with is down, even if the numbers of aliens have grown.

Whitehorse is no longer recognizable as the town it was before. With the integration of the newcomers, the gradual transformation is now complete. Shops owned by the Tuinnar and the Yerick have transformed the downtown core, many of them widening doorways and changing architecture to suit our new alien friends and their taste. Some of the changes are subtle—lights that shine slightly cooler than normal, counters that are a little higher than normal. Other changes are more drastic as our alien guests make things their own—automated steel doors, liquid metal doorways, or wide-open stores protected by clear shield enclosures.

It's more than architecture though; it's the populace. We still don't have a public transportation system, so most people walk. Of course, the occasional high-tech car, truck, bike, or giant rolling armored personnel carrier makes an appearance, but mostly it's pedestrians. A mixture of humans, Tuinnar, Yerick, and the occasional Kapre or other exotic alien wander the streets. Everyone but the smallest child carries a weapon or two on them at all times, a hard-edged wariness in their movements.

Three days of relative peace and quiet as the downtown changes quickly under the combined efforts of the populace and the System. Three days till the alarm goes out. Practiced movements clear the streets within minutes as hunters head to their posts and civilians hunker down for the danger to pass. Those that don't know what the alarms are are quickly told. No one is surprised, but this time, it's not a Swarm. This time, it's something more dangerous.

"How many?" I ask when I finally make my way to the wall at Robert Service Way.

Roxley, Capstan, Jim, and more of the usual suspects are here, waiting. Interestingly, Vir and Amelia aren't, but I guess they're at one of the other posts. Not that we intend to fight. If we have to, we're truly hosed.

"Most of the Company," Roxley answers.

"Not military," I reply.

"One hundred twenty-three, boy-o," Ali answers loudly for everyone's sake. I'm glad he did. I'm sure there are others who had no clue as well.

"That's quite a few," I mutter. They outnumber the full complement of our hunters, Adventurers, and guards. Not to mention the fact that their lieutenants and sergeants probably out-level the majority of people here. Heck, some of their privates are probably just as strong as ours.

"Not unexpected. A show of force might bend us to their will without a fight," Capstan rumbles. "My people will not fight a losing battle, Lord Roxley."

"Not a lord anymore," Roxley absently corrects while he stares at screens only he can see. "And I understand. I will not be placing any of our people in that position."

That quiets the group, and we end up standing around in silence, many pondering his words. It's not as if we've spread the full plan around much. I stare at my minimap, watching the dots shift and move, telling a story of what is to come.

***

The Envoy stands at the front of the column, Labashi and Hondo next to her. The gleaming group of black-suited Hakarta move in well-ordered columns on foot, a pair of large, hovering vehicles with an intimidatingly large gun trailing behind them. A series of smaller vehicles follow the mobile artillery pieces, each of those vehicles wielding their own smaller but just as worrying weaponry. Not as many vehicles as you'd expect, but the data Ali sends me about them tells the real story. Each of those vehicles are hand-crafted and fully registered, built up lovingly and carefully tendered by mechanics. They're the equivalent of any four mass-manufactured vehicle and probably have a few tricks Ali isn't aware of. The entire column moves in lockstep formation, taking their time and letting the sheer force of their presence do all the talking.

The column comes to a halt a distance away, and the Envoy walks forward flanked by her minions, ahead of the company of armed and armored Hakarta. She comes to a final stop a hundred meters from the wall. Well within range if we decided to shoot. She doesn't need to worry though. We aren't going to be the first one to shoot and she knows it.

A brief hesitation, then Roxley steps forward, dropping over the wall onto the ground. I follow him a second later, Ali floating down alongside me. The others, the rest of the team, stay above since this conversation… well, it's just going to be a few of us.

"Mr. Roxley," Lady Priya says coolly. "We are here to take the city."

"As the humans say, the gloves have come off, have they?" Roxley looks at me. "Why do you say that? It seems silly to take them off, especially in these climates."

"I think it's got to do with the way people challenged each other to duels before," I blithely answer, ignoring the Envoy.

I see the Weaponmaster twitch at the blatant disrespect. He steps forward and is held back by the slightest shake of the Envoy's head.

"Your actions do you no favors for when the city is taken," Lady Priya says. "Your obstinance and childish actions will, in fact, reflect badly on your people."

"Don't do me any favors," Roxley says, that sardonic smile on his lips. "If you take the city, I will not survive. Having me alive does your Duchess no good. Though perhaps you will return me in chains to my former Duke. I'm sure he would be happy to extract his own form of vengeance."

"Are you intending to fight?" Hondo steps forward, and now the Envoy doesn't stop him. His lips twist, sneering. "You have not the people to stop Labashi and his men. And if you think you can beat me—"

"Actually, that'd be me," I interrupt Hondo, walking to the side to give myself space. Sabre's wrapped around me, protective armor and its shield and mine enclosed around me.

"You?" Hondo smirks, holding his hand out to the side. The polearm, a too-familiar polearm, appears. "I beat you without breaking a sweat last time."

"Me. You know, you guys are very predictable. Is it because you don't think we're worth it?" I ask, shaking my head. "Did you not think we'd take steps to deal with you? We knew you'd do this. It was a predictable play. So we needed a counter for it."

"Your trip to the icefields. Yes, we know. You gained a few Levels, but you failed in acquiring the loot you needed to hire your own mercenary company. Insufficient funds for the fight. Pity about the deposit," Lady Priya says, shaking her head. "Did you really think that would work?"

"Not really. Be nice if we did, but not really." I turn to Labashi, my eyes glinting. "Major, what would it cost for you to fight an Elder Dragon?"

"We would not," Labashi says. Droll and bored though his tone might be, I see him glance up and to the side. "Are we expecting one?"

I fix my gaze on the lady. "Depends on what the Envoy decides."

"If you've done with the melodrama, perhaps you'd care to inform us of what you did?" the Envoy says.

I chuckle softly. I let the silence extend for a bit, waiting, waiting, waiting until just before she's about to speak again. "We planted a bomb in the Dragon's lair. Left enough material in it so that when it explodes, it'll leave a ton of evidence of who did it." Before they can object, I continue. "And no, it isn't powerful enough to kill it. Heck, it probably won't do much more than annoy it. But it's planted right in the center of the Dragon's hoard, and the explosion should, at least, damage that.

"Way I understand it, Dragons aren't particularly forgiving when things happen to their hoard. I wonder what it'd do to any person, city, or entity that would dare damage its hoard?"

"We have nothing to do with that," Lady Priya says, but I can see her heart isn't in it. She understands.

"No. And you're welcome to take the city. But the moment you do, I'm pulling the trigger."

"And you doom yourself and your friends."

"Yes, there is that wrinkle. But since you and the System decided to come to Earth, every day seems to be the day I'm going to die. At least this way I get to say I punched a Dragon in the nose," I say, keeping my voice light and flat. I have to, because under all this, my rage has begun to froth. "And before you ask, my friends know. We all signed up for this."

"And the civilians? The humans you are looking to protect?" Lady Priya turns, staring at Roxley. "Your people?"

"Adventurer Lee told me once of a period of time in human history called the Cold War. Two superpowers facing off against each other but living in peace and prosperity for many years. All because of something called mutually assured destruction." Roxley sighs. "But you are right. I could not do this to my people.

"That's why Adventurer Lee has the trigger."

Oh shit.

Hondo doesn't ask for permission, moving in a flash. He crosses toward me, swinging his polearm in a strike meant to decapitate me. If not for the fact that I've layered my shields, he would have. My reflexive jerk doesn't get me out of the way of the initial strike, Sabre's shield flickering and failing as the blow lands.

The second attack I manage to block, my sword catching his polearm, sparks flashing as the blades clash. I keep my sword in hand, calling forth another with Thousand Blades to block the next strike with my other hand, then it just becomes a flurry of strikes. Between the blades, my shielding, and Sabre's armor, I manage to get away without getting hurt too badly during the initial rush.

I trigger the sonic pulser, the shrieking throwing Hondo off for a microsecond as the Tuinnar refuses to let up. Long enough for the missiles to launch. This close, Ugly slices a couple apart, but this time, all that means is that their payload explodes closer than I'd like. Hondo still takes the majority of the coating, but I get splashed too, the mixture slowing me down as I scramble aside. I circle away from Hondo, pulling myself apart from the little of the insta-concrete as I call forth my last additional blade.

Even as Hondo breaks free, I'm triggering Blade Strikes with all three weapons, arcs of power cutting through the air, each wrapped in the icy-glow of the Freezing Blades spell. The Tuinnar dances through the first two cuts but gets hit by the third, slowing down slightly. Then again and again as I layer attack after attack. Each attack slows him a little more, evening out the fight.

Slowed down or not, he still makes his way to me, thrusting with the polearm and forcing me to give up my attacks. I can keep up with him now, I'm even a little faster, but he's still more skilled. A strike I never see coming, a projection of attacks that chip away the shield, then a powered cut that rips right through it and the chest armor leaves me sprawled out next to the Envoy. I catch his last attack with my blade, shifting it aside just enough that it plunges into the right of my chest and not left.

I grab the weapon, trying to stop the Weaponmaster from pulling it out. I succeed, mostly because Ugly's not trying to do that. He twists, opening my wound wider and making me choke on blood, pain racking my body. I can feel Frenzy wanting to activate, to take over my body and finish this fight, but I push it aside. Not. Yet.

When the blade comes out, pulled from my weak fingers, I scream and gurgle in pain. Polearm raised, Hondo begins his final strike, not even bothering to use a Skill to finish me off. Only a last-minute twitch in his body and a weak deflection by me keeps it from decapitating me, instead leaving a long cut along my face that I barely feel. The polearm stays buried in the ground next to my face as the Tuinnar arches his back in pain.

"That's for Bill," Ingrid snarls, pulling her daggers from his body. "And that's for Luthien." Another Skill-aided stab, the Assassin now fully in view.

Hondo is too high level for her to sneak up on while he's paying attention, but during the fight and just before he finished me? Obviously she's good enough to do that. Even with her Skills and her attacks, the son of a bitch is still standing.

Hondo Ehrish (Weaponmaster Level 39, Master of Blades and Guns, Slayer of Orcs, Goblins and Unika, Destroyer of Monsters, The Unbroken Warrior)

HP: 1,775/4,340
MP: 1,183/1,900

Recovering from the attack, Hondo shows his mettle as he shrugs off the freezing, poison, and shock effects, and strikes with the body of his polearm as he levers it out of the ground. The haft hammers into her center, the muted crack of the blow landing and the much louder snap of broken bones resounding through the road. The blow sends the Assassin spinning through the air to land, crumpled. The way she's twisted, the angle of her back speaks of very bad things.

I struggle to my knees, grip Hondo by the top of his armor before he can continue his attack, and pull him toward me as I crumple backward. Hondo releases his polearm to lash out with a fist, cracking my helmet. Another strike smashes into my face again, throwing my head back against the ground and splitting my head protection. A third punch crashes through the helmet, and I feel my nose break along with one of my cheekbones.

"A sneak attack, human? Is that all you have? Tricks and subterfuge? Answer me!" Hondo punctuates the last few sentences with blows, pummeling my face and cracking bones, sending my health spinning down.

"Can't. Concentrating," I manage to spit out.

There. Right there. I find what I'm looking for in him, around him, and all around us. Holding tight to the connection I can feel through my Elemental Affinity, I give it a nudge. Just the way I learnt to do. Just a little.

My words only briefly confuse Hondo, but it does resolve his desire to finish this. He raises his hand, the fist glowing red with an activated Skill. Even as he throws the attack, I get my feet on his hips and I kick upward with both feet with all the strength I can muster. The shove sends him flying through the air, higher and faster than even my System-aided muscles should have been able to do so.

The Elemental connection frays, threatening to disappear as he moves away faster than a speeding bullet. I hold on as tight as I can to the connection, my eyes fixed on his disappearing body. I hold on to the connection with everything I have, my eyes fixed on the glowing tendril that spools out from my body with every second.

In seconds, he's out of sight and the connection snaps, leaving me groaning as the rebound pounds into my head. Everything disappears for a second, backlash and damage from the fight dogpiling my consciousness and shoving it under the bus after having their way with it. It's only the automated software in Sabre that injects me with healing potions and slowly brings me back to consciousness, my health given a temporary boost. Ali is whooping it up, laughing his ass off.

"What did you do?" The Envoy strides up to me, her eyes wide.

Hondo is gone, arcing through the air to land somewhere. Enhanced or not, it'll take him a long time to get back.

I look up, coughing hard as my body heals the open wounds and spraying Lady Priya's beautiful green gown with a touch of blood. I reach out with a bloody hand, gripping hers for a second before she pulls it away with a sniff as she steps back. Done.

"Friction. Boy-o killed the friction all around the lunk." Ali laughs, shaking his head.

"You…" The Envoy pulls her hand back, murder in her eyes.

"*Enough!*" the command, sent with all the force of personality and Skill that Roxley can wield, freezes everyone for a second. "Enough, Lady Priya. Attack again and I will not stay my hand."

Lady Priya nods jerkily, stepping away from me as she looks back toward Hondo. I can see the wheels turning in her mind. "Something this intricate would not be reliant on the Adventurer alone for its final success."

"Got it in one, lady," Ali says. "There are a few people with the trigger, including John. Killing him won't remove the threat."

I can see Lady Priya working the plan over, working the angles. I would say something, anything, but I'm finding it hard to breathe, let alone speak.

"A few more things to note. We have just marked you and the Weaponmaster. When the Adventurer or any of the others die, the explosion will trigger thanks to a deadman switch that now implicates you and Hondo directly. Along with the Adventurers, of course," Roxley says, walking forward.

"My Duchess—"

"Will not want to trade yours and the Weaponmaster's services for the shell of a border town on a new Dungeon world. The trade-off is inequitable," Roxley states.

"Splashdown, boy-o. Roxley needs to get this finished."

I'd say something, anything, but my breathing is rough. The wound he opened in me is stopping me from speaking, and all my spells, all my attacks have drained my Mana. I mentally trigger a second dose of the instant heals, knowing the backlash will harm my regeneration but needing to be healed right now. At least enough…

"Enough…" I croak before spitting out globs of congealed blood. "Leave. And stop bothering us."

"I will…"

Roxley steps forward, approaching the Envoy and lowering his voice. He speaks in Tuinnar, and for a second, I can't understand it. Then Ali translates and the words sounds familiar, even if they don't make sense.

"Parley... parsley... party." I find myself giggling slightly, the world swimming in and out of focus.

"Redeemer?" Capstan walks over to me, squatting and frowning. He pokes at my wounds, then he growls, picking me up even as the sound of trees crashing erupts from the forest.

Hondo comes rushing in, looking pissed. Before he can reach us, a wolf hits him low, hamstringing the Weaponmaster. As he stumbles, a flash of fire erupts, sending him sprawling. Even as he struggles to his feet, Lana is walking out from the treeline, unloading blast after blast from her shotgun. She hits him a few times before he dodges, only to be met by Mikito. They dance, polearms clashing and striking in circles of death that are dodged by millimeters.

"Hondo!"

The command freezes the Weaponmaster and he disengages, stepping back swiftly. Mikito, crouched low, is holding out her naginata, watching the Weaponmaster warily as she bleeds from a cut along her leg.

"We are under the rules of parley," the Envoy says.

I relax into the big, furry pillow carrying me. Finally.

Chapter 20

Double dosing the healing potions added to the poison effects and the damage put me down for hours. If I had to guess, the accumulated stress of the past few months didn't help either. Double dosing harmed the System-gifted regeneration so sufficiently that it was supposedly touch-and-go for a few minutes, the continual bleeding and poison effects dragging me down. Good thing both a pre-System doctor and Nelia were on-hand at the wall.

I get filled in on the blanks a little later. When Hondo attacked me, the Hakarta didn't join in because they were only hired to attack the city. A finely-cut line by Labashi, but one he insisted on holding. The Envoy didn't dare move since Roxley had headed her off, and everything happened so fast, she never got a chance to renegotiate the deal with Labashi.

"So they left?" I murmur to Roxley, who has come to visit me in the apartment. I'm fully dressed and seated on a comfy sofa, staring at the Elf.

"Yes. The parley was successful. We reached an agreement that will ensure that Whitehorse will stay under my control," Roxley says slowly. "I had to make certain concessions."

I frown, staring at the Tuinnar. "Why?"

"You know why. The threat could only hold them for so long. We still needed to get a signal to the bomb, and once they blocked that, we'd be back to square one. We had a small window of opportunity where the cost of taking us on outweighed the compromises they had to make," Roxley says, his voice calm and collected.

"What did you give them?" I reply, my voice tight with doubt.

"Me. I am Lord Graxan Roxley of the Yukon now, or will be soon," Roxley answers. "I answer to the Duchess as the ruler of Whitehorse, Fairbanks, and Juno. All the lands between are claimed by us, and we will expand until we have it in fact, as well as name."

I blink, trying to understand why they'd hire him. After all this. "Why?"

"It seems the Duchess admires men with spirit and the ability to thwart her. Rather than destroy us, she prefers to co-opt useful assets. Our continued rebuttals of her attempts have moved us into the asset column."

"So they won," I hiss as the initial shock wears off. "You gave them everything. Just for a job."

Roxley is calm, though there's a touch of wariness in his eyes and stance. One that most would miss, but I've been around the damn elf long enough. "There was no other way to win. We were never going to stand them off, never win fully. You cannot have expected your plan to last forever."

"No, but we could have found another solution, another way around. Earned the Credits to hire our own forces."

"At what cost? Putting the city's progress back months, years? This way, I have control, the ability to ensure that nothing happens that I do not want. The city will grow, prosper, and at a higher, better rate than before," Roxley insists, leaning forward. "This is the best way."

"Best?" I laugh bitterly, shaking my head. "Best. For you perhaps, Lord Roxley."

"Damn it, John, for the city. This way, we'll be able to pay you and Lana back for your loan from the foundation. We'll be able to build the city up and make it safe. Make it a real place to live in again," Roxley says, reaching out a hand for me. "You have to trust me on this."

I pull away from the reaching hand and point at the door, my voice low and hoarse with controlled emotions. "We're done here."

"John…"

"Go."

Roxley walks to the door, where he pauses and turns to me, his voice low and raw with emotion. "Damn you, John. Your naiveté, your insistence at finding your own way will kill you. And others eventually. I made the right choice."

I don't answer, turning away to stare at a wall.

Roxley stands there in silence for a second before he speaks again, his voice calm and controlled. "There was one other thing. Hondo is furious that you managed to disgrace him like you did. They will return in six months to check on the city. It is best you not be here then."

In the silence of the empty apartment, a pain in my gut, an emptiness in my chest consumes me. I reach for my anger, that comforting old friend, and find it elusive, hiding. I shut my eyes and curse myself for trusting as I work on blocking the pain away. No one to blame here. No one but me. I should have known better.

Lana finds me later, lying on the couch and staring at the ceiling. She squats next to me, placing a hand on my arm. "I'm sorry. Ali told me that Roxley told you."

"Huh?"

"John…" Lana looks at me, concern in those violet eyes that I love to stare at. She squeezes my arm till I give her my attention. "Are you okay?"

"No," I answer truthfully, my lips twisting in bitter recrimination. "I should have known. Eric warned me. Should have known…"

"It's not that simple," Lana says, squeezing my arm again. "You know that."

"You on his side now?"

"I'm on the truth's side."

"Huh." I stare at her, that gnawing pit in my stomach aching, and I snap. "Fine. Just go."

"John…"

"Just leave me alone," I say before reining in my temper a bit. I hold up a hand placatingly as I grind out the words. "Not that I… well, not… I just need to be alone. Please. Not trying to be an ass, just not in the place to be good company."

Lana compresses her lips, obviously struggling not to say something as she searches my face. Finally, she stands. "I'll be around. You don't have to do this, you know, not alone."

I give her a quick nod. She's right. But just because she's right and I can now acknowledge that doesn't mean I'm ready yet to take help. Finally she leaves me to brood alone in the darkness. Except for Ali, who I have to threaten to banish before he shuts up. So many deaths, just to find ourselves under her thumb anyway. No control, no say, just another group of slaves to an uncaring Lord and the System.

I sit and think, wondering about the choices I made and the lives I've sacrificed. All for this bittersweet victory.

Epilogue

Congratulations! The planet you know as Earth is now a fully integrated Dungeon World.

We're impressed. 9.69% of you humans managed to survive the transition period. Some of you even managed to develop some impressive cities in this year. All survivors have now been Credited a one-time survival bonus of 20,000 Credits.

As a new Dungeon World, there might be some little irregularities with regard to zone levels and monster spawns. Expect new and exciting immigrants as Mana flows stabilize. We hope you'll accept them with open arms and provide the necessary information and goods to make their experience in your Dungeon World a pleasant one.

Once again, welcome to the Galactic Council!

Cheering and screaming resounds through the city as bottles of beer, wine, and champagne are popped and shared. Humans, Yerick, Tuinnar, and Kapre all rejoice as the notifications appear, celebrating their survival. The humans most of all, as the Credits appear in our System accounts.

On a stage, Roxley is chatting with the General Council members, shaking hands and passing words of congratulations. Seated on Sabre, a short distance away, I watch the celebrations, plates of food flowing out from the Nugget and other establishments, as the band plays and dancers take to the street. It looks as though it'll be one hell of a wild party.

I watch it for a moment more, drinking in the scene and parking the celebration in my memory. I even drink a mug of beer that gets passed to me.

When the initial jubilation dies down, I tap my new helmet control, letting my new headgear form around me.

I'm not angry—well, not much—about how it all panned out. Betrayed and hurt, but not angry. Not anymore. If I could go back… but I can't. So it is what it is, and Roxley is right—the city is in better hands with him than before.

"You know, we could wait a day," Ali says longingly as I swing Sabre around, the silent Mana engine pulling us forward on the road out of town.

We could. We could stay, enjoy the party, bask in the celebration. Even let a few people know that we're leaving. I'm sure some of them want to say goodbye, might have words or gifts to commemorate my leaving. But this way is better—less emotion, less awkwardness. I don't want, I don't need, their thanks. What I did, I did for myself. My dad never really had much to say that was worthwhile, but one thing I do remember—if you're going to do something good, you don't ask for thanks and you don't expect gratitude. You do it because it's right.

Fourth Avenue is clear all the way to the wall as everyone is downtown already. The guards are a little surprised to see me leave. I offer them a nod and ignore their questioning looks as I slip out.

"Seems a pity to miss out on a party like that. Maybe meet another cute girl…" Ali continues while I ignore him.

Today, now, is the perfect time. If I need to go, best just go. The city will survive. While I might dislike what Roxley did, he's unlikely to screw the city over too greatly. Not any more than he has already. In the end, what I told the council holds true. Better the devil you know.

As we crest the hill that leads out of Whitehorse, I stare at the group awaiting me. My eyes narrow, noting a rather familiar bike-like item that Mikito sits on, before traveling to Lana, who's busy scratching a puppy on its belly. I open my mouth before spinning around, glaring at Ingrid as she sneaks up on me.

She sighs, clearly disappointed. "How'd you know?"

"The extra bike. Also, you're getting predictable," I answer.

She smirks at me.

"What are you all doing here?" I let my gaze travel over the equipment they've got secured to the bikes and the puppies, noting how they're set up for quick release in case of trouble.

"What do you think, you big idiot?" Lana says, shaking her head as she walks up to me. When she gets close, she kicks my foot sharply. It's hard enough to hurt, a bit, even through the armor. "You thought we were going to let you leave? Just like that?"

"Lana…"

"I have nothing left here. No business, no family. Just memories of a life that…" Lana stops, choking a bit. "I'm coming, John."

As my eyes travel to Mikito, she mouths, "Baka."

Even I'm not so stupid as to try to dissuade her. What Lana said goes doubly for her.

"Trust me, I'd rather be home. But considering I stabbed the asshole in the kidneys and he didn't die, I figure I need to not be here when he's back," Ingrid says.

"How did you know?" I mutter.

Ali just grins at me. Of course. Betrayed again. Except this time, I find I'm not angry.

"We going or we going to cry about our feelings more?" Ali says, prodding me along.

In answer, I start Sabre rolling down the road. Howard crouches, and Lana smoothly grabs his collar, swinging herself on him. In moments, the entire party is moving down the snow-covered highway, heading south. I cast one last glance backward, at Whitehorse and the world I left behind, before I look back at the road and pick up speed. I find myself smiling as I stare at the road, feeling some of the worries, the burdens I've carried fall away. There's an open road and a new world out there. And I still have a promise to keep.

"So where are we going?"

The End

John and company will be back in

Cities in Chains (Book 4 of the System Apocalypse) with more problems!

Author's Note

This concludes the first arc of the System Apocalypse and ends our time in Whitehorse. Cities in Chains, the System Apocalypse Book 4 starts a new, exciting arc set outside of the Yukon and can be bought here:

- Cities in Chains (Book 4 of the System Apocalypse)

  https://readerlinks.com/l/729263

I'd like to reiterate that I am grateful for the support all of you have provided. While I'd still be telling myself John's story, I certainly wouldn't be spending time writing it. ☺

If you enjoyed reading the book, please do leave a review and rating. It helps sales and yes, that's the reason I write!

In addition, please check out my other series, Adventures on Brad (a more traditional LitRPG fantasy), Hidden Wishes (an urban fantasy GameLit series), and A Thousand Li (a cultivation series inspired by Chinese wuxia and xianxia novels).

To support me directly, please go to my Patreon account:

https://www.patreon.com/taowong

For more great information about LitRPG series, check out the Facebook groups:

- LitRPG Society

  https://www.facebook.com/groups/LitRPGsociety/
- LitRPG Books

  https://www.facebook.com/groups/LitRPG.books/

About the Author

Tao Wong is an avid fantasy and sci-fi reader who spends his time working and writing in the North of Canada. He's spent way too many years doing martial arts of many forms, and having broken himself too often, he now spends his time writing about fantasy worlds.

For updates on the series and other books written by Tao Wong (and special one-shot stories), please visit the author's website:

http://www.mylifemytao.com

Subscribers to Tao's mailing list will receive exclusive access to short stories in the Thousand Li and System Apocalypse universes.

Or visit his Facebook Page: https://www.facebook.com/taowongauthor/

About the Publisher

Starlit Publishing is wholly owned and operated by Tao Wong. It is a science fiction and fantasy publisher focused on the LitRPG & cultivation genres. Their focus is on promoting new, upcoming authors in the genre whose writing challenges the existing stereotypes while giving a rip-roaring good read.

For more information on Starlit Publishing, visit their website: https://www.starlitpublishing.com/

You can also join Starlit Publishing's mailing list to learn of new, exciting authors and book releases.

Glossary

Erethran Honor Guard Skill Tree

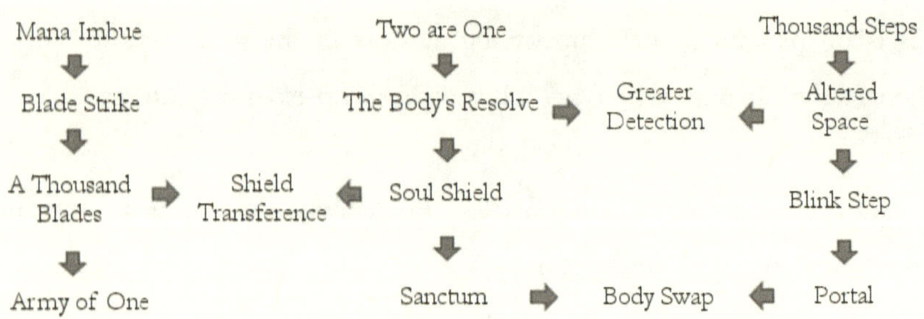

John's Skills

Mana Imbue (Level 1)

Soulbound weapon now permanently imbued with mana to deal more damage on each hit. +10 Base Damage (Mana). Will ignore armor and resistances. Mana regeneration reduced by 5 Mana per minute permanently.

Blade Strike (Level 2)

By projecting additional mana and stamina into a strike, the Erethran Honor Guard's Soulbound weapon may project a strike up to 20 feet away.
Cost: 35 Stamina + 35 Mana

Thousand Steps (Level 1)

Movement speed for the Honor Guard and allies are increased by 5% while skill is active. This ability is stackable with other movement related skills.
Cost: 20 Stamina + 20 Mana per minute

Altered Space (Level 2)

The Honor Guard now has access to an extra-dimensional storage location of 30 cubic feet. Items stored must be touched to be willed in and may not include living creatures or items currently affected by aura's that are not the Honor Guard's. Mana regeneration reduced by 10 Mana per minute permanently.

Two are One (Level 1)

Effect: Transfer 10% of all damage from Target to Self

Cost: 5 Mana per second

The Body's Resolve (Level 3)

Effect: Increase natural health regeneration by 35%. On-going health status effects reduced by 33%. Honor Guard may now regenerate lost limbs. Mana regeneration reduced by 15 Mana per minute permanently.

Greater Detection (Level 1)

Effect: User may now detect System creatures up to 1 kilometer away. General information about strength level is provided on detection. Stealth skills, Class skills and ambient mana density will influence the effectiveness of this skill. Mana regeneration reduced by 5 Mana per minute permanently.

A Thousand Blades (Level 1)

Creates two duplicate copies of the user's designated weapon. Duplicate copies deal base damage of copied items. May be combined with Mana Imbue and Shield Transference. Mana Cost: 3 Mana per second

Soul Shield (Level 2)

Effect: Creates a manipulable shield to cover the caster's or target's body. Shield has 1,000 Hit Points.

Cost: 250 Mana

Blink Step (Level 2)

Effect: Instantaneous teleportation via line-of-sight. May include Spirit's line of sight. Maximum range—500 meters.

Cost: 100 Mana

Frenzy (Level 1)

Effect: When activated, pain is reduced by 80%, damage increased by 30%, stamina regeneration rate increased by 20%. Mana regeneration rate decreased by 10%

Frenzy will not deactivate until all enemies have been slain. User may not retreat while Frenzy is active.

Cleave (Level 2)

Effect: Physical attacks deal 60% more base damage. Effect may be combined with other Class Skills

Cost: 25 Mana

Instantaneous Inventory (Maxed)

Allows user to place or remove any System-recognized item from Inventory if space allows. Includes the automatic arrangement of space in the inventory. User must be touching item.

Cost: 5 Mana per item

Elemental Strike (Level 1 - Ice)

Effect: Used to imbue a weapon with freezing damage. Adds +5 Base Damage to attacks and a 10% chance of reducing speed by 5% upon contact. Lasts for 30 seconds.

Cost: 50 Mana

Tech Link (Level 2)

Effect: Tech Link allows user to increase their skill level in using a technological item, increasing input and versatility in usage of said items. Effects vary depending on item. General increase in efficiency of 10%. Mana regeneration rate decreased by 10%

Designated Technological Items: Neural Link, Sabre

Spells

Improved Minor Healing (III)

Effect: Heals 35 Health per casting. Target must be in contact during healing. Cooldown 60 seconds.

Cost: 20 Mana

Improved Mana Dart (IV)

Effect: Creates four darts out of pure Mana, which can be directed to damage a target. Each dart does 15 damage. Cooldown 10 seconds

Cost: 25 Mana

Enhanced Lightning Strike

Effect: Call forth the power of the gods, casting lightning. Lightning strike may affect additional targets depending on proximity, charge and other conductive materials on-hand. Does 100 points of electrical damage.

Lightning Strike may be continuously channeled to increase damage for 10 additional damage per second.

Cost: 75 Mana.

Continuous cast cost: 5 Mana / second

Lightning Strike may be enhanced by using the Elemental Affinity of Electromagnetic Force. Damage increased by20% per level of affinity

Greater Regeneration

Effect: Increases natural health regeneration of target by 5%. Only single use of spell effective on a target at a time.

Duration: 10 minutes

Cost: 100 Mana

Fireball

Effect: Create an exploding sphere of fire. Deals 150 points of fire damage to those caught within. Sphere of fire expands to 3 meters radius (on average). Cooldown 60 seconds.

Cost: 100 Mana

Polar Zone

Effect: Create a thirty meter diameter blizzard that freezes all targets within one. Does 10 points of freezing damage per minute plus reduces effected individuals speed by 5%. Cooldown 60 seconds.

Cost: 200 Mana

Greater Healing

Effect: Heals 75 Health per casting. Target does not require contact during healing. Cooldown 60 seconds per target.

Cost: 50 Mana

Mana Drip

Effect: Increases natural health regeneration of target by 5%. Only single use of spell effective on a target at a time.

Duration: 10 minutes

Cost: 100 Mana

Freezing Blade

Effect: Enchants weapon with a slowing effect. A 5% slowing effect is applied on a successful strike. This effect is cumulative and lasts for 1 minute. Cooldown 3 minutes

Spell Duration: 1 minute.

Cost: 150 Mana

Sabre's Load-Out

Omnitron III Class II Personal Assault Vehicle (Sabre)

Core: Class II Omnitron Mana Engine

CPU: Class D Xylik Core CPU

Armor Rating: Tier IV (Modified with Adaptive Resistance)

Hard Points: 5 (5 Used)

Soft Points: 3 (2 Used)

Requires: Neural Link for Advanced Configuration

Battery Capacity: 120/120

Attribute Bonuses: +35 Strength, +18 Agility, +10 Perception

Inlin Type II II Projectile Rifle

Base Damage: N/A (Dependent Upon Ammunition)

Ammo Capacity: 45/45

Available Ammunition: 250 Standard, 150 Armor Piercing, 200 High Explosive, 25 Luminescent

Ares Type II Shield Generator

Base Shielding: 2,000 HP

Regeneration Rate: 50/second unlinked, 200/second linked

Mkylin Type IV Mini-Missile Launchers

Base Damage: N/A (dependent on missiles purchased)

Battery Capacity: 6/6

Reload rate from internal batteries: 10 seconds

Available Ammunition: 12 Standard, 12 High Explosive, 12 Armor Piercing, 4 Napalm

Type II Webbing Mini-Missile

Base Damage: N/A

Effect: Disperses insta-webbing upon impact or on activation. Dispersal covers 3 cubic feet.

Cost: 500 Credits

Shinowa Type II Sonic Pulser

Base Damage: 25 per second

Additional Effect: Disrupts auditory sense of balance on opponent during use.

Effects have a small chance of continuing after use.

Cost: 25,000 Credits

Other Equipment

Tier II Sword (Soulbound Personal Weapon of an Erethran Honor Guard)

Base Damage: 71

Durability: N/A (Personal Weapon)

Special Abilities: +10 Mana Damage, Blade Strike

Silversmith Mark II Beam Pistol (Upgradeable)

Base Damage: 18

Battery Capacity: 24/24

Recharge Rate: 2 per hour per GMU

Cost: 1,400 Credits

Tier IV Neural Link

Neural link may support up to 5 connections.

Current connections: Omnitron III Class II Personal Assault Vehicle

Software Installed: Rich'lki Firewall Class IV, Omnitron III Class IV Controller

Ferlix Type II Twinned-Beam Rifle (Modified)

Base Damage: 57

Battery Capacity: 17/17

Recharge rate: 1 per hour per GMU (currently 12)